D1666527

*The Scriptures used in this book are from the New International Version and typically italicized. Words in parentheses (and not italicized) are the interpretation of the author. The author also bolds and underlines Scriptures for the emphasis he believes of special importance.

FORWARD

I have written this book to help Christians and interested persons
Understand what the Scriptures teach about "The Time of the END".
Christ Jesus gave us The Book Of Revelation and all of Scripture,
So that we could understand what He wanted us to know
About The Time of the END.
He said about the Book of Revelation:

'Blessed is the one who reads the words of this prophecy,
And blessed are those who hear it
And take to heart what is written in it,
Because the time is near.' *(Revelation 1:3)*

Christ Jesus also said that the Holy Spirit will tell us what is yet to come.
(John 16:13)

The Book of Revelation is the primary book describing The Time of the END.
However, in the gospels of Matthew, Mark and Luke Christ Jesus gives
The Signs of the End of the Age.
In these books He gives us the Beginning of Birth Pains,
And the "Season," "The Lesson from the Fig Tree,"
That will immediately precede The Great Tribulation.
He tells us that the generation that is living in the time of this "Season"
Will not pass away until The Great Tribulation occurs.

Other books of the New Testament give insight to The Time of the END,
And also, the Old Testament Prophets and the Psalms
Have much to say about this subject;
Books written hundreds of years before the birth of Christ Jesus.
The fact of Israel's becoming a nation again in 1948,
As was foretold by Scripture , speaks for itself.
Once one becomes aware of what God has to say through His Word,
About The Time of the END,
We are better able to interpret the time we are living in, in relationship to it.

This book is a journey through what God has to say about The Time of the END.
I give my interpretation as to what I believe it means.
However, the pertinent Scriptures are quoted
So the reader can make their own interpretation.
God clearly wants His people to be prepared for The Time of the END.
Christ Jesus said about this:

No one knows about that day or hour,
Not even the angels in heaven, nor the Son, but only the Father.
Be on guard! Be alert!

The Time Of The END

You do not know when the time will come.
It's like a man going away:
He leaves his house in charge of his servants, each with his assigned task,
And tells the one at the door to keep watch.

Therefore keep watch
Because you do not know when the owner of the house will come back--
Whether in the evening or at midnight, or when the rooster crows, or at dawn.
If he comes suddenly, do not let him find you sleeping.

What I say to you, I say to everyone: 'Watch!' *(Mark 13:32-37)*

It is plain from what Christ Jesus said,
That we are to actively anticipate His return, and the "Season" that precedes it.
To do this we must understand all that He had to say on the subject.

It is also clear from reading the Scriptures concerning The Time of the END,
That many, who name His name, are not ready for His return
And are caught unprepared, to their great harm.

It is my prayer, that you I are prepared, ready, alert, on guard and watching,
As Christ Jesus teaches us to be.

INTRODUCTION

The Self-Existent God, who has forever been, the I am;
Who spoke the material world into existence with His Word;
The God who is LIFE itself;
Who created and sustains all living things;
The God who is Love and Light;
Who is all knowing, all seeing, present everywhere and all powerful;

The God who created mankind in His image, body, mind, soul and spirit;
Who gave mankind Paradise, a place of perfection before their fall from grace;
The God who is going to restore His people, His Bride, back to His Paradise;

The God who knows the number of hairs on your head;
Who wrote the number of your days in His book before you were born;
Who knew you before you were born;
Who made you fearfully and wonderfully;
Who knows every thought you ever had;
And every thing you have ever done;

The God who loved you enough to give His life for you;
Who was crucified from the foundation of the earth;
Who endured the cross of Calvary to purchase forgiveness for your sins;
Who continually speaks to every living person;
Who sent His Holy Spirit to all who receive Him,
To teach them the Way, the Truth and the LIFE,
The only Way, the only Truth, and the only LIFE.

This God, the only God, has determined The Time of the END.

He has determined the day, the hour, the minute and the second
Of His second coming and every event that precedes it.
He has provided His written Word to mankind so they would not be ignorant;
That they might know the heart and mind of God;
And all He has done and is going to do;
That each person might choose to accept His Christ, Jesus, as their Lord and Savior.
That each person might choose eternal LIFE rather than eternal death.

The only thing standing in your way of receiving Christ Jesus is the liar, Satan.
The powerful (compared to man) angel, created by God for greatness,
Who chose to abandon his high position in Heaven
For the irrational idea that he could be like God.
He looked at himself in a mirror
And could see the incredibly beautiful being God created him to be,
So in his vanity and pride he decided that he wanted to be worshiped;
Mankind became the object of his deception.

The Time Of The END

He realized that he could get mankind to worship him,
Like puppets on strings,
By appealing to their vanity and pride.
Deceiving mankind into believing the LIE,
That they, like him, could be like God.

From the beginning of "Time", Satan has been deceiving mankind with his LIE.
At the same time God has personally spoken the Truth
To every person who ever lived.
Each person has had the opportunity to believe Satan or God.

Satan, like a peacock, showy and strutting, masquerading as an angel of light.
Deceiving mankind into reducing their lives
To the cesspool of the lust of the flesh, the lust of the eyes,
And the pride of what they possess and have done.

God, however, is not interested in the accomplishments of mankind.
He has only one interest, an eternal interest;
The condition of the heart of every living person.
That is all that is of importance to God.
Mankind's accomplishments are meaningless to Him.
God knows that there is LIFE in Himself alone and so does Satan.
Satan knows he is doomed to eternal death.
However, in his evil, twisted, wicked mind,
He is determined to take as many people to hell with him as he can.

So there, the stage is set for your life.
The only decision you have to make of any comparative importance at all,
Is where will you spend eternity?
Will you believe the LIE, packaged by Satan,
Appealing to your vanity and pride,
Or the Truth spoken by the Word of God
And His speaking to you personally by His Holy Spirit.

The God of Heaven, offers love, peace and joy in the here and now
As well as the by and by.
He offers you His Holy Spirit to live inside you;
Christ in you the hope of glory,
And the wonderful LIFE to be lived in the here and now in His Spirit.
He wants to take you into realms of His glory
That you have never dreamed of,
In the here and now.

The choice is yours!

CONTENTS

Chronology Of Events Preceding The Great Tribulation

The Time Of The END

The Time Of The END

THE SIGNS OF THE END OF THE AGE

Christ Jesus gives the Signs of the End of the Age in three of the Gospels,
Matthew, Mark and Luke.
These signs include two types of events, The Beginning of Birth Pains
And The Lesson From The Fig Tree (the Season of the last generation).
So although He does not give the day or the hour
That The Great Tribulation will begin,
Or the "abomination that causes desolation" that precedes it,
He does give the signs of the "Season" just before.
We begin looking at these signs from the Gospel of Matthew.

Matthew 24

Jesus left the temple and was walking away
When his disciples came up to him to call his attention to its buildings.

'Do you see all these things?' he asked. 'I tell you the truth,
Not one stone here will be left on another; every one will be thrown down.'

[A similar occurrence happens at the end of "Time"
When Babylon and all the cities of earth are pounded into dust
By one hundred pound hail stones, and no man made thing is left standing.]

As Jesus was sitting on the Mount of Olives, the disciples came to him privately.
'Tell us,' they said, 'when will this happen,
And what will be the sign of your coming and of the end of the age.'

Jesus answered: 'Watch out that no one deceives you.
For many will come in my name, claiming, 'I am the Christ,'
And will deceive many.
You will hear of wars and rumors of wars,
But see to it that you are not alarmed.
Such things must happen, but the <u>end</u> is still to come.
Nation will rise against nation, and kingdom against kingdom.
There will be famines and earthquakes in various places.
<u>All these are the beginning of birth pains</u>.

Then you will be handed over to be persecuted and put to death
And you will be hated by all nations because of me.
<u>At that time many will turn away from the faith</u>
<u>And will betray and hate each other,</u>
And many false prophets will appear and deceive many people.

Because of the increase of wickedness, the love of most will grow cold,

The Time Of The END

But he who stands firm to the <u>end</u> will be saved.

*And this gospel of the kingdom will be preached in the whole world
As a testimony to all nations, and then the <u>end</u> will come.*

**So when you see standing in the holy place
The abomination that causes desolation,**
*Spoken through the prophet Daniel—let the reader understand—
Then let those who are in Judea flee to the mountains.
Let no one on the roof of his house go down to take anything out of the house.
Let no one in the field go back to get his cloak.
How dreadful it will be in those days for pregnant women and nursing mothers!
Pray that your flight will not take place in winter or on the Sabbath.*

*[In these verses, 16-20, Christ speaks of events that are true of the end of time
As well as when Titus, the Roman general, came and destroyed Jerusalem in 70
A.D.]*

For then there will be great distress,
**Unequaled from the beginning of the world until now--
And never to be equaled again.**

*If those days had not been cut short, no one would survive,
But for the sake of the elect those days will be shortened.*

*At that time if anyone says to you, 'Look, here is the Christ!' or
'There he is!' do not believe it.
For false Christs and false prophets will appear
And perform great signs and miracles
To deceive even the elect—if that were possible.
See, I have told you ahead of time.*

*So if anyone tells you, 'There he is, out in the desert,' do not go out; or
'Here he is, in the inner rooms,' do not believe it.
For as the lightning comes from the east and flashes to the west,
So will be the coming of the Son of Man.*

Wherever there is a carcass, there the vultures will gather.

Immediately after the distress of those days

*The sun will be darkened, and the moon will not give its light;
The stars will fall from the sky,
And the heavenly bodies will be shaken.*

At that time the sign of the Son of Man will appear in the sky,

The Time Of The END

And all the nations of the earth will mourn.

They will see the Son of man coming on the clouds of the sky,
With power and great glory.
And he will send his angels with a loud trumpet call, and they will gather his elect
From the four winds, from one end of the heavens to the other.

Now learn this lesson from the fig tree:
As soon as its twigs get tender and its leaves come out,
You know that summer is near.
Even so, when you see all these things, you know that it is near
Right at the door.
I tell you the truth, this generation will certainly not pass away
Until all these things have happened.
Heaven and earth will pass away, but my words will never pass away.

The Beginning Of Birth Pains
Jesus gives a list of the things that He calls the beginning of birth pains,
That will lead up to The Great Tribulation:

- Many will come claiming to be the Christ;
- There will be wars and rumors of wars;
- Nation will rise up against nation, kingdom against kingdom;
- There will be famines and earthquakes.

These signs have occurred periodically since the ascension of Christ Jesus.
However, we can anticipate that there will be a uniqueness to them
At the end of the age.

At the end of the birth pains comes the "Season"
That precedes the "abomination that causes desolation",
The apostasy and rebellion that occurs within the Church of God,
Which allows the Beast (Antichrist) to set up his "image" in the holy place
(the Church)
And requires that everyone worship him.
Then comes The Great Tribulation.

The Lesson From The Fig Tree, The "Season"
Jesus gives the lesson from the fig tree
In which He describes the "Season" of time that will immediately precede
The "abomination that causes desolation" and The Great Tribulation:

From Matthew:
- Christians will be persecuted and put to death;
- They will be hated by all nations because they belong to Christ;

The Time Of The END

- Many Christians will turn away from the faith and betray and hate each other (the apostasy and rebellion);
- Many false Christs and false prophets will appear and perform signs and miracles to deceive even the elect—if that were possible (which it is not).
- Because of the increase of wickedness the love of most will grow cold,
- But those who stand firm to the end will be saved.

Additional Lessons From The Gospel Of Mark:
- Christians will be handed over to local councils and flogged in Churches.
- Christians will be brought before governors and kings as a witness to them.
- The gospel will be preached to all nations.
- Whenever Christians are arrested and brought to trial, they are not to worry about what to say because the Holy Spirit will speak through them and for them.
- Brother will betray brother to death, and a father his child.
- Children will rebel against their parents and have them put to death.
- All men will hate those who belong to Christ, but those who stand firm will be saved.

Additional Lessons From The Gospel Of Luke:
- Saints will be sent to prison.
- When brought to trial Christ will give His saints words and wisdom that none of their adversaries will be able to contradict.
- Saints will be betrayed by parents, brothers, relatives and friends, but not a hair of their head will perish.
- The saints must be careful, or their hearts will be weighed down with dissipation, drunkenness and anxieties of life, and the day will close on them unexpectedly like a trap. For it will come upon all those who live on the face of the whole earth.
- We must always be on the watch and pray that we may be able to escape all that is about to happen; to escape The Great Tribulation and stand before the Son of Man.

The lessons from the fig tree describe the "Season"
That will immediately precede the "Apostasy," the "Rebellion,"
That takes place in the "Church" of God;
That results in the "abomination that causes desolation;"
Then comes The Great Tribulation.
Every Christian will be able to know and understand this "Season".
Jesus says that the generation that experiences these "signs"
Will not pass away until The Great Tribulation occurs.

The "fig tree" is also representative of Israel as a nation.
The nation Israel, is at this time, "leafed out," from its former barrenness.

The Last Generation
We must understand that the generation Christ Jesus speaks about
Is the last generation, at the end of the 6,000 years of Scriptural history,

At a time when Israel has been reconstituted as a nation;
Which are the two prophetic requirements that set up the end times,
That have not been present ever before.

Then, that generation, is positioned for the end time events to occur in their life.
After The Battle of Armageddon, will come the day of rest,
The thousand year millennium,
Where God will rest from His 6,000 years of dealings with mankind.

Christ Jesus promised that the Holy Spirit will tell us what is yet to come.
(John 16:13)
The end time events will not take the The Bride of Christ, by surprise.

Many Will Come Claiming To Be The Christ
Christ Jesus says that during the "Season" that precedes The Great Tribulation
No one should believe anyone who says
That He can be found anywhere on the earth.
The return of Christ Jesus, His second coming, will be no mystery;
The heavens will be ablaze.
At the end of The Great Tribulation and before the Battle of Armageddon
He will come and the whole world will see Him.
At the trumpet call of God, He will come on the clouds with power and great glory;
Gathering his elect from heaven and earth.

The Gospel Of The Kingdom Preached To The Whole World
Christ Jesus says that the Gospel of the Kingdom of God
Will be preached to the whole world and then the end will come.
This may not entirely be done through the evangelism of the saints,
Because an angel is sent at the beginning of The Great Tribulation
To preach the gospel to every living person.
Every person on earth will have heard the gospel before the end comes.

The Abomination That Causes Desolation
Jesus says that,
So when you see standing in the holy place
The abomination that causes desolation,
Spoken of through the prophet Daniel--
Let the reader understand--
Then let those who are in Judea flee to the mountains. (Matthew 24:15)

14

The Time Of The END

- The Beast, the Antichrist, sets up his "image", "the abomination that causes desolation" in the holy place, the Church.
- This situation has been brought about by an apostasy and rebellion in the Church against God, brought about by the deception of the devil.
- This is the time when every living person must make a choice for Christ Jesus or for the devil.
- Then, after a brief period of time The Great Tribulation begins.

The Bride of Christ In The Desert

Christ Jesus gives a single brief description of the Bride of Christ in the desert, the "Woman" of Revelation 12:1:

Wherever there is a carcass, there the vultures will gather. (Matthew 24:28)

In other words wherever the body and blood of Christ are lifted up and celebrated, There the vultures, the eagles, the Bride of Christ will be gathered.

The Great Tribulation

Christ Jesus gives a description of The Great Tribulation:
For then there will be great distress,
Unequaled from the beginning of the world until now--
And never to be equaled again.
If those days had not been cut short, no one would survive,
But for the sake of the elect those days will be shortened. (Matthew 24:21-22)

Jerusalem will be trampled on by the Gentiles
Until the times of the Gentiles are fulfilled. (Luke 21:24)
[This passage parallels Revelation 11:2]

There will be signs in the sun, moon and stars.
On earth, nations will be in anguish and perplexity
At the roaring and tossing of the sea.
Men will faint from terror, apprehensive of what is coming on the world,
For the heavenly bodies will be shaken. (Luke 21:25-26)

If Those Days Had Not Been Shortened

Christ Jesus speaks of the unequaled distress of The Great Tribulation;
That if those days had not been shortened,
No one on earth would have remained living.
But for the sake of the elect those days were shortened.
I believe that it was because of the Bride of Christ (the elect) in the desert
That those days were shortened.
I say this because those days were not shortened for the saints who were beheaded;
They died for Christ.

The Time Of The END

The days were shortened for the elect, the Bride of Christ, living in the desert
As they were the only elect, still living on earth at that time, who would benefit.

False Prophets And False Christs Will Appear

During and just after the time that the Beast, the Antichrist
Sets up the "abomination that causes desolation"
And before the beginning of The Great Tribulation,
There will be false prophets and false Christs
Who will appear and perform great signs and miracles to deceive even the elect--
If that were possible (which it is not).
The signs and wonders are aimed at getting every living person to worship the Beast
And to receive his "mark."
Nevertheless, those who believe the Word of God,
Will understand what is happening and determine to die for Christ,
The only option for them at that time.

The Return of Christ Jesus

Just before The Battle of Armageddon
When Satan and the armies of the world are defeated,
Christ returns:

Immediately after the distress of those days (The Great Tribulation)
The sun will be darkened, and the moon will not give its light;
The stars will fall from the sky,
And the heavenly bodies will be shaken.

At that time the sign of the Son of Man will appear in the sky,
And all the nations of the earth will mourn.
They will see the Son of man coming on the clouds of the sky,
With power and great glory.
And he will send his angels with a loud trumpet call, and they will gather his elect
From the four winds, from one end of the heavens to the other.
(Matthew 24:29-31)

No One Knows The Day Or The Hour (Matthew 24:36-51)

No one knows about that day or hour,
Not even the angels in heaven, nor the Son, but only the Father.

As it was in the days of Noah, so it will be at the coming of the Son of Man.
For in the days before the flood, people were eating and drinking,
Marrying and giving in marriage, up to the day Noah entered the ark;
And they knew nothing about what would happen
Until the flood came and took them all away.
That is how it will be at the coming of the Son of man.

Two men will be in the field; one will be taken and the other left.
Two women will be grinding with a hand mill; one will be taken and the other left.

Therefore keep watch,
Because you do not know on what day your Lord will come.

But understand this: If the owner of the house had known
At what time of night the thief was coming,
He would have kept watch and would not have let his house be broken into.
So you also must be ready,
Because the Son of man will come at an hour when you do not expect him.

Who then is the faithful and wise servant,
Whom the master has put in charge of the servants in his household
To give them their food at the proper time?
It will be good for that servant whose master finds him doing so when he returns.
I tell you the truth, he will put him in charge of all his possessions.

But suppose that servant is wicked and says to himself,
'My master is staying away a long time,'
And he then begins to beat his fellow servants and to eat and drink with drunkards.
The master of that servant will come on a day when he does not expect him
And at an hour he is not aware of.
He will cut him to pieces and assign him a place with the hypocrites,
Where there will be weeping and gnashing of teeth.

Christ Jesus says that no one knows the day or the hour,
However, he has already said that we should recognize the "Season".

The warning of Christ Jesus:
Keep watch and be ready,
Because you do not know on what day your Lord will come.
The Word of God is an open book
And makes plain what the Lord requires for each of us to be ready.

Those who are not ready when He comes, will be cut to pieces,
And find themselves with the hypocrites,
Where there will be weeping and gnashing of teeth.

As It Was In The Days Of Noah
Christ Jesus says, that as it was in the days of Noah,
So it will be when He comes again.
In the days of Noah:
The Lord saw how great man's wickedness on the earth had become,
And that every inclination of the thoughts of his heart was only evil all the time.

The Time Of The END

The Lord was grieved that he had made man on the earth,
And his heart was filled with pain. (Genesis 6:5-6)

Now the earth was corrupt in God's sight and was full of violence.
God saw how corrupt the earth had become,
For all the people on earth had corrupted their ways.
So God said to Noah,'I am going to put an end to all people,
For the earth is filled with violence because of them.' (Genesis 6:11-13)

For most people The Time of the End will be like the days of Noah.
The worldly, godless people had no idea that the flood was coming.
They watched as Noah built the ark over a long period of time,
Just as people today watch God build His Church.
Noah preached to his generation,
Just as the Church of God preaches to this generation.
Worldly people will have no idea that the end is coming until it is upon them,
And The Great Tribulation begins.

One will be taken and one will be left;
One will be taken into the desert as part of the Bride of Christ,
And one will be left to endure the Tribulation.

THE PARABLE
OF THE TEN VIRGINS

Matthew 25:1-13

At that time the kingdom of heaven will be like ten virgins
Who took their lamps and went out to meet the bridegroom.
Five of them were foolish and five were wise.
The foolish ones took their lamps but did not take any oil with them.
The wise, however, took oil in jars along with their lamps.
The bridegroom was a long time in coming,
And they all became drowsy and fell asleep.

At midnight the cry rang out: 'Here's the bridegroom! Come out to meet him!'

Then all the virgins woke up and trimmed their lamps.
The foolish ones said to the wise, 'Give us some of your oil;
Our lamps are going out.'

'No,' they replied, 'there may not be enough for both us and you.
Instead, go to those who sell oil and buy some for yourselves.'

But while they were on their way to buy oil, the bridegroom arrived.
The virgins who were ready went in with him to the wedding banquet.
And the door was shut.

Later the others also came . 'Sir! Sir!' they said. 'Open the door for us!'

But he replied, 'I tell you the truth, I don't know you.'

Therefore keep watch, because you do not know the day or the hour.

This is a parable of The Time of the END; about "virgins," "oil" and "knowing."
The ten were all virgins; that is people washed in the blood of the Lamb; forgiven.
Which is the only way that any of us can become virgins in the eyes of God.
The virgins all had some oil in their lamps,
But the only the wise had enough in jars,
To sustain them for the extended period of time that would be required.
They all became drowsy and fell asleep.
At the announcement of the coming of the Bridegroom (Christ Jesus)
They all lit their lamps.

At that time, the foolish virgins realized that they did not have enough oil.
They were not prepared for the occasion.
They ask the wise virgins for some of their oil.

However, the wise refused
Because they said that they may not have enough for all of them.
The wise virgins tell the foolish ones to go and buy oil for themselves.

The foolish virgins go to buy oil.
In the meantime the Bridegroom arrives and there can be no delay;
The five virgins who were ready went in with Him and the door was shut.

Later the five foolish virgins came to the door
And implored the Bridegroom to let them in.
But He replied, that He did not "know" them.

They did not "know" Him because they had not allowed
Christ Jesus to write upon their hearts and upon their minds,
Because then, they would have "known" Him;
He would have been their teacher according to Jeremiah 31:31-34.
This "knowing" comes by Christ in us our teacher;
Putting His law in our minds and writing it upon our hearts;
It is the anointing, of The Anointed One that teaches us to "know" Him;
It is the oil, a type of the Holy Spirit; Christ in us the hope of glory.
Christ Jesus said,

Now this is eternal life:
That they may know you, the only true God,
And Jesus Christ, whom you have sent. (John 17:3)

The oil to the five virgins in this case was as critical
As "first love" was to the church of Ephesus.
It is a matter of spiritual LIFE or death before the Christ of God.

THE PARABLE OF THE TALENTS

Matthew 25:14-30
This parable concerns the status of three servants of Christ Jesus
At The Time of the END.

Again, it will be like a man going on a journey,
Who called his servants and entrusted his property to them.
To one he gave five talents of money,
To another two talents, and to another one talent,
Each according to his ability.
Then he went on his journey.
The man who had received the five talents
Went at once and put his money to work and gained five more.
So also, the one with the two talents gained two more.
But the man who had received the one talent went off,
Dug a hole in the ground and hid his master's money.

After a long time the master of those servants returned
And settled accounts with them.
The man who had received the five talents brought the other five.
'Master,' he said, 'you entrusted me with five talents.
See, I have gained five more.'

His master replied, 'Well done, good and faithful servant!
You have been faithful with a few things;
I will put you in charge of many things.
Come and share your master's happiness!'

The man with the two talents also came.
'Master,' he said, 'you entrusted me with two talents;
See, I have gained two more.'

His master replied, 'Well done, good and faithful servant!
You have been faithful with a few things;
I will put you in charge of many things.
Come and share your master's happiness!'

Then the man who had received the one talent came.
'Master,' he said, 'I knew that you are a hard man,
Harvesting where you have not sown
And gathering where you have not scattered seed.
So I hid your talent in the ground.
See, here is what belongs to you.'

His master replied, 'You wicked, lazy servant!

So you knew that I harvest where I have not sown
And gather where I have not scattered seed?
Well then, you should have put my money on deposit with the bankers,
So that when I returned I would have received it back with interest.

Take the talent from him and give it to the one who has the ten talents.
For everyone who has will be given more, and he will have an abundance.
Whoever does not have, even what he has will be taken from him.
And throw that worthless servant outside, into the darkness,
Where there will be weeping and gnashing of teeth.'

Christ Jesus on The Day of Pentecost poured out His Holy Spirit
On those who believed in Him,
And He has been doing that same thing from that time on;
Giving gifts to men:

Now to each one the manifestation of the Spirit is given for the common good.
To one there is given through the Spirit the message of wisdom,
To another the message of knowledge by means of the same Spirit,
To another faith by the same Spirit,
To another gifts of healing by that one Spirit,
To another miraculous powers,
To another prophecy,
To another the ability to distinguish between spirits,
To another the ability to speak in different kinds of tongues,
And to still another the interpretation of tongues.
All these are the work of one and the same Spirit,
And he gives them to each one, just as he determines. (1 Corinthians 12:4-11)

It is the intent of Christ Jesus
That each of His servants would receive his gift(s) (talent)
And use that gift(s) (talent) to bear fruit for the Kingdom of God.
Those who use their gift(s) (talent) as Christ intended are commended.
Those who do not use their gift(s) are condemned.

Christ Jesus said:

You did not choose me, but I chose you to go and bear fruit--
Fruit that will last. (John 15:16)

I am the true vine and my Father is the gardener.
He cuts off every branch in me that bears no fruit,
While every branch that does bear fruit he trims clean
So that it will be even more fruitful. (John 15:1-2)

THE PARABLE OF THE WEDDING BANQUET

Matthew 22:1-14

Jesus spoke to them again in parables, saying:
'The kingdom of heaven is like a king
Who prepared a wedding banquet for his son.
He sent his servants to those who had been invited to the banquet
To tell them to come, but they refused to come.

Then he sent some more servants and said,
'Tell those who have been invited that I have prepared my dinner:
My oxen and fattened cattle have been butchered, and everything is ready.
Come to the wedding banquet.'

But they paid no attention and went off—one to his field, another to his business.
The rest seized his servants, mistreated them and killed them.
The king was enraged.
He sent his army and destroyed those murderers and burned their city.

Then he said to his servants,
'The wedding banquet is ready but those I invited did not deserve to come.
Go to the street corners and invite to the banquet <u>anyone</u> *you find.'*
So the servants went out into the streets
And gathered all the people they could find, both good and bad,
And the wedding hall was filled with guests.
But when the king came into see the guests,
He noticed a man there who was not wearing wedding clothes.
'Friend,' he asked, 'how did you get in here without wedding clothes?'
The man was speechless.

Then the king told the attendants,
'Tie him hand and foot, and throw him outside, into the darkness,
Where there will be weeping and gnashing of teeth.

For many are invited, but few are chosen.'

God the Father has been inviting people to the wedding of His Son
From the beginning of time.
In the Old Testament, the people doing the inviting were the prophets of old.
The people invited were the people of God, but most of them refused to come.
The people of God mistreated and killed many of the prophets
That God sent to invite them.

The Time Of The END

John the Baptist came inviting the people of God to the wedding banquet,
And many came to him in the desert confessing their sins
Being baptized; cleansing themselves.
The ones who refused the invitation were the religious leaders of Israel.
John the Baptist was killed for standing for God.

Christ Jesus came inviting the people of God to His wedding banquet.
A few of the people of God received the invitation and received Christ.
However, the religious leaders did not receive their invitation;
They were jealous of Christ Jesus and were responsible for His death.

Because of their treatment of the Son of God;
Because they did not respond to the day of their visitation, their invitation;
Their religious rites were taken from them, their temple destroyed,
And they were dispersed to the nations until 1948.

Because the people of God refused the invitation to the wedding banquet
God sent evangelists to the Gentiles;
He sent them to the street corners, to people good and bad.
Because His wedding banquet hall will be filled.

Today, the Father continues to invite the people of God
And whosoever will come, to the wedding banquet.
However, there will be those to busy to come,
Too involved with the things of this world.
There will be those who resent those who invite them to come
And they will mistreat and kill them.

Nevertheless, the wedding banquet will take place,
And everyone who has a heart for God and His Son will be there.
They will have purchased wedding clothes.
They will be clothed in the righteousness of Christ.
No one will be allowed into the wedding banquet without wedding clothes.
In The Time of the END, just as in all preceding times,
Many will have been called, but few will be chosen.

NOT EVERYONE WHO SAYS LORD, LORD WILL ENTER THE KINGDOM OF HEAVEN

Matthew 7:21-23
Not everyone who says to me, 'Lord, Lord' will enter the kingdom of heaven,
But only he who does the will of my Father who is in heaven.
Many will say to me on that day,
'Lord, Lord, did we not prophesy in your name,
And in your name drive out demons and perform many miracles?'
Then I will tell them plainly, 'I never knew you.
Away from me you evil doers!'

Christ Jesus says that MANY will say to Him on that day,
'Lord, Lord, did we not prophesy in your name,
And in your name drive out demons and perform many miracles?'
Yet, the Christ of God will tell them that He never KNEW them,
And calls them EVIL DOERS.

This is one of the most shocking Scriptures in the Bible.
First of all there are not a few, but many in this condition.
These people are exercising gifts that can only be given by the Spirit of God.
They are prophesying, driving out demons, and performing miracles;
They are doing those things that the Scriptures admonish the saints to do.
Yet Christ Jesus does not KNOW them,
And calls them evil doers.

This Scripture teaches us that we can be saved,
Baptized (immersed) in the Spirit;
Christ can put His laws in our minds and write them on our hearts,
Which enables us to KNOW Him;
Yet we can FAIL to do His will.

This FAILURE has everything to do with motives.
If our motive in doing what Scripture calls us to do
Is not done solely out of love for and to please the Christ of God,
Then we are not doing the will of God, no matter what it is.
Doing the will of God is ultimately important.

Scripture teaches that the GIFTS and CALL of God are without repentance.
In other words God gives GIFTS and CALLINGS to men and women as He sees fit.
However, how they use these GIFTS and CALLINGS is in the hands of the person.
If these GIFTS and CALLINGS are not carried out

The Time Of The END

In LOVE for God and His people, then they are EVIL.

MOTIVE is everything.
If they are done to exalt the person or for monetary gain they are EVIL.

The GIFTS and CALLINGS of God must be done to exalt Christ alone;
They are from Christ, and must exalt Him only.
When they are done to exalt a person this is a LIE
And therefore, perverse and EVIL.

When the GIFTS and CALLINGS of God are used to exalt a person,
That person is following in the foot steps of Satan,
A created being who desires to be exalted and worshiped;
This is a LIE.
Everything he has was given to him by God,
Therefore, for him to take credit for attributes he was given by God,
Is a LIE, EVIL, and condemns that person to eternal death.

THE SHEEP AND THE GOATS

Matthew 25:31-46

Jesus said:

When the Son of Man comes in his glory, and all the angels with him,
He will sit on his throne in heavenly glory.
All the nations will be gathered before him,
And he will separate the people one from another
As a shepherd separates the sheep from the goats.
He will put the sheep on his right and the goats on his left.

Then the King will say to those on his right,
'Come you who are blessed by my Father;
Take your inheritance,
The kingdom prepared for you since the creation of the world.
For I was hungry and you gave me something to eat,
I was a stranger and you invited me in,
I needed clothes and you clothed me,
I was sick and you looked after me,
I was in prison and you came to visit me.'

Then the righteous will answer him,
'Lord, when did we see you hungry and feed you,
Or thirsty and give you something to drink?
When did we see you a stranger and invite you in,
Or needing clothes and clothe you?
When did we see you sick or in prison and go to visit you?'

The King will reply, 'I tell you the truth,
Whatever you did for one of the least of these my brothers of mine,
You did for me.'

Then he will say to those on his left,
'Depart from me, you who are cursed, into the eternal fire
Prepared for the devil and his angels.
For I was hungry and you gave me nothing to eat,
I was thirsty and you gave me nothing to drink,
I was a stranger and you did not invite me in,
I needed clothes and you did not clothe me,
I was sick and in prison and you did not look after me.'

They also will answer,
'Lord, when did we see you hungry or thirsty or a stranger
Or needing clothes or sick or in prison, and did not help you?'

He will reply, 'I tell you the truth,

The Time Of The END

Whatever you did not do for one of the least of these,
You did not do for me.'

Then they will go away to eternal punishment, but the righteous to eternal life.

This parable teaches the sobering reality
Of the love, righteousness and justice of God, the King.
It demonstrates that Christ Jesus completely identifies
With each of His created children, whether they know Him or not,
And all of their needs are of paramount importance to Him.

To supply the needs of others is to supply for Christ Jesus;
To ignore the needs of others is to ignore Christ Jesus Himself.

To be as selfless as Christ Jesus calls us to be, requires that we have His heart;
That we have Christ living inside of us;
That we have been crucified with Christ and no longer live,
But Christ lives in us;
That we do not belong to this world but to His Kingdom,
And we love His children as much as He does.

Christ Jesus is telling us that our eternal destination
Rests on the condition of our heart;
We must have His heart, nothing less will do.

ADMONISIONS OF CHRIST JESUS

(From the Book of Revelation)

"**Blessed** is the one who reads the words of this prophecy,
And **blessed** are those who hear it
And take to heart what is written in it,
Because the time is near."
(Revelation 1:3)

"Behold I am coming soon!
Blessed is he who keeps the words
Of the prophecy in this book."
(Revelation 22:7)

"Behold, I am coming soon!
My reward is with me,
And I will give to everyone according to what he has done.
I am the Alpha and the Omega,
The First and the Last, The Beginning and the End.

Blessed are those who wash their robes,
That they may have the right to the tree of life
And may go through the gates into the city.

I Jesus, have sent my angel
To give you this testimony for the churches.
I am the Root and the Offspring of David,
And the bright Morning Star."

The Spirit and the bride say, "Come!"
And let him who hears say, "Come!"
Whoever is thirsty, let him come;
And whoever wishes, let him take the free gift
The water of life.

I warn everyone who hears the words
Of the prophecy of this book:
If anyone adds anything to them,
God will add to him the plagues in this book.
And if anyone takes words away from this book of prophecy,
God will take away from him his share in the tree of life
And in the holy city, which are described in this book.
He who testifies to these things says,
"Yes, I am coming soon."
(Revelation 22:12-20)

OVERVIEW OF THE BOOK OF REVELATION

Many have viewed the Book of Revelation as a mystery
That few, if any, can understand.
However, Christ Jesus says:

"Blessed" is the one who reads the words of His prophecy.
And Blessed are those who hear it and take to heart what is written in it.

In other words, this book was definitely meant to be read and understood,
Because one cannot take to heart that which he does not understand.
Those who take into their heart what Christ Jesus says,
And apply it to their lives, they will be "Blessed."

The Book of Revelation is the revelation of Christ Jesus to the apostle, John,
For seven churches of that day and to the Church of Christ Jesus for all time.
It is also written to warn all mankind of what lies ahead,
Whether in their life time or not.

Christ Jesus said that He was coming soon,
And He has come soon to everyone who has ever lived.
The life span of each one of us is short
And then we all die and meet our Maker;
To eternal glory or eternal damnation.

He is also **COMING SOON** at the end of the ages.
He is coming to judge the people of the earth,
And to reward those who have been faithful to Him.

We have had approximately 6,000 years of Scriptural history.
We are about ready for the 1,000 year millennial rest,
Where Christ Jesus rules and reigns on earth for 1,000 years.

The apostle Peter said that to God a day is like a thousand years.
God created the earth in six days and rested on the seventh.
So God has worked with mankind for approximately six days, six thousand years,
And it is about time for His rest, for a thousand years,
The millennial reign of Christ.

The Book of Revelation is the revelation of Christ Jesus,
Revealing the condition of His Church at that time
And what will happen at the culmination of the history of mankind:

Christ Jesus Reveals the following:
Seven letters to seven churches in the time of the apostle John;

The Time Of The END

Five of which were in dire trouble, and two of which were commended.

The faithfulness of the "Church of Christ," the "Woman;" the Bride of Christ,
Against which, the gates of hell will not prevail,
And the rebellion of most of mankind against God and His Christ.

The "Woman," the end times Bride of Christ
Who ministers on earth, in the fullness of Christ for three and one half years,
Prior to The Great Tribulation
And then is taken into the desert and protected by God during The Great Tribulation.
At the end of The Great Tribulation she along with all the redeemed, marries Christ
And lives happily ever after with Him in Paradise.

The Harlot, Babylon, Satan's bride;
The personification of all those who reject God and His Christ;
Who indulge in every evil practice;
Reveling in the lust of the flesh, the lust of the eyes and the pride of life.
She is completely destroyed at the end of The Great Tribulation,
Along with all who follow her.

The fallen angel, Satan, the serpent, the dragon, the devil who's objective is
To seduce all of mankind into worshiping him,
And thereby causing them to reject God and seal their doom along with him.
Through his supernatural deception,
He succeeds in causing most of people of the world to follow him.
The only ones able to resist his deception are the followers of Christ;
Who, by Christ in them, and His supernatural enablement, reject this deception.
Satan and his fellow, fallen angels are finally thrown into the Lake of Fire by God
Where they live in eternal torment with all who followed them.

The nations of the world,
Every tribe, people and language, under the deception of Satan,
Worshiping Satan and his Beast and the "image" of the Beast;
Receiving his "mark" on their foreheads and hands;
The ultimate, and unforgivable rebellion against God.
The nations of the world finally come together to fight against Christ Jesus
At The Battle of Armageddon and are defeated
By the breath of His mouth and the brightness of His appearing.

The heart of God,
That every person would come to know Him,
Repent and receive the forgiveness that he offers.
The arms of God are open at this time to all who will receive His Christ;
Who will allow the blood of Christ Jesus to wash them clean;
Who will receive Christ Jesus, the Way, the Truth and the LIFE.

SYNOPSIS
OF THE BOOK OF REVELATION

THE REVELATION OF JESUS CHRIST (Revelation 1:1-20)
The Book of Revelation begins
With Christ Jesus sending an angel to the apostle John who is imprisoned
On the island of Patmos,
To reveal Himself in His glorified state;
And to tell him what will take place at The Time of the End.

SEVEN LETTERS TO SEVEN CHURCHES (Revelation 2, 3:1-22)
Christ Jesus gives John seven letters to seven churches
In which he describes their current condition
And exhorts them to repent of their misdeeds.
Only two of the seven are commended.
These letters represent the condition of the Church at that time,
And are also warnings for all future churches.

Jesus declares of Himself:

'I am the Alpha and the Omega,' says the Lord God,
'Who is, and who was, and who is to come, the Almighty.' *(Revelation 1:8)*

Christ Jesus is alive today and sits at the right hand of God in Heaven.
He was the One who came to the world as a baby in a stable at Bethlehem;
The One who ministered for three and one half years in Israel,
Healing the sick and raising the dead, in the power of the Holy Spirit;
The One who was himself, raised from the dead by God;
Who revealed Himself to many and then ascended into Heaven;
The One who promised to come again, soon.

John is then shown a scroll in the right hand of God.
The scroll contains the prophecy of The Time of The END.
The Lamb of God opens the scroll.

Within the Scroll, are the end time events
Which are not always in chronological order.
The following is what I believe the chronology to be:

The Chronology Of The Events
Preceding The Great Tribulation

THE THRONE IN HEAVEN (Revelation 4)
The awesome throne in Heaven is revealed to John.
He sees the twenty-four elders and the four living creatures
Who are continually giving glory to God.

THE SCROLL AND THE LAMB (Revelation 5)
John is shown a scroll in the hand of God
But no one in Heaven or earth is able to open it.
Then the Lamb of God, Christ Jesus, comes forth
As the only one who is able to open the scroll.

THE END TIMES MINISTRY OF THE BRIDE OF CHRIST
(Revelation 12)
The Bride of Christ is the "Woman" who ministers in the fullness of Christ,
For three and one half years prior to The Great Tribulation,
A mirror of the ministry of Christ Himself.
She confirms a covenant with Christ for seven years,
Three and one half years before The Great Tribulation,
And three and one half years in the desert,
After the worship of God is ended by the Beast (the Antichrist).
This is according to the prophecy of Daniel 9:27.

The MEASURING ROD (Revelation 1:1-2)
Prior to the beginning of The Great Tribulation,
The Apostle John is given a measuring rod to measure the temple of God,
The temple being the "Church" of God,
And the altar, and to count the worshipers there.
In other words, John is to determine by measure the portion of the Church
That is truly committed to Christ Jesus.
Those who have entered the Holy Place and the Holy of Holies.
But John is told to exclude the Outer Court; to not even measure it,
Because it has been given to the Gentiles, the non-believers,
Who will trample on it for three and one-half years,
The time of The Great Tribulation.
The Outer Court represents those who claim the name of Christ
But have not come to "know" Him.

THE WOMAN AND THE DRAGON (Revelation 12:1-17)
The Woman, The Bride of Christ, is pregnant by Christ
With the fruit of her ministry, a male child.
The dragon tries to kill the Woman's male child
But it is snatched up to Heaven.
The dragon then tries to kill the Woman
But she is given two wings of a great eagle

And taken into a desert place and protected by God.
Satan is cast out of Heaven and is enraged, knowing his time is short.
His first objective is to get ride of the rest of the off-spring of the Woman--
Those who obey God's commandments and hold to the testimony of Jesus;
Those who have remained in the Outer Court.

THE LAMB AND THE 144,000 (Revelation 14:1-5)

John looks and sees the Lamb (Christ Jesus) standing on mount Zion
And with Him are are 144,000
Who have his name and His Father's name on their foreheads.
They sing a new song no one else could learn.
They have kept themselves pure and have not defiled themselves with women.
They follow the Lamb wherever He goes.
The were purchased from among men
And offered as firstfruits to God and to the Lamb.
No lie is found in their mouths; they are blameless.
I believe that this is the male child, that was snatched up to God,
The firstfruits of the Bride of Christ in union with Christ Jesus.

144,000 SEALED (Revelation 7:1-8)

John sees four angels at the four corners of the earth,
Holding back the four winds of the earth
To prevent the wind from blowing on land or sea.
He calls to the angels given the power to harm the land and the sea,
And tells them not to harm anything
Until the seal of God is put on the foreheads of the servants of God.
Then 144,000 are sealed from the twelve tribes of Israel;
This is the Israel of God not simply natural Israel.
This is the male child of the "Woman" in Rev. 12 and Christ Jesus.

The Chronology Of Events
From The Beginning Of The Great Tribulation
To Its End

THE APOSTACY / THE REBELLION

The apostasy begins before and includes the time of the coming of the Beast
(the Antichrist).
The apostle Paul says that the Spirit of God says plainly
That in the last times some will abandon the faith
And follow deceiving spirits and things taught by demons. (1 Timothy 4:1-2)

The Time Of The END

In Daniel 8:10-14, Daniel also sees the apostasy that Paul speaks of;
Daniel calls it a rebellion.
It is a rebellion against Christ and His Word.
Because of this, God allows the Beast to stop the worship of God
(The daily sacrifice).
It is this rebellion that allows the Beast, the Antichrist, to place
The "abomination that causes desolation", which is his "image",
In the "Church" of God.
And require that all people worship this "image".

THE BEAST OUT OF THE SEA (Revelation 13:1-10)
John sees a Beast, the Antichrist coming out of the sea;
Out of the midst of the people of the world.
The Beast has ten horns and seven heads, with ten crowns on his horns,
And each head had a blasphemous name.
The dragon gives his power to the Beast.
The Beast has a fatal wound that is healed,
And the whole world is astonished by this apparent miracle and follows the Beast.

The Beast is given a mouth to utter proud words and blasphemies
And is given authority (by God) for three and one-half years.
He is given power to make war against the saints and to defeat them.
These are those in the Outer Court that John did not measure.
And he is given authority over every tribe, people, language and nation.
All the inhabitants of the earth will worship the Beast--
All those whose names have not been written in the Book of LIFE.

THE BEAST OUT OF THE EARTH,
THE FALSE PROPHET (Revelation 13:11-18)
John then sees another beast coming out of the earth.
He has two horns like a lamb, but he speaks like a dragon.
He has all the authority of the first Beast and acts on his behalf.
He makes the people of the earth worship the first Beast
Whose fatal wound was healed.
The False Prophet performs great and miraculous signs,
Causing fire to come down from heaven to earth that everyone can see.
Because of the signs he performs on behalf of the Beast,
He deceives the people of the earth.

The False Prophet orders people to set up an "image" in honor of the Beast
Who was fatally wounded by the sword yet lived.
He was given power to give breath to the "image",
So that it could speak and cause all who refused to worship the "image" to be killed.

He forces everyone, regardless of social or economic status

To receive a "mark" on his right hand or forehead,
So that no one can buy or sell unless he has the "mark" of the Beast.
This "mark" is the name of the Beast and the number of his name.
His number is 666.

THE ETERNAL GOSPEL PROCLAIMED (Revelation14:6-7)

Then John sees another angel flying in the air.
The angel loudly proclaims the eternal gospel
To all the people on the earth.
Every nation, tribe, and language.
He tells everyone to fear God and give Him glory
Because the time of His judgment is at hand.
He tells the people to worship Him who created all that is.
Every living person is given the opportunity to accept Christ Jesus
As their Savior and Lord.

WARNING AGAINST WORSHIPING THE BEAST OR RECEIVING HIS MARK (Revelation14:9-13)

John sees a third angel loudly warning everyone on earth
Not to worship the Beast or to receive his "mark."
He tells them that if they do so they will suffer the wrath of God.

THE TWO WITNESS (Revelation 11:3-14)

God places two witnesses in the street of Jerusalem,
Who prophesy for 1,260 days, three and one-half years,
The time of The Great Tribulation.
These two witnesses call down all the judgments of God upon the earth,
Just like God through Moses called down the plagues upon Egypt.

THE FIRST THROUGH THE SIXTH SEALS OPENED

THE LAMB OPENS THE FIRST SEAL (Revelation 6:1-2)

Christ Jesus is the rider on the white horse
With a bow and a crown,
Riding out as a conqueror bent on conquest.
Christ Jesus said that the gates of hell would not prevail against His Church.
He came to destroy the works of the devil, to set His people free.
He has been gathering His people to Himself since His resurrection;
Those who hear and respond to His voice.
This effort now intensifies in the three and one-half years
Prior to The Great Tribulation.

THE LAMB OPENS THE SECOND SEAL (Revelation 6:3-4)
The fiery red horse is given the power
To take peace from the earth.
From the time of the resurrection of Christ the world has had little peace.
This lack of peace intensifies until the beginning of The Great Tribulation
When there is no peace at all.

THE LAMB OPENS THE THIRD SEAL (Revelation 6:5-6)
As the Lamb opens the Third Seal, John sees a black horse.
Its rider is holding a pair of scales in his hand.
A voice declares, a days wages will only buy a quart of wheat
Or three quarts of barley.
God sends a famine upon the earth to all who have rejected His Christ.
The voice also says, do not touch the oil and the wine.
I believe that this means
That he is not to touch the Bride of Christ in the desert.

THE LAMB OPENS THE FOURTH SEAL (Revelation 6:7-8)
With the opening of the Fourth Seal John sees a pale horse.
Is rider is named Death, and Hades was close behind.
He is given the power to kill by sword, famine and plague,
And by the wild beasts of the earth.

THE LAMB OPENS THE FIFTH SEAL (Revelation 6:9-11)
As the Fifth Seal is opened John sees under the altar of God
The souls of those who have been slain up to and including the present time
Because of the Word of God and the testimony of their faithfulness to God.
The slain ask God,
How long before He judges the people of the earth for their treachery.
They are told it will be when the last of their brothers has been killed.

THE LAMB OPENS THE SIXTH SEAL (Revelation 6:12-17)
As the Lamb opens the Sixth Seal there is a great earthquake.
The sun turns black and the moon turns blood red.
The stars in the sky fall to the earth, like figs from a shaken tree.
The sky rolls up like a scroll,
And every mountain and island are removed from their places.

THE SEVENTH SEAL AND THE GOLDEN SENSOR (Revelation 8:1-5)
When the Seventh Seal is opened
There is silence in heaven for about half an hour.
John sees seven angels standing before God who are given seven trumpets.
Another angel who has a golden censer,
Comes and stands at the altar, before the throne.
The angel fills the censer with fire from the altar, and hurls it to the earth

This causes peals of thunder, rumblings, flashes of lightning and an earthquake.

THE TRUMPET JUDGMENTS (Revelation 8:6-13, 9:1-21)

The first angel sounds his trumpet, and there is hail and fire mixed with blood,
That is hurled down upon the earth.
A third of the earth and a third of the trees are burned up,
And all the green grass is burned up. (Revelation 8:6-7)

The second angel sounds his trumpet,
And what appeared to be a huge mountain,
On fire was thrown into the sea.
A third of the sea turned to blood,
A third of the sea creatures died,
And a third of the ships on the sea were destroyed. (Revelation 8:8-9)

The third angel sounds his trumpet, and a enormous star like a blazing torch,
Came from the sky and fell on a third of the rivers and springs of waters;
The name of the star is Wormwood.
A third of the waters turn bitter, and many people die from them.
(Revelation (8:10-11)

The fourth angel sounds his trumpet,
And a third of the sun and moon are struck, so that a third of them turns dark.
A third of daytime is now dark and also a third of the night. (Revelation 8:12-13)

As John continues to watch, he hears an angel in the sky calling out in a loud voice;
'Woe! Woe! To the people of the earth,
Because of the trumpet blasts about to be sounded by the next three angels!'

The fifth angel sounds his trumpet,
And John sees a star that has fallen from the sky to the earth.
The star is given the key to the shaft of the Abyss.
He opens the Abyss and smoke rises from it like a enormous furnace.
The sun and sky are darkened by the smoke.
Out of the smoke come locusts that descend upon the earth,
And they are given power similar to scorpions.
They were instructed not to harm the grass of the earth or any plant or tree,
But only people who do not have the seal of God on their foreheads.

The locusts are given the power to torture the people for five months
But not to kill them.
The pain inflicted on the people was like that of a scorpion sting.
During this time men seek death, but are unable to die.

The locust have the appearance of horses ready for battle.
They wore what looked like gold crowns on their heads,
And their faces were like those of humans.
Their hair was like a woman's and their teeth were like lions.
They wore breastplates of iron, and the sound of their wings
Was like the the thundering of horses and chariots rushing into battle.
Their tails had the sting of scorpions,
And they tormented the people for five months.
Their king was the angel of the Abyss.
His name in Hebrew is Abaddon, and in Greek, Apollyon. (Revelation 9:1-12)

The first woe is finished, but two more are about to come.

The sixth angel blew his trumpet,
And John hears a voice coming from the horns of the golden altar before God.
It says to the sixth angel, with the trumpet,
'Release the four (fallen) angels who are bound at the great river Euphrates.'
God had kept these four (fallen) angels for this exact hour, day, month and year,
To kill a third of the people of the earth.
Their were two hundred million mounted troops with them.

The horses and riders that John saw in his vision
Were fiery red, dark blue, and yellow like sulfur.
The heads of the horses were like the heads of lions;
Out of their mouths came fire, smoke and sulfur.

A third of mankind was killed by the three plagues of fire, smoke and sulfur.

The power of the horses was in their mouths and tails;
Their tails were like snakes with heads that inflict injury.
Even after seeing the terrible judgment of God upon the people and the earth,
Those who were not killed by the plagues would still not repent of their deeds;
They continued to worship demons,
And idols of gold and silver, bronze and stone and wood.
Idols that are merely the work of the hands of men, that cannot hear, see or walk.
They would not repent of their murders, magic arts, thefts
Or their sexual immorality. (Revelation 9:13-21)

THE ANGEL WITH THE LITTLE SCROLL (Revelation 10:1-11)
After this John sees another mighty angel coming down out of Heaven;
Robed in a cloud, with a rainbow above his head;
His face was like the sun, and His legs were like fiery pillars.
This is Christ Jesus who John saw in Revelation Chapter 1.
He held a little scroll open in His hand.

The Time Of The END

Christ Jesus says that there will be no more delay,
The mystery of God will be accomplished.
Just as has been foretold by Scripture.
John is told to eat the little scroll, which he does.
It is sweet in his mouth but turns his stomach sour;
Just as the promises of God are sweet to those who believe
But the judgment of God is an terrible for those who do not.

THE LAST SEVEN PLAGUES (Revelation 15)
Next come the last seven plagues.
John sees those who have been victorious over the Beast.
Then out of the temple come the seven angels with the last seven plagues.
They hold seven bowls filled with the wrath of God.
The temple is filled with smoke from the glory of God,
And no one can enter the temple until the seven plagues are completed.

THE SEVEN BOWLS OF GOD'S WRATH (Revelation 16)
The angels are told to pour out the seven bowls of God's wrath on the earth.

The first angel pours out his bowl and painful sores break out on those
Who have received the "mark" of the Beast. (Revelation 16:2)

The second angel pours out his bowl and the sea turns to blood
And every living thing in the sea dies. (Revelation 16:3)

The third angel pours out his bowl on the rivers and springs of water
And they be come blood.
The people of the earth have shed the blood of the saints of God
And God has given them blood to drink. (Revelation 16:4-7)

The fourth angel pours out his bowl on the sun
And this causes the sun to scorch people with fire.
The people curse the name of God, but refuse to repent. (Revelation 16:8-9)

The fifth angel pours out his bowl on the throne of the Beast
And darkness covers it.
Men gnaw their tongues in agony and curse the God of Heaven
Because of their pains and sores, but they refuse to repent. (Revelation 16:10-11)

The sixth angel pours out his bowl on the river Euphrates,
And this allows the kings from the East to cross it with their army.
Evil spirits come out of the mouth of the Beast and the False Prophet
And go to the kings of the earth, performing miraculous signs,
And gathers them to The Battle of Armageddon
The Great Day of God Almighty. (Revelation 16:12-16)

The seventh angel pours out his bowl
And a voice from the temple declares, "It is done!"
The city Babylon breaks into three parts
And the cities of the nations collapse.
One hundred pound hailstones crush the cities and their inhabitants,
And the people of the earth curse God. (Revelation 16:17-21)

THE TWO WITNESSES ARE KILLED AND COME BACK TO LIFE
(Revelation 11:7-14)
It is now the end of The Great Tribulation
And the two witnesses have finished their ministry.
For three and one half years they have represented God
And have called down from Heaven all the tribulations upon the earth and its people.
The Beast comes up from the Abyss and is allowed to kill them.
Their bodies lie in the street of Jerusalem for three and one-half days.
The people of the earth celebrate their deaths,
However, a voice comes out of Heaven and says: "Come Up Here!"
And the breath of life comes into them, they stand to their feet,
And rise up to Heaven in a cloud.
At the same time a severe earthquake shakes the city, Jerusalem.
A tenth of the city collapses, and seven thousand people are killed.

THE WOMAN ON THE BEAST (Revelation 17)
John is shown the "great prostitute," Babylon
Who has dominating influence over the peoples of the world.
He is told he will see her punishment,
Because she has committed adultery with the kings of the earth,
And the people of the earth are intoxicated with the wine of her adulteries.
John is taken away in the Spirit into a desert.
There he is shown the woman dressed like a queen
Sitting on a scarlet beast covered with blasphemous names.
She held a cup filled with abominable things, the filth of her adulteries.

She was drunk with the blood of God's saints, from the beginning of time, until now;
The blood of those whose lives were a testimony for Christ Jesus.
This title was written on her forehead:

MYSTERY BABYLON, THE MOTHER OF PROSTITUTES
AND OF THE ABOMINATIONS OF THE EARTH.

John was astonished at her sight.
The angel explains to John that this woman obtains her influence from
The Beast that comes out of the Abyss.
The Beast who the kings of the earth give their power and authority.
God allows them to have power and authority for one hour.

They use this power and authority to make war against the Lamb, Christ Jesus,
But the Lamb overcomes them, because He is the King of kings and Lord of lords.
The Beast and the kings of the earth come to hate the prostitute
And destroy her with fire, because God has put this in their hearts to do so.
The woman is the great city, Babylon, who rules over the kings of the earth;
The greatest city of the greatest nation on earth,
As she has always been throughout history;
Satan's harlot bride.
And she goes the way of all her predecessors, all the "Babylons" before her;
Complete destruction, by the hand of God.
God has told His people earlier, to come out of her.

THE FALL OF BABYLON (Revelation 18)

John sees another angel come down out of Heaven declaring the fall of Babylon.
She boasted that she was a queen and would never be a widow.
But now she is totally destroyed, never to rise again.
In one hour she has come to nothing.

There was **never** a city like this city, and who lived in such luxury;
Who exerted such power over all the rulers and people of the earth.
On her hands is the blood of the prophets and the saints
And all who have been killed on the earth.

THE RIDER ON THE WHITE HORSE (Armageddon)

(Revelation19:11-21)
Heaven opens and John sees a white horse.
It's rider is called Faithful and True and whose name is the Word of God.
The nations of the world have gathered to fight against Him,
Under the deception of the Beast;
But He strikes them down with the sword of His mouth,
And the carnivorous birds then gorge themselves on their flesh.

THE SEVENTH TRUMPET (Revelation 11:15-19)

The seventh angel sounds his trumpet and voices in Heaven declare:
"The kingdom of the world has become the kingdom of our Lord
And of His Christ.
And He will reign forever and ever."
The Great Tribulation is over with the sounding of the Seventh Trumpet;
With the defeat of Satan and the kings of the earth at The Battle of Armageddon;
With the fall of Babylon The Great Prostitute.

THE GREAT MULTITUDE IN WHITE ROBES (Revelation 7:9-17)

John sees a great multitude that no one could count,
Standing before the throne of God and before the Lamb.

They are from every nation, tribe, people and language.
They are wearing white robes and holding palm branches, and praising God.
John asks the angel who they are,
And he is told that they are those who have come out of The Great Tribulation.
They have washed their robes in the blood of the Lamb.
Christ Jesus leads them to springs of Living Water,
And they serve Him day and night, forever.

THE WEDDING SUPPER OF THE LAMB (Revelation 19:7)
All of Heaven rejoices because Christ Jesus now rules and reigns on the earth.
The thousand years of rest, the millennium,
Begins with the wedding supper of the Lamb,
For His Bride has made herself ready.
The Bride includes the saints of all ages.

SATAN IS BOUND FOR A THOUSAND YEARS (Revelation 20:1)
A mighty angel comes down out of Heaven, seizes Satan,
And binds him with chains in the Abyss for a thousand years.

CHRIST RULES AND REIGNS FOR A THOUSAND YEARS
(Revelation 20:4-5)
The dead in Christ rise,
Those who's names are contained in the Lambs Book of LIFE,
And they rule and reign with Him for a thousand years.

SATAN'S DOOM (Revelation 20:7-10)
At the end of the thousand years Satan is released for a short time.
He proceeds to deceive the nations and to gather them against God
And to surround His City.
However, fire from Heaven comes down and destroys Satan
And all those who followed him.
He is then thrown into the Lake of Fire, forever.

THE DEAD ARE JUDGED (Revelation 20:11-15)
John sees a white throne and Him who sits on it.
He sees the dead of all social status, standing before the throne,
And the books were opened.
Another book was opened, the Book Of LIFE.
The dead are judged according to what they had done as recorded in the books.
Those whose names were not found in the Lamb's Book Of LIFE
Were thrown into the Lake of Fire, the second and final death.

THE NEW JERUSALEM (Revelation 21)

At the end of the thousand years
God creates a new Heaven and a new earth.
The first heaven and the first earth have passed away.
The Holy City, the New Jerusalem comes down out of Heaven as a Bride
Dressed beautifully for her Husband.
And Christ Jesus and His Bride live happily ever after.

THE RIVER OF LIFE (Revelation 22:1-6)

The angel shows John the River of LIFE, crystal clear,
Flowing from the throne of God,
Down the middle of the great street of the City of God.
The River nourishes the Tree of LIFE on each side of the River.
The leaves of the Tree are for the healing of the nations.
All of the saints in Heaven have drunk the Water of LIFE,
From the River of LIFE.

JESUS COMING SOON! (Revelation 22:7-21)

The Book of Revelation ends with Christ Jesus declaring that He is coming soon!
He says that His reward for the faithful is with Him,
And that those will be blessed who keep the words of His prophecy.
Blessed are those who wash their robes in the blood of the Lamb
And have the right to the Tree of LIFE.
Whoever is thirsty, let him take the free gift of the Water of LIFE.

THE REVELATION OF JESUS CHRIST

Prologue - Revelation 1:1-3
The revelation of Jesus Christ, which God gave him
To show his servants what must soon take place.
He made it known by sending his angel to his servant John,
Who testifies to everything he saw--
That is, the word of God and the testimony of Jesus Christ.

Blessed is the one who reads the words of this prophecy,
And blessed are those who hear it
And take to heart what is written in it,
Because the time is near.

Christ Jesus came to the apostle John for the specific purpose
Of telling him what must soon take place.
He did not want any of His servants to be in doubt
As to what would happen when they died.
And what would happen when God wrapped up "Time"--
When "Time" came to an END.

Soon, of course, was much longer than many expected;
It was the apostle Peter who said that to the Lord,
A day was like a thousand years.
We have had approximately 6,000 years of Scriptural history.
Just as in "Creation" God worked for six days and rested the seventh,
So God is about to rest from His dealings with mankind.
The sixth day of his dealing with mankind is about over.
So that when Christ Jesus was speaking with John,
He saw that only two days, two thousand years, were left until His return,
Which was to Him, soon.

Many have viewed the Book of Revelation as a mystery
That few if any can understand.
However, Christ Jesus says:

"Blessed" is the one who reads the words of His prophecy.
And "Blessed are those who hear it and take to heart what is written in it."
In other words, this book was definitely meant to be read and understood,
Because one cannot take to heart that which he does not understand.
Those who take into their heart what Christ Jesus says,
And apply it to their lives, they will be "Blessed."

46

Greetings and Doxology – Revelation 1:4-5
John, to the seven churches in the province of Asia:
Grace and peace to you from him who is, and who was, and who is to come,
And from Jesus Christ, who is the faithful witness,
The firstborn from the dead,
And the ruler of the kings of the earth.

Christ Jesus, through the apostle John is addressing His revelation
To the seven churches in the province of Asia:

John pronounces grace and peace to the churches
From the only person who can grant those things, Christ Jesus.
The One who is, and who was, and who is to come.
The Self-Existent One, who came as The Christ, who is coming again, soon;
Who is the sevenfold Spirit of God, seated on His Throne.

Christ Jesus is the faithful witness, the embodiment of God,
God In the flesh, the perfect revelation of God,
Who revealed the character and nature of God to the world;
The Christ, The Messiah, The Anointed One.

Christ Jesus is the firstborn from the dead;
The first person to die and go to Heaven.

Christ Jesus is the ruler of the kings of the earth.
Satan and all of his realm can do nothing without permission from Christ Jesus.

Love Is The Motivation Of Christ – Revelation 1:5-6
To Him who loves us and has freed us from our sins by his blood,
And made us to be a kingdom and priests to serve his God and Father--
To Him be glory and power for ever and ever! Amen.

Everything that Christ Jesus has done from the beginning
Is out of His love for His people, His Bride.
He was slain from the foundation of the earth;
Before creation took place,
He knew the price that He would have to pay to redeem His Bride.
It would cost Him His life,
Because the only thing that could redeem His Bride was His own blood.

After Adam and Eve fell from the grace of God
All humankind was born into sin
And the only effective agent that could wash away this sin
Was the blood of the only sinless One, Christ Jesus.
Those who allow Christ Jesus to wash away their sins

The Time Of The END

Are brought into the everlasting Kingdom of God;
They are made to be priests in that Kingdom;
To serve the One true God and Father of all.
To Him there is glory and power for ever and ever! Amen.
As there has been from eternity past.

He Is Coming Again On The Clouds – Revelation 1:7

Look, he is coming with the clouds,
And every eye will see him,
Even those who pierced him;
And all the peoples of the earth will mourn because of him.
So shall it be! Amen.

He will come again on the clouds,
And every person on earth will see Him
All those who pierced Him with their sin.
The whole world will mourn when they see Him
Because it is too late to repent and they know their destination.
This is the unfortunate way that it will be at The Time of the END.

Christ Jesus Is The Alpha and The Omega, The Beginning And The End – Revelation 1:8

'I am the alpha and the Omega,' says the Lord God,
'Who is, and who was, and who is to come, the Almighty.'

Christ Jesus is the beginning of all things as Creator
And the end of all things pertaining to earth as Judge;
Who came as a helpless child;
Who revealed the glory of God as the Christ;
Who is coming again at the end of the age to wrap up "Time;"
The Almighty.

One Like a Son of Man – Revelation1:1-20)

I, John, your brother and companion in the suffering
And kingdom and patient endurance that are ours in Jesus,
Was on the island of Patmos because of the word of God and the testimony of Jesus.

*On the Lord's Day **I was in the Spirit**,*
And I heard behind me a loud voice like a trumpet, which said:

'Write on a scroll what you see and send it to the seven churches:
To Ephesus, Smyrna, Pergamum, Thyatira, Sardis, Philadelphia and Laodicea.'

I turned around to see the voice that was speaking to me.

The Time Of The END

And when I turned I saw seven golden lampstands,
And among the lampstands was someone 'like a son of man,'
Dressed in a robe reaching down to his feet
And with a golden sash around his chest.
His head and hair were white like wool, as white as snow,
And his eyes were like blazing fire.
His feet were like bronze glowing in a furnace,
And his voice was like the sound of rushing waters.
In his right hand he held seven stars,
And out of his mouth came a sharp double-edged sword.
His face was like the sun shining in all its brilliance.

When I saw him, I fell at his feet as though dead.
Then he placed his right hand on me and said:
'Do not be afraid.
I am the First and the Last.
I am the Living One;
I was dead, and behold I am alive for ever and ever!
And I hold the keys of death and Hades.

Write, therefore, what you have seen,
What is now and what will take place later.

The mystery of the seven stars that you saw in my right hand
And of the seven golden lampstands is this:

'The seven stars are the angels of the seven churches,
And the seven lampstands are the seven churches.'
(Revelation 1:1-20)

Christ Jesus reveals this great revelation to the apostle John.
John, a companion in suffering with all the Church of Christ.
The Church which is part of God's Kingdom;
Those, who with patient endurance live for Christ in a wicked world.

John was a prisoner on the island of Patmos
Because he defended the Word of God and testified for Jesus.
There are always consequences for standing for Christ,
In a world controlled by the devil.

On the Lord's Day, John was in the Spirit;
Caught-up in the Spirit, so that the natural world around him disappeared.
In this state he hears behind him a loud voice like a trumpet,
Which told him to write letters to seven churches.

When he turned around to see who was speaking to him,

The Time Of The END

THE REVELATION OF JESUS CHRIST

He sees seven golden lampstands
And among the lampstands someone who looked in form like a normal man.
However, he was supernatural in every other respect.
He had a robe that reached down to His feet
And a golden sash around His chest, speaking of His Kingship.
His head and hair were white, speaking of the holiness of God.
And His eyes were like blazing fire, the all consuming fire of God;
All seeing and meaning certain judgment for sin.
His feet were like bronze glowing in a furnace,
Speaking of His ultimate power and authority.
His voice was like the sound of rushing waters,
Like the sound of the River of LIFE that flows continually from the throne of God;
Like the sound of standing near Niagara Falls.

Christ Jesus holds His Church leaders in His right hand
From which no one can remove them.
Out of His mouth comes a sharp double-edged sword,
Speaking of the absolute Truth of the Word of God.
His face was like the sun shining in all its brilliance;
Speaking of the absolute holiness of God.

When John sees the risen Christ, he falls to the ground as though dead;
The manifest presence of God is overwhelming, rendering him powerless.
No one can stand in His presence, unless He allows it.

Christ Jesus stabilizes John by placing his right hand on him
And tells John not to be afraid.
Christ Jesus tells John that He is the First and the Last,
The Self-Existent One, the Eternal One, with no beginning and no end.
He says that He is the Living One,
The One from whom all LIFE emanates.
He died for the sins of all mankind but is now alive forever.
Christ Jesus holds the keys of death and Hades;
He determines who lives and who dies, who goes to heaven and who goes to hell,
Based on His all knowing, perfect love;
Who desires that every person choose the LIFE He offers.

John is told to write down what he has seen,
What is currently taking place, and what will take place later.
Christ Jesus tells John that the seven stars
Are the "angels," or leaders of the seven churches,
And the seven lampstands are the seven churches.

TO THE CHURCH IN EPHESUS

Revelation 2:1-7

To the angel of the church in Ephesus write:

These are the words of him who holds the seven stars in his right hand
And walks among the seven golden lampstands:

I know your deeds, your hard work and your perseverance.
I know that you cannot tolerate wicked men,
That you have tested those who claim to be apostles but are not,
And have found them false.
You have persevered and have endured hardships for my name,
And have not grown weary.

Yet I hold this against you:
You have forsaken your first love.
Remember the height from which you have fallen!

Repent and do the things you did at first.
If you do not repent, I will come to you and remove your lampstand from its place.
But you have this in your favor:
You hate the practices of the Nicolaitans, which I also hate.

He who has an ear, let him hear what the Spirit says to the churches.
To him who overcomes, I will give the right to eat from the tree of life,
Which is in the paradise of God.

Christ Jesus tells John to write to the leader of the church in Ephesus;
That it is He who holds the church leaders in His hand,
And walks among the churches.

He tells the Ephesus church leader the things that the church is doing right:
They have worked hard and have persevered;
They cannot tolerate wicked men;
They have tested those who claim to be apostles but are not,
And have found them liars.
They have persevered and have endured hardships for Christ Jesus,
And have not grown weary;
They hate the practices of the Nicolaitans,

However, Christ Jesus holds this against them:

You have forsaken your first love!

He tells them to remember the height from which they have fallen!

The Time Of The END

Repent and do the things you did from the first,
When they first came to know Him.

The relationship between Christ Jesus and His Church
Is an intimate personal relationship;
It is a love affair, and not a relationship of simply works!
It is like the relationship between a man and a woman when it is as God intended.
It is like the exhilaration that young lovers have when they first fall in love;
Mind, soul and spirit, they are consumed with love for each other;
It is all they can think and talk about.
They long to be with the other person, to be apart is a hardship.
They have intimate and wonderful conversations about everything under the sun.
They trust and rely upon each other;
They are honest and transparent with each other.
Christ Jesus is saying to the church in Ephesus,
This is what you have lost and must regain, if you are to belong to Me.

Then He issues a sever warning:
If they do not repent, He will come and remove their lampstand from its place;
They will be removed from the Kingdom of God, and from before His throne,
Which is where the lampstands of all God's churches reside.
We understand from this that "first love" is of ultimate importance.

Christ Jesus then tells them that they have in their favor
That they hate the practices of the Nicolaitans,
Who think they can live in their worldliness and idolatry
And still belong to Him.

He tells the church at Ephesus, if you have an ear, hear what I am telling you.
To those who hear, respond and overcome this world and its ways;
Which are dominated by the deception of Satan,
He will give the right to eat from the Tree of LIFE
Which is nourished by the River of LIFE, that contains the Water of LIFE,
That can only be found in the Paradise of God.

Today, we must have ears that hear what the Spirit is saying to us.
Only by our diligence will we maintain the fervency of our first love for Christ;
Only by allowing Christ to live in and through us.
We must hate what Christ hates.
Then we will maintain our lampstand before the throne of God.
Then we will have the right to eat from the Tree of LIFE.

TO THE CHURCH IN SMYRNA

Revelation 2:8-11

To the angel of the church in Smyrna write:

These are the words of him who is the First and the Last,
Who died and came to life again.
I know your afflictions an your poverty--
Yet you are rich!
I know the slander of those who say they are Jews and are not,
But are a synagogue of Satan.
Do not be afraid of what you are about to suffer.
I tell you, the devil will put some of you in prison to test you,
And you will suffer persecution for ten days.
Be faithful, even to the point of death,
And I will give you the crown of life.

He who has an ear, let him hear what the Spirit says to the churches.
He who overcomes will not be hurt at all by the second death.

The church in Smyrna is afflicted
By those who claim to belong to Christ but do not.
It is a fact that the true church is always afflicted by the false church,
Just as it was in the time of Christ.
The church in Smyrna is being slandered by the church of Satan
That pretends to be a church of Christ Jesus.
They are in poverty, yet are rich in God.
They are going to suffer at the hand of the false church and be put in prison,
But if they are faithful, even to the point of being killed,
They will receive the crown of LIFE and avoid eternal death.

Today, we also must have ears that hear what the Spirit is saying to us.
We must remember that the only entity
That stands in the way of Satan's complete domination of the world
Is the Church of Christ Jesus.
Because of this, the Church is the focus of Satan's deception,
The rest of the whole world belongs to him.
The synagogue of Satan, the false church,
Believes that it represents God, but it is deceived, just as it was in the time of Christ.
It believes it can embrace God and the world at the same time, which it cannot.
The Church of Christ Jesus today faces the same trial,
There is nothing new under the sun.
The human condition, in the natural, is one boring repetition after another,
Of mankind rejecting God and His Christ, under the deception of Satan.
The result is hell for all, but those who receive Christ Jesus and live for Him.

TO THE CHURCH IN PERGAMUM

Revelation 2:12-17

To the angel of the church in Pergamum write:

These are the words of him who has the sharp, double-edged sword.
I know where you live—where Satan has his throne.
Yet you remain true to my name,
You did not renounce your faith in me,
Even in the days of Antipas, my faithful witness,
Who was put to death in your city—where Satan lives.

Nevertheless, I have a few things against you:
You have people there who hold to the teaching of Balaam,
Who taught Balak to entice the Israelites to sin by eating food sacrificed to idols
And by committing sexual immorality .
Likewise you also have those who hold to the teaching of the Nicolaitans.
Repent therefore!
Otherwise, I will soon come to you and will fight against them
With the sword of my mouth.

He who has an ear, let him hear what the Spirit says to the churches.
To him who overcomes, I will give some of the hidden manna.
I will also give him a white stone with a new name written on it,
Known only to him who receives it.

The sharp double-edged sword is the Word of God, who is Christ Jesus
The impeccable judge of all things.

The church of Pergamum is in the city where Satan resides and has his throne.
In spite of this, the church of Pergamum has remained true to Christ Jesus,
Even though their leader was put to death by Satan's emissaries,
The false church.

However, within the Pergamum church, there are those deceived,
Who hold to the teaching of Balaam
And are involved in idol worship and sexual immorality.
Some also, are involved with the teaching of the Nicolaitans
And their idol worship and worldliness.
Christ Jesus warns them that unless they repent,
He will come and fight against them,
Revealing them for what they are.
Christ Jesus calls for those of us who have an ear,
To hear what He is saying to the churches.
Those who overcome the deception of Satan,
Will receive some of the hidden manna, the Bread of LIFE.

The Time Of The END

They will also receive a white stone with a new name written on it,
Known only to him who receives it.
The white stone represents the holiness that Christ Jesus imparts to His own;
The new name is symbolic of the intimate and personal relationship
Between each saint and Christ Jesus.
Each of us will have a name (a nick name given us by Christ),
That is only known by Christ and ourselves.

Today, there are those who believe they can follow Christ Jesus
And do as they please
From the very beginning of the Church
There have been those claim they can live as they please
And remain in the favor of God.
This, is of course, a lie from the deception of the devil.

TO THE CHURCH IN THYATIRA

Revelation 2:18-29

To the angel of the church in Thyatira write:

These are the words of the Son of God, whose eyes are like blazing fire
And whose feet are like burnished bronze.
I know your deeds, your love and faith, your service and perseverance,
And that you are now doing more than you did at first.

Nevertheless, I have this against you:
You tolerate that woman, Jezebel, who calls herself a prophetess.
By her teaching she misleads my servants into sexual immorality
And the eating of food sacrificed to idols.

I have given her time to repent of her immorality, but she is unwilling.
So I will cast her on a bed of suffering,
And I will make those who commit adultery with her suffer intensely,
Unless they repent of her ways.

I will strike her children dead.
Then all the churches will know that I am he who searches hearts and minds,
And I will repay each of you according to your deeds.

Now I say to the rest of you in Thyatira,
To you who do not hold to her teaching
And have not learned Satan's so called deep secrets
(I will not impose any other burden on you):
Only hold on to what you have until I come.

To him who overcomes and does my will to the end,
I will give authority over the nations--

He will rule them with an iron scepter;
He will dash them to pieces like pottery--

Just as I have received authority from my Father.
I will also give him the morning star.
He who has an ear, let him hear what the Spirit says to the churches.

Christ Jesus says to the leader of the church of Thyatira,
That His words are the words of the Son of God,
Whose all seeing eyes blaze with His holiness;
Who's feet are like burnished bronze,
Speaking of His absolute power and authority.

The Time Of The END

Christ Jesus tells them He knows everything they have done and continue to do,
That they are now doing more that ever before.

However, in their midst of the church is a woman, Jezebel
(A Satan deceived, rebellious woman)
Who the church has allowed a place of authority;
Who claims and pretends to be a prophetess;
Who is misleading His servants into sexual immorality and idol worship.
Christ Jesus has given her a time to repent, but she refuses.
She is about to be afflicted with great suffering,
Along with all those who have committed adultery with her.
Christ Jesus will strike her children (those who have followed her teaching) dead,
To let all the churches know that He searches hearts and minds
And repays each person according to what they have done.

Christ Jesus says to those who have not been seduced by Jezebel
And who have not involved themselves with her teaching
And Satan's so called deep secrets
(Satan always pretends to have something more than God),
He will not impose any other burden on them.
He tells them to hold on to what they have (the WAY, the TRUTH and the LIFE),
Until He comes for them.

Those who overcome the deception of Satan and do the will of Christ,
Will be given the authority of Christ over the nations,
They will rule them with an iron scepter (the absolute power and authority of Christ),
They will dash them to pieces like pottery
(The nations will be rendered absolutely powerless and submissive
Because of presence of Christ in the people of God).

Christ Jesus says that just as He received authority from His Father,
He is going to give that same authority to His people.
He is also going to give the Morning Star, which is Himself, Christ in us.
All of us who have an ear, let us hear what the Spirit (Christ)
Says to each one of us and to every church that claims His name.

Today, like the church in Thyatira, we must persevere.
We must not be mislead by false prophets within the Church.
We must avoid even the appearance of what is not acceptable to God.
We also, will be rewarded for what we have done whether good or bad.
We can overcome by the power of Christ in us
And rule and reign with Christ when He comes.

TO THE CHURCH IN SARDIS

Revelation 3:1-6

To the angel of the church in Sardis write:

These are the words of him who holds the seven spirits of God and the seven stars.
I know your deeds;
You have a reputation of being alive, but you are dead.
Wake up! Strengthen what remains and is about to die,
For I have not found your deeds complete in the sight of my God.
Remember, therefore, what you have received and heard;
Obey it, and repent.
But if you do not wake up,
I will come like a thief, and you will not know at what time I will come to you.

Yet you have a few people in Sardis who have not soiled their clothes.
They will walk with me, dressed in white, for they are worthy.

He who overcomes will, like them, be dressed in white.
I will never erase his name from the book of life,
But will acknowledge his name before my Father and his angels.
He who has an ear, let him hear what the Spirit says to the churches.

Christ Jesus embodies the seven fold Spirit of God,
He holds the angels, the leaders of His church, in His hands.
He knows the deeds of the church in Sardis, which is thought to be alive
By those who look through the eyes of man;
But in reality, in the eyes of God, they are dead.

Christ Jesus tells them to wake up,
And strengthen what remains and is about to die.
He does not find their deeds complete in the eyes of God.
He tells them to remember what they have received and heard;
To repent, of their current situation
And obey what they have received and heard.
If they do not, He warns them that He will come like a thief;
They will not know when He will come.

The few saints in Sardis who have not soiled their clothes
By disobeying what they have received and heard,
Will walk with Christ, dressed in white (His righteousness) for they are worthy.
All those who overcome the deception of Satan,
Will be like them, dressed in white;
Their names will never be erased from the Book of LIFE,
And Christ Jesus will acknowledge their names before His Father and His angels.
All of us who have an ear, let us hear what the Spirit (Christ) says to the churches.

The Time Of The END

Today, each one of us must be alive in and to God;
We must have zeal and fervency toward God;
The Scriptures teach that Christ's zeal for God consumed Him;
That the Kingdom of God is apprehended by forceful men and women,
Who have set their hearts and minds to please Christ Jesus.
We must obey what we have received and heard.
If we do not, we will be surprised by the coming of Christ.
If we are not prepared to meet Him, there will be terrible consequences.
Yet, all we have to do, is to continue to drink of His Living Water,
Continue to put our faith, hope and trust in Him.
To love Him with all our heart, soul, mind and strength.
Then He belongs to us and we belong to Him
And we can live in the peace of God that passes all human understanding.

TO THE CHURCH IN PHILADELPHIA

Revelation 3:7-13

To the angel of the church in Philadelphia write:

These are the words of him who is holy and true,
Who holds the key of David.
What he opens, no one can shut;
And what he shuts, no one can open.

I know your deeds.
See, I have placed before you an open door that no one can shut.
I know that you have little strength,
Yet you have kept my word and have not denied my name.
I will make those who are of the synagogue of Satan,
Who claim to be Jews though they are not, but liars--
I will make them come and fall down at your feet
And acknowledge that I have loved you.
Since you have kept my command to endure patiently,
I will also keep you from the hour of trial
That is going to come upon the whole world
To test those who live on the earth.

I am coming soon.
Hold on to what you have, so that no one will take your crown.
He who overcomes I will make a pillar in the temple of my God.
Never again will he leave it.
I will write on him the name of my God
And the name of the city of my God, the new Jerusalem,
Which is coming down out of heaven from my God;
And I will also write on him my new name.

He who has an ear, let him hear what the Spirit says to the churches.

Christ Jesus is holy and true and holds the key of David
(The key to the throne of David, the key to Heaven).
He has the absolute authority over what is shut and what is open.
When He shuts something, it is shut and no one can open it,
And when He opens something, it is open, and no one can shut it.
He holds the keys to death, hell and the grave,
By His perfect knowledge, He determines who goes to Heaven and who goes to hell.

He knows the deeds of the church at Sardis and of every church today.
For the church at Sardis, He has placed before them, an open door
That no one can shut, even though they have little strength,
Because they have kept His Word and have not denied His name.

The Time Of The END

Christ Jesus is going to make those who are of the synagogue of Satan,
Who claim to be Jews (Christians) though they are not, but liars;
He is going to make the liars fall down at the feet of the saints
And acknowledge that He loved them.

Because the saints have kept His command to endure patiently,
Christ Jesus is going to keep them from the hour of trial
That is going to come upon the whole world to test those who live on the earth.

[All of a sudden Christ Jesus has jumped to the end of "Time,"
And is talking about The Great Tribulation;
The hour of TRIAL that is going to TEST the whole earth.
This is a promise that those who are true to Him
Will not go through The Great Tribulation.]

Christ Jesus says again, He is coming soon.
He warns His saints to hold on to what they have,
So that no one will take their crown.
If we follow Christ according to His Word, no one can take our crown.
However, we can give away our crown if we give in to the deception of Satan.

Christ Jesus promises that those who overcome,
He will make a pillar in the temple of His God,
Never to leave it for all eternity.
He will write on each saint the name of His God
And the name of the City of His God, the New Jerusalem,
Which will come out of Heaven from God.
Each saint will also have the new name of Christ Jesus written upon him.
Those of us who have an ear, let us hear what the Spirit is saying to His church.

Today, Christ Jesus offers each one of us an open door that no one can shut.
We too must resist the false church,
Those who claim to belong to Christ but do not.
We are near to the end of "Time,"
And many of us will be alive when the TRIAL comes upon the earth.
If we are faithful to Christ Jesus we can rest in His peace, without fear.
We can be a pillar in the temple of God
And have His new name written upon us.

TO THE CHURCH IN LAODICEA

Revelation 3:14-22

To the angel of the church of Laodicea write:

These are the words of the Amen, the faithful and true witness,
The ruler of God's creation.
I know your deeds, that you are neither cold nor hot.
I wish you were either one or the other!
So, because you are lukewarm—neither hot nor cold--
I am about to spit you out of my mouth.

You say, 'I am rich, I have acquired wealth and do not need a thing.'
But you do not realize that you are wretched, pitiful, poor, blind and naked.
I counsel you to buy from me gold refined in the fire, so you can become rich;
And white clothes to wear, so you can cover your shameful nakedness;
And slave to put on your eyes, so you can see.

Those whom I love I rebuke and discipline.
So be earnest, and repent.
Here I am! I stand at the door and knock.
If anyone hears my voice and opens the door,
I will come in and eat with him, and he with me.

To him who overcomes,
I will give the right to sit with me on my throne,
Just as I overcame and sat down with my Father on his throne.
He who has an ear, let him hear what the Spirit says to the churches.

Christ Jesus declares that He is the Amen (It will be as I say!),
The faithful and true witness during His time on earth,
And through His people, upon His resurrection,
The ruler of God's creation as the King of kings and Lord of lords.

He knows that the church of Laodicea is neither hot or cold toward Him,
And wishes that they were either one or the other,
As they would be easier to deal with that way.
Because they are lukewarm, Christ Jesus is about to spit them out of His mouth,
And sever relationship with them altogether;
The cold of course are already lost.

The Laodicean church says of themselves that they are rich and in need of nothing.
However, Christ Jesus finds them wretched, pitiful, poor, blind and naked.
God's view is diametrically the opposite of the church's view of themselves.
Christ Jesus counsels the church to come to Him and buy gold refined in the fire;
Allowing the Holy Spirit to put His laws in their minds

And write them upon their hearts.
Then they would become rich in Christ by the power of His Holy Spirit;
They would have gold refined in the fire of His Holy Spirit;
Then the would have white clothes to wear, to cover their shameful nakedness;
Then they would have salve to put on their eyes, so that they could see.
They would have actions and deeds motivated by the Holy Spirit.

Christ Jesus declares that He rebukes and disciplines those He loves;
He always warns them when they have gone astray.
He admonishes them to be earnest and repent;
Their very lives are at stake, eternally.
Christ Jesus stands at the door of every person who claims His name and knocks.
Those who hear, open the door to Him, and He comes in and eats with them,
And has intimate communion with them.

To those who overcome this world and its ways
He will give the right to sit with Him on His throne,
Just as He sits at the right hand of God the Father on His throne.
Those of us who have an ear, let us hear what the Spirit is saying to His church.

Today, unlike the church of Laodicea, we must be hot for God,
Full of the fire and passion of His Holy Spirit;
An all consuming zeal for God;
Possessing gold refined in the fire of God;
Having actions and deeds that we can present to Christ Jesus,
That have been accomplished through Christ in us.

THE THRONE IN HEAVEN

Revelation 4

After this I looked, and there before me was a door standing open in heaven.
And the voice I had first heard speaking to me like a trumpet said,
'Come up here, and I will show you what must take place after this.'
At once I was in the Spirit,
And there before me was a throne in heaven with someone sitting on it.
And the one who sat there had the appearance of jasper and carnelian.
A rainbow, resembling an emerald, encircled the throne.

Surrounding the throne were twenty-four other thrones,
And seated on them were twenty-four elders.
They were dressed in white and had crowns of gold on their heads.
From the throne came flashes of lightning, rumblings and peals of thunder.
Before the throne, seven lamps were blazing.
These are the seven spirits of God.
Also before the throne there was what looked like a sea of glass, clear as crystal.

In the center, around the throne, were four living creatures,
And they were covered with eyes, in the front and back.
The first living creature was like a lion, the second was like an ox,
The third had a face like a man, the fourth was like a flying eagle.
Each of the four living creatures had six wings
And was covered with eyes all around, even under his wings.
Day and night they never stop saying:

'Holy, holy, holy is the Lord God Almighty,
Who was, and is and is to come.'

Whenever the living creatures give glory, honor and thanks
To him who sits on the throne and who lives for ever and ever,
The twenty-four elders fall down before him who sits on the throne,
And worship him who lives for ever and ever.
They lay their crowns before the throne and say:

'You are worthy, our Lord and God,
To receive glory and honor and power,
For you created all things, and by your will they were created
And have their being.'

Supernaturally, John looks and sees before him a door standing open in Heaven.
The voice that first spoke to him like a trumpet says:
"Come up here and I will show you what must take place after this."
Immediately he was in the Spirit;
That is he was no longer aware of anything in the natural;

64

The Time Of The END

He entered the realm of the Spirit of God.
Before him was a throne in heaven with someone sitting on it.
And the One who sat there had the appearance of being composed of specific jewels.
A rainbow encircled the throne, the sign given to Noah after the flood.

Surrounding the throne were twenty-four other thrones,
And seated on them were twenty-four elders.
Probably the twelve apostles and those who have led God's people
From the time of their deaths until the present time.
They were dressed in white (the righteousness of the saints)
And had crowns of gold on their heads (the crown of salvation, Psalm 149:4).
Seven lamps blazed before the throne, representing the sevenfold Spirit of God.
Before the throne was what looked like a sea of glass, clear as crystal.
This signifies the transparent nature of Heaven;
Where nothing is hidden and Christ Jesus is its light
Which penetrates everywhere unhindered.

In the center, around the throne, are the four living creatures.
They are covered with eyes, in front and back,
Representing the all seeing nature of God.
The first living creature was like a lion, The second like an ox,
The third had the face like a man, the fourth was like a flying eagle.
Each of the four living creatures had six wings
And was covered with eyes all around, even under his wings.

Each supernatural creature takes on a characteristic of Christ Jesus:
The Lion of the tribe of Judah; the Ox: One who labored among men;
A face like a man representing the One who took on the form of a man,
And flying like an eagle representing the unrestricted, supernatural freedom
He had and brought to those who received Him.
The six wings represent the number of man; six, being identified as the Son of Man,
Yet, the supernatural Son of God, and not being tied to earth.

Day and night the four living creatures never stop saying:
'Holy, holy, holy is the Lord God Almighty
Who was, and is, and is to come.'

**The four living creatures represent the marvelous,
Incomparable work of Christ.**
As they glorify and thank Christ Jesus on His throne,
The ever living One
The twenty-four elders are compelled to do likewise.
They lay their crowns before the throne signifying
That it is because of Christ, and Him alone that they have their crowns.
They declare that Christ Jesus alone is worthy
To receive glory and honor and power.

The Time Of The END

He is the One who created all things
And by the will of Christ Jesus all things have their being
And are sustained by Him.

THE SCROLL AND THE LAMB

Revelation Chapter 5

As the scene of the throne of Heaven remains open to John,
He sees in the right hand of Him who sits on the throne, a scroll,
With writing on both sides, and sealed with seven seals.
There appears a mighty angel proclaiming in a loud voice,

'Who is worthy to break the seals and open the scroll?'

However, no one in heaven or on earth or under the earth
Could open the scroll or even look inside it.
Because this scroll contains The Time of The END,
And the judgment of God upon the earth and its inhabitants.
Only one person is able to look into it to see what it contains;
The One who created "Time."
He is the only one worthy to do this,
Because He is the One who gave ALL.

John weeps because it appears that no one is found to be worthy
To open the scroll or look inside.
Then an elder speaks to John and says,

'Do not weep!
See, the Lion of the tribe of Judah, the Root of David, has triumphed.
He is able to open the scroll and its seven seals.' (Revelation 5:5)

John then sees a Lamb, looking as if it had been slain,
Standing in the center of the throne,
Encircled by the four living creatures and the elders.
He had seven horns and seven eyes,
Which are the Seven Spirits of God sent out into the earth.

The elder stepped up to the throne
And took the scroll from the right hand of Him who sat on the throne.
And when he had taken it, the four living creatures and the twenty-four elders
Fell down before the Lamb.
Overwhelmed by His glory and presence.
Each one had a harp and they were holding golden bowls full of incense,
Which are the prayers of the saints.
And they sang a new song.

'You are worthy to take the scroll and to open its seals.
Because you were slain, and with your blood you purchased men for God
From every tribe and language and people and nation.

The Time Of The END

You have made them to be a kingdom and priests to serve our God,
And they will reign on the earth.' (Revelation 5:9-10)

John then looked... *and heard the voice of many angels,*
Numbering thousands upon thousands, and ten thousand times then thousand.
They encircled the throne and the living creatures and the elders,
In a loud voice the sang:

'Worthy is the Lamb, who was slain,
To receive power and wealth and wisdom and strength
And honor and glory and praise!'

He hears... *every creature in heaven and on earth and under the earth*
And on the sea, and all that is in them singing:

'To him who sits on the throne and to the Lamb
Be praise and honor and glory and power for ever and ever!'

The four living creatures said, 'Amen,' and the elders fell down and worshiped.
(Revelation 5:11-14)

The blood of Christ Jesus is the agent that purchases those who believe.
The only access to Christ Jesus and eternity in Heaven is His blood.
The Israelites in the time of Moses,
Placed the blood of a lamb on the top and sides of the door
So that the Death Angel passed over them and left them alive.
Likewise, each one of us must repent of our sin
And apply the blood of Christ to our lives,
So that the eternal death
That awaits all who do not receive Christ
Passes over us.

We who receive Christ Jesus and apply His blood to our lives
Have been made by Christ to be a Kingdom and Priests to serve God,
And we will reign with Him forever.

In Heaven, all of creation, continually worships God and His Christ, forever.
We will live continually in the Anointing of The Anointed One;
The glory realm of God, where His love, joy, and peace reign.

Today, we should be living in the continual anointing of The Anointed One;
Continually praising God and giving Him all glory;
Living in His glory realm where His love, joy and peace reign.

THE MEASURING ROD

John is given a measuring rod to measure the Church of Christ Jesus.

Revelation 11:1-2

I was given a reed like a measuring rod and was told,
'Go and measure the temple of God
And the altar, and count the worshipers there.
But exclude the outer court; do not measure it,
Because it has been given to the Gentiles.
They will trample on the holy city for 42 months (three and one-half years).'

John is told to take a measure, to count those
Who have entered into the Holy Place and the Holy of Holies.
However, he is to exclude the Outer Court,
Those who have not met the requirements of a priest;
Those who have remained in the Outer Court
Will be given over to the Gentiles, the non-believers,
Who will trample on the Outer Court 42 months.
The time of The Great Tribulation.

An understanding of the Old testament Temple is require here.
A priest in the Old Testament could only enter the Holy Place
By changing his clothes (a type of putting on Christ),
By being washed with water (a type of water baptism),
Sprinkled with blood (a type of the covering of the blood of Christ),
And by being "anointed" with oil, (a type of the Holy Spirit).

In the New Testament we are the "priests" of God.
We require the reality of the "types" of the Old Testament.
Those who remain in the Outer Court have not fulfilled the requirements of a priest.
They are those who find themselves in The Great Tribulation.
They are spoken of as:

The rest of her offspring (of the woman)--
Those who obey God's commandments and hold to the testimony of Jesus.
(Revelation 12:17)

These people are "The Great Multitude In White Robes" shown to John:

After this I looked and there before me was a great multitude
That no one could count, from every nation, tribe, people and language,
Standing before the throne and in front of the Lamb.
They were wearing white robes and were holding palm branches in their hands.
And they cried out in a loud voice:

'Salvation belongs to our God, who sits on the throne, and to the Lamb.'

All the angels were standing around the throne and around the elders
And the four living creatures.
They fell down on their faces before the throne and worshiped God, saying:

'Amen! Praise and glory and wisdom and thanks and honor and power
And strength be to our God for ever and ever. Amen!'

Then one of the elders asked me,
'These in white robes—who are they, and where did they come from?'
I answered, 'Sir, you know.'

And he said, 'these are they who have come out of the great tribulation;
They have washed their robes and made them white in the blood of the Lamb.
Therefore, they are before the throne of God
And serve him day and night in his temple;
And he who sits on the throne will spread his tent over them.
Never again will they hunger; never again will they thirst.
The sun will not beat upon them nor any scorching heat.

For the Lamb at the center of the throne will be their shepherd;
He will lead them to springs of living water.
And God will wipe away every tear from their eyes.' (Revelation 7:9-17)

During The Great Tribulation these people wash their robes
In the blood of the Lamb.
They have given their lives for Christ; they have been beheaded for Christ;
They have not worshiped the Beast, or received his "mark;"
Therefore, they were killed by the Beast.

Now, Christ Jesus leads them to springs of Living Water
They had not received before.
Christ Jesus immerses them in the Springs of Living Water,
Which comes form the River of LIFE, the Holy Spirit,
That flows from the throne of God.
Now, He honors them by allowing them to be before His throne day and night,
And to serve Him for eternity.

The Book of Daniel is also instructive about the events in this period of time.
Daniel sees a horn (the Beast) that was waging war against the saints
And defeating them. (Daniel 7:21)

The saints will be handed over to him (the Beast) for three and one half years.
(Daniel 7:25)

It (the kingdom of the Beast) *grew until it reached the host of the heavens,*
And it threw some of the starry host (leaders of the Church) *down to the earth*

The Time Of The END

And trampled on them.
It set itself up to be as great as the Prince of the host (Christ Jesus);
It took away the daily sacrifice (not allowing worship of Christ Jesus)
From him (Christ),
And the place of his sanctuary (the Church) *was brought low.*
Because of rebellion,
The host of the saints and the daily sacrifice (worship of Christ)
Were given over to it (the kingdom of the Beast).
It prospered in everything it did, and truth was thrown to the ground.
Then I heard a holy one speaking, and another holy one said to him,

'How long will it take for the vision concerning the daily sacrifice ,
The rebellion that causes desolation, and surrender of the sanctuary
And of the host that will be trampled underfoot?'

He said to me,
'It will take 2,300 evenings and mornings;
Then the sanctuary will be reconsecrated.' (Daniel 8:10-14)

The kingdom of the Beast grows in power
And seduces some of the leaders of the Church of Christ Jesus,
And throws them to the ground.
The Beast sets himself up to be as great as Christ Jesus
And forbids the worship of Christ Jesus.
Because of the rebellion, the apostasy of the saints, the Beast is allowed to do this.

The apostle Paul says of The Time of The END:
The Spirit clearly says that in later times some will abandon the faith
And follow deceiving spirits and things taught by demons. (1 Timothy 4:1)

The truth of Christ Jesus is thrown to the ground.
The Church of Christ Jesus is trampled underfoot for 1,150 days,
Approximately, three and one half years.
Then Christ returns and His sanctuary is reconstituted.

Continuing from the Book of Daniel:
Then I, Daniel, looked, and there before me stood two others,
One on this bank of the river and one on the opposite bank.
One of them said to the man clothed in linen,
Who was above the waters of the river,
'How long will it be before these astonishing things are fulfilled?'

The man clothed in linen, who was above the waters of the river,
Lifted his right hand and his left hand toward heaven,
And I heard him swear by him who lives forever, saying,

The Time Of The END

'It will be for time, times and half a time (three and one-half years).
When the power of the holy people has been broken,
All these things will be completed.'

I heard, but I did not understand.
So I asked, 'My lord, what will the outcome of all this be?'

He replied, 'Go your way, Daniel, because the words are closed up and sealed
Until the time of the end.
Many will be purified, made spotless and refined,
But the wicked will continue to be wicked.
None of the wicked will understand, but those who are wise will understand.

From the time that the daily sacrifice is abolished
And the abomination that causes desolation is set up, there will be 1,290 days.
Blessed is the one who waits for and reaches the end of the 1,335 days.'

At the end of The Great Tribulation which lasts three and one-half years,
The power of the holy people
(Those who refuse to worship the Beast and to receive his "mark,"
And die as a result), is broken;
The last of them are killed and the END is reached.

Daniel is told to go his way as these things are for the distant future,
The Time of The END.
Many in the Church of Christ Jesus will be purified, made spotless and refined,
But the wicked (those who reject God and His Christ)
Will continue in their wickedness.
None of the wicked will anticipate the impending END,
But the wise; those who belong to Christ Jesus,
Will understand and anticipate the END.

THE END TIMES MINISTRY OF THE BRIDE OF CHRIST

Revelation 12:1-17

A great and wondrous sign appeared in heaven:
A woman clothed with the sun, with the moon under her feet
And a crown of twelve stars on her head.
She was pregnant and cried out in pain as she was about to give birth .

This "Woman" is the Bride of Christ.
She is clothed with the sun, which speaks of her ministering
In the fullness of Christ.
She has the moon under her feet,
Which speaks of all those who are the reflection of Christ supporting her.
She has a crown of twelve stars on her head, which speaks of the Israel of God,
The "Church", The Bride of Christ, is the Israel of God.
She has confirmed the "Covenant" with Christ Jesus spoken of in Daniel 9:27.
She has been ministering for three and one half years
A mirror of the ministry of Christ Jesus.
Then the apostasy, rebellion occurs in the "Church" of God.
Because of this, the Beast is allowed by God to put an end
To the worship of Christ Jesus.
He sets up his "image" in the sanctuary of God;
The "abomination that brings desolation" (Daniel 9:27).
The "Woman" is then taken into the desert,
To a place prepared for her by God where she is taken care of for 1,260 days,
The time of The Great Tribulation.

This is the Woman of Song of Songs 6:10:

Who is this that appears like the dawn,
Fair as the moon, bright as the sun,
Majestic as the stars in procession?

It is the remnant of the people of God spoken of in Isaiah 28:5-6:

In that day the Lord Almighty will be a glorious crown,
A beautiful wreath for the remnant of his people.
He will be a spirit of justice to him who sits in judgment,
A source of strength to those who turn back the battle at the gate.

The Time Of The END

She is Zion in Isaiah 60:1-3:

Arise, shine, for you light has come,
And the glory of the Lord rises upon you.
See, darkness covers the earth
And thick darkness is over the peoples.
But the Lord rises upon you
And his glory appears over you.
Nations will come to your light,
And kings to the brightness of your dawn.

She is Zion in Isaiah 62:1-3:

For Zion's sake I will not keep silent,
for Jerusalem's sake I will not remain quiet,
Till her righteousness shines out like the dawn
Her salvation like a blazing torch.
The nations will see your righteousness,
And all kings your glory;
You will be called by a new name
That the mouth of the Lord will bestow.
You will be a crown of splendor in the Lord's hand,
A royal diadem in the hand of your God.

What is the nature of the ministry of the Bride of Christ?
Malachi 4:5 gives an indication:

See, I will send you the prophet Elijah
Before the great and dreadful day of the Lord comes.
He will turn the hearts of the fathers to their children,
And the hearts of the children to their fathers;
Or else I will come and strike the land with a curse.

God does not send the literal prophet of Elijah;
Just as He sent John the Baptist in the Spirit of Elijah,
He sends the Bride of Christ, in the Spirit of Elijah.

THE WOMAN AND THE DRAGON

Revelation Chapter 12

Then another sign appeared in heaven:
An enormous red dragon with seven heads and ten horns
And seven crowns on his heads.
His tail swept a third of the stars out of the sky and flung them to the earth.
The dragon stood in front of the woman who was about to give birth,
So that he might devour her child the moment it was born.
She gave birth to a son, a male child,
Who will rule all the nations with an iron scepter.
And her child was snatched up to God and to his throne.
The woman fled into the desert to a place prepared for her by God,
Where she might be taken care of for 1,260 days.(Revelation 12:1-6)

The "dragon", Satan has swept a third of the stars out of the sky;
He has deceived and perverted a third of the leaders of the "Church" of God,
And caused the "apostasy", the "rebellion" in the "Church,"
That allows the Beast to set up his "image" in the "Church,"
The "abomination that causes desolation".

The "Woman", the Bride of Christ is pregnant by Christ
With the fruit of her ministry, a male child.
Satan, the red dragon, stands in front of her so that he might devour her child.
However, God snatches the child up to His throne,
And the Woman, The Bride of Christ, is taken into the desert,
To a place prepared for her by God where she is taken care of for 1,260 days,
The time of The Great Tribulation.

In the Millennium the male child will rule the nations, along side of Christ,
With an iron scepter.

And there was war in heaven.
Michael and his angels fought against the dragon,
And the dragon and his angels fought back.
But he was not strong enough, and they lost their place in heaven.
The great dragon was hurled down--
That ancient serpent called the devil or Satan, who leads the whole world astray.
He was hurled to the earth, and his angels with him.

Then I heard a loud voice in heaven say:
'Now have come the salvation and the power and the kingdom of our God,
And the authority of his Christ.
For the accuser of our brothers who accuses them before our God day and night,
Has been hurled down.
They overcame him by the blood of the Lamb

The Time Of The END

And by the word of their testimony;
They did not love their lives so much as to shrink from death.
Therefore rejoice, you heavens and you who dwell in them!
But woe to the earth and the sea,
Because the devil has gone down to you!
He is filled with fury, because he knows that his time is short.' (Revelation 12:7-12)

Until this time God has allowed Satan to rule over the earth
With the exception of the Bride of Christ.
In Heaven, Satan, is continually bringing accusation against God's people.
However, Satan, could not prevent the ministry of the Bride of Christ.
When he tries to devour the fruit of her ministry, the male child,
God snatches the child up to Heaven.
The Bride and the male child have overcome Satan and his deception
By the blood of the Lamb and the word of their testimony,
Just as the saints of all ages have.
Many giving their lives for Christ Jesus.

This is the beginning of the end for Satan.
He and his fallen angels are forced to the earth by the Heavenly angels.
This begins the period of The Great Tribulation,
Where an angry Satan, knowing his time is short,
Is allowed to perpetrate the full extent of his evil upon an unbelieving mankind;
Those who have rejected God and His Christ.

When the dragon saw that he had been hurled to the earth, he pursued the woman
Who had given birth to the male child.
The woman was given the two wings of a great eagle,
So that she might fly to the place prepared for her in the desert,
Where she would be taken care of for a time, times and half a time,
Out of the serpent's reach.
Then from his mouth the serpent spewed water like a river,
To overtake the woman and sweep her away with the torrent.
But the earth helped the woman by opening up its mouth and swallowing the river
That the dragon had spewed out of his mouth.
Then the dragon was enraged at the woman
And went off to make war against the rest of her offspring--
Those who obey God's commandments and hold to the testimony of Jesus.
And the dragon stood on the shore of the sea.

The dragon is hurled to the earth
And the first thing that he does is to pursue the woman.
Why is this?
Because as the representative of God on earth, the Bride of Christ;
She is the only one who stands in the way of his complete rule!
When she is out of the way he controls the earth and all its inhabitants.

The Time Of The END

God Almighty has allowed this.
The Bride of Christ has finished her ministry on earth.
Now the people of the earth who have rejected God, Christ Jesus and His Bride,
Receive what their wickedness demands, the judgment of God.

The "Woman" is given two wings of a great eagle and flown into the desert
To a place God has prepared for her, out of the reach of Satan,
Where He protects her for three and one half years.
The other time when God delivered His people on the wings of an eagle
Was when He delivered the children of Israel out of Egypt.

Satan spews out of his mouth a river of death,
But God opens up the earth and swallows up the river.

The dragon is enraged at the "Woman" and his failure to kill her.
He now goes off to make war against the rest of her off-spring--
Those who obey God's commandments and hold to the testimony of Jesus.

The Bride of Christ has just ministered on earth, in the fullness of Christ.
Those who receive Christ Jesus in His fullness, who become ONE with Him
Are part of the Bride.
These are those who have been crucified with Christ and no longer live
But Christ lives in them.
They have died to this world and its ways
And have given their lives completely to Christ Jesus, holding nothing back.
They have become ONE with Christ Jesus.
Many, however, who name the name of Christ,
Do not respond to the ministry of the Bride, and even persecute her.
They have made a confession of faith and hold to the testimony of Christ Jesus
But do not become ONE with Him;
They remain in the Outer Court, and do not enter the Holy Place.
These are left behind.
It is against these that the dragon makes war;
These are killed (beheaded) by the dragon and his representative, the Beast,
When they maintain, their confession of faith.
When the last of these are killed, Christ Jesus returns.

[There are those who claim the name of Christ
Who believe that The Book of Revelation is an allegory, just a symbolic story.
When they realize that it is a reality and that they are in the midst of it,
They come to their senses and stand and die for Christ.]

The dragon stands on the shore of the sea,
Looking at the mass of humanity that he is about to deceive
And send to their eternal death, into the Lake of Fire;
The same place that he knows is his destination.

THE LAMB AND THE 144,000

Revelation 14:1-5

Now the scene changes and John is shown the 144,00.

Then I looked, and there before me was a Lamb, standing on Mount Zion,
And with him 144,000 who had his name
And his Father's name written on their foreheads.
And I heard a sound from heaven like the roar of rushing waters
And like a loud peal of thunder.
The sound I heard was like that of harpists playing their harps.
And they sang a new song before the throne
And before the four living creatures and the elders.

No one could learn the song except the 144,000
Who had been redeemed from the earth.
These are those who did not defile themselves with women,
For they kept themselves pure.
They follow the Lamb wherever he goes.
They were purchased from among men
And offered as firstfruits to God and the Lamb.
No lie was found in their mouths; they are blameless.(Revelation 14:1-5)

The 144,000 is the male child that is the firstfruits
Of the ministry of the "Woman," the Bride of Christ.
They have the name of the Lamb and His Father on their foreheads;
The forehead being the most prominent place of marking on a human.
They are "marked" or sealed to God.
They sing a song that no one else can sing.
They have never been with a woman.
No lie is in their mouths, they are blameless.
Such will be 144,000 young men "snatched up to God,"
Just prior to the beginning of the Great Tribulation.

144,000 SEALED

Revelation 7:1-8

After this I saw four angels standing at the four corners of the earth,
Holding back the four winds of the earth
To prevent any wind from blowing on the land or on the sea or on any tree.
Then I saw another angel coming up from the east,
Having the seal of the living God.
He called out in a loud voice to the four angels
Who had been given power to harm the land and the sea.

'Do not harm the land and the sea: or the trees
Until we put a seal on the foreheads of the servants of our God.'

Then I heard the number of those who were sealed:
144,000 from all the tribes of Israel.

From the tribe of Judah 12,000 were sealed
From the tribe of Reuben 12,000 were sealed
From the tribe of Gad 12,000 were sealed.
From the tribe of Asher 12,000 were sealed.
From the tribe of Naphtali 12,000 were sealed.
From the tribe of Manasseh 12,000 were sealed.
From the tribe of Simeon 12,000 were sealed.
From the tribe of Levi 12,000 were sealed.
From the tribe of Issachar 12,000 were sealed.
From the tribe of Zebulun 12,000 were sealed.
From the tribe of Joseph 12,000 were sealed.
From the tribe of Benjamin 12,000 were sealed.

This is the "male child," sealed and snatched up to God.
These young men are not necessarily Jewish,
But are part of the Israel of God, the New Jerusalem, God's Church.

THE APOSTASY / THE REBELLION

1 Timothy 4:1-2
The Spirit clearly says that in later times some will abandon the faith
And follow deceiving spirits and things taught by demons.
Such teaching comes through hypocritical liars,
Whose consciences have been seared as with a hot iron.

The Book of Daniel is also instructive about the events in this period of time.
Daniel sees a horn (the Beast) that was waging war against the saints
And defeating them. (Daniel 7:21)

The saints will be handed over to him (the Beast) for three and one half years.
(Daniel 7:25)

It (the kingdom of the Beast) *grew until it reached the host of the heavens,*
And it threw some of the starry host (leaders of the Church) *down to the earth*
And trampled on them.
It set itself up to be as great as the Prince of the host (Christ Jesus)*;*
It took away the daily sacrifice (the worship of Christ Jesus)
From him (Christ),
And the place of his sanctuary (the Church) *was brought low.*
Because of rebellion,
The host of the saints and the daily sacrifice (worship of Christ)
Were given over to it (the kingdom of the Beast).
It prospered in everything it did, and truth was thrown to the ground.
Then I heard a holy one speaking, and another holy one said to him,

'How long will it take for the vision concerning the daily sacrifice ,
The rebellion that causes desolation, and surrender of the sanctuary
And of the host that will be trampled underfoot?'
He said to me,
'It will take 2,300 evenings and mornings;
Then the sanctuary will be reconsecrated.' (Daniel 8:10-14)

The kingdom of the Beast grows in power
And seduces some of the leaders of the Church of Christ Jesus,
And throws them to the ground.
The Beast sets himself up to be as great as Christ Jesus
And forbids the worship of Christ Jesus.
Because of the rebellion, the apostasy of the saints, the Beast is allowed to do this.
The Beast sets up his "image" in the Church of God,
The "abomination that causes desolation."

The truth of Christ Jesus is thrown to the ground.
The Church of Christ Jesus is trampled underfoot for 1,150 days,

The Time Of The END

Approximately, three and one half years.
Then Satan is defeated and Christ returns and His sanctuary is reconstituted.

The Man Of Lawlessness (2 Thessalonians 2:1-12)

Concerning the coming of the Lord Jesus Christ
And our being gathered to him, we ask you brothers,
Not to become easily unsettled or alarmed by some prophecy, report or letter
Supposed to have come from us, saying that <u>the day of the Lord</u> has already come.

Don't let anyone deceive you in any way, for <u>that day</u> will not come,
*Until <u>the rebellion occurs</u> and **the man of lawlessness** is revealed,*
The man doomed to destruction.
He opposes and exalts himself over everything that is called God or is worshiped,
And even sets himself up in God's temple, proclaiming himself to be God.

Don't you remember that when I was with you I used to tell you these things?
And now you know what is holding him back,
So that he may be revealed at the proper time.
For the secret power of lawlessness is already at work;
But the one who now holds it back will continue to do so
<u>Till he</u> (the Holy Spirit) <u>is taken out of the way</u>.
*And then the **lawless one** will be revealed,*
Whom the Lord Jesus will over throw with the breath of his mouth
And destroy by the splendor of his coming.

*The coming of the **lawless one** will be in accordance with the work of Satan*
displayed in all kinds of <u>counterfeit</u> miracles, signs and wonders,
And every sort of evil that deceives those who are perishing.
They perish because they refused to love the truth and so be saved.

*For this reason God sends them **a powerful delusion***
*So that they will believe **the lie***
And so that all will be condemned who have not believed the truth
But have delighted in wickedness.

According to the apostle Paul,
The Great Day Of The Lord will not come until the man of lawlessness,
The Beast, the Antichrist is revealed.
At that time the Holy Spirit is taken out of the way
And Satan, through the Antichrist, has complete rule over mankind.
Just prior to this, the rebellion within the Church occurs,
And the Beast is sets up his "image" in the Church of God,
Claiming to be God and deceiving mankind
With <u>counterfeit</u> miracles, signs and wonders.
God allows this powerful delusion for those who have delighted in wickedness.

81

THE BEAST OUT OF THE SEA

Revelation 13

And I saw a beast coming out of the sea.
He had ten horns and seven heads, with ten crowns on his horns,
And on each head a blasphemous name.
The beast I saw resembled a leopard, but had feet like those of a bear
And a mouth like that of a lion.
The dragon gave the beast his power and his throne
And great authority.

One of the heads of the beast seemed to have had a fatal wound,
But the fatal wound had been healed.
The whole world was astonished and followed the beast.
Men worshiped the dragon because he had given authority to the beast,
And they also worshiped the beast and asked,
'Who is like the beast? Who can make war against him?'

The beast was given a mouth to utter proud words and blasphemies
And to exercise his authority for forty-two months.
He opened his mouth to blaspheme God, and to slander his name
And his dwelling place and those who live in heaven.

He was given power to make war against the saints and to conquer them.
And he was given authority over every tribe, people, language and nation.
All the inhabitants of the earth will worship the beast--
All whose names have not been written in the book of life belonging to the Lamb
That was slain from the creation of the world.

He who has an ear let him hear.

If anyone is to go into captivity, into captivity he will go.
If anyone is to be killed with the sword, with the sword he will be killed.

This calls for patient endurance and faithfulness on the part of the saints.

The apostle John sees a Beast coming out of the sea;
He sees the son of Satan coming out of the masses of the people of the earth.
As Christ Jesus is to God the Father so the Beast is to Satan.
The Beast is the Man of Lawlessness
That the apostle Paul speaks of in 2 Thessalonians 2.

He has ten horns and seven heads, representing nations and heads of authority.
The Beast has ten crowns on his horns, and on each head a blasphemous name.
The crowns are representative of authority over a specific people group
And the heads have a name that speaks against God.

The Time Of The END

This Beast is a composite of the beasts that Daniel is shown in Daniel 7:2-7,
Resembling a leopard with feet like a bear and a mouth like a lion.
The dragon (Satan) gives the Beast, the Antichrist his power, throne
And great authority,
Just as the God gave Christ Jesus His power, throne and authority.

One of the heads of the Beast seemed to be fatally wounded,
But the fatal wound was healed,
Causing the whole godless world to be astonished and to follow the Beast,
Ultimately to hell.
This is Satan's attempt to mimic the death, burial and resurrection of Christ Jesus.

The whole world worships the dragon (Satan) and the Beast.
The world cannot comprehend anyone who can come against the power of the Beast.
They have completely forgotten the God of Heaven, the Almighty.

Satan gives his Beast a mouth to utter proud words and to malign God,
Calling what is good evil and what is evil, good.
They slander the name of God, Christ Jesus, Heaven itself,
And those who live in Heaven.
God Almighty gives Satan and his Beast three and one-half years
To wreck havoc on a world that has disavowed the true and Living God.

They are also given power to make war against the remaining saints
And to conquer them.
Prior to this time they did not have this power;
They were constrained by the Holy Spirit.

Satan and his Beast are given by God,
Authority over every tribe, people, language and nation
Because they have turned away from the God of Heaven.

Every person on earth worships the Beast,
All those whose names have not been written in the Lamb's Book of LIFE.
The Lamb who was slain from the creation of the world,
To save all those who turn to Him in faith.

Satan now has the worship he wanted from the time he fell from God's grace.
He masquerades as an angel of light and seduces the whole world,
Except those who belong to Christ Jesus.

If anyone can hear the voice of God, let him hear and respond.
Now is the time to give your heart to the One who holds the keys to death and hell.
To the One who is the Way, the Truth and the LIFE;
The One who offers eternal LIFE to those who repent and turn to Christ Jesus.
Everyone else is lost and destined for hell.

The Time Of The END

Those saints who find themselves in The Great Tribulation
Must patiently endure what lies in front of them.
They will be killed, but their faith, and their willingness to die for Christ,
Will save them from eternal death.

THE BEAST OUT OF THE EARTH, THE FALSE PROPHET

Revelation 13:11-18

Then I saw another beast, coming out of the earth.
He had two horns like a lamb, but he spoke like a dragon.
He exercised all the authority of the first beast on his behalf,
And made the earth and its inhabitants worship the first beast,
Whose fatal wound had been healed.
And he performed great and miraculous signs,
Even causing fire to come down from heaven to earth in full view of men.

Because of the signs he was given power to do on behalf of the first beast,
He deceived the inhabitants of the earth.
He ordered them to set up an image in honor of the beast
Who was wounded by the sword and yet lived.
He was given power to give breath to the image of the first beast,
So that it could speak
And cause all who refused to worship the image to be killed.

He also forced everyone, small and great, rich and poor, free and slave,
To receive a mark on his right hand or on his forehead,
So that no one could buy or sell unless he had the mark,
Which is the name of the beast or the number of his name.

This calls for wisdom.
If anyone has insight, let him calculate the number of the beast,
For it is man's number.
His number is 666.

The False Prophet Enters the Scene

The Apostle John sees another beast coming out of the earth.
He had two horns like a lamb, but speaks like a dragon.
He is the False Prophet of the Beast and has all his authority.
The False Prophet forces the people of the earth worship the Beast,
Whose fatal wound had been healed.
The False Prophet gives breath to the "image" of the Beast,
So that the "image" can speak.
He also requires that all who refuse to worship the "image" of the Beast to be killed.

The False Prophet forces everyone,
Regardless of social status, rich or poor, free and slave,
To receive the "mark" of the Beast on their right hand or forehead.
This "mark" signifies the complete ownership of the person,

Body, soul, mind and spirit, by Satan.
Now, no one can buy or sell anything unless he has the "mark,"
Which is the name of the beast or the number of his name.

This Calls For Wisdom

The apostle John pauses and says this calls for wisdom.
He says that if anyone has insight, let him calculate the number of the beast.
This number has only to do with man deceived by Satan and nothing to do with God.
The number itself is an affront to God, as Satan intended.
It is man glorifying himself and bringing damnation upon himself as Satan intended.
Just as Christ Jesus identified Himself with mankind for their salvation,
So Satan identifies himself with mankind for their damnation.

THE ETERNAL GOSPEL PROCLAIMED

Revelation 14:6

Again the scene changes for the Apostle John.

Then I saw another angel flying in midair,
And he had the eternal gospel to proclaim
To those who live on earth—to every nation, tribe, language and people.
He said in a loud voice, 'Fear God and give him glory,
Because the hour of his judgment has come.
Worship him who made the heavens,
The earth, the sea, and the springs of water.' (Revelation 14:6-7)

Here, God in His great mercy, before the Great Tribulation begins,
Announces the "eternal gospel", the "good news" to every living person,
Inviting them to receive the Christ of God as their Savior and Lord.

The angel loudly proclaims the eternal gospel
To all the people on the earth.
Every nation, tribe, and language.
He tells everyone to fear God and give Him glory
Because the time of His judgment is at hand.
He tells the people to worship Him who created all that is.
Every living person is given the opportunity to accept Christ Jesus
As the Savior and Lord.

WARNING AGAINST WORSHIPING THE BEAST
OR RECEIVING HIS MARK

Revelation 14:9-12

A third angel followed them and said in a loud voice:
'If anyone worships the beast and his image
And receives his mark on the forehead or on the hand,
He, too, will drink of the wine of God's fury,
Which has been poured full strength into the cup of his wrath.

He will be tormented with burning sulfur
In the presence of the holy angels and of the lamb.
And the smoke of their torment rises forever and ever.
There is no rest day or night for those who worship the beast and his image,
Or for anyone who receives the mark of his name.'

This calls for patient endurance on the part of the saints
Who obey God's commandments and remain faithful to Jesus.

Then I heard a voice from heaven say,
'Write: Blessed are the dead who die in the Lord from now on.'

'Yes,' says the Spirit, 'they will rest from their labor,
For their deeds will follow them.'

John sees a third angel loudly warning everyone on earth
Not to worship the Beast or to receive his "mark."
He tells them that if they do so they will suffer the wrath of God.
And will be tormented eternally.

The angel says that those saints who find themselves in The Great Tribulation
Will need patient endurance.
If they do not worship the Beast or receive his "mark,"
They will be killed by the Beast and his followers.
In order to be faithful to Christ Jesus they will have to die for Him.

The Spirit of God, says that those who die in the Lord
From the beginning of The Great Tribulation on, are blessed.
They will rest from their labor and their deeds will follow them.
The willingness of these saints to die for Christ during The Great Tribulation
Puts them in a special category in God.
They are with Christ Jesus continually in Heaven.

THE TWO WITNESSES

Revelation 11:1-14

And I will give power to my two witnesses, and they will prophesy for 1,260 days,
Clothed in sackcloth.
These are the two olive trees and the two lampstands
That stand before the Lord of the earth.
If anyone tries to harm them, fire comes from their mouths
And devours their enemies.
This is how anyone who wants to harm them must die.
These men have power to shut up the sky so that it will not rain
During the time they are prophesying;
And they have power to strike the earth with every kind of plague
As often as they want.

Now when they have finished their testimony,
The beast that comes up from the Abyss will attack them,
And overpower and kill them.
Their bodies will lie in the street of the great city,
Which is figuratively called Sodom and Egypt,
Where also their Lord was crucified.
For three and half days men from every people tribe, language and nation
Will gaze on their bodies and refuse them burial.
The inhabitants of the earth will gloat over them and will celebrate
By sending each other gifts,
Because these two prophets had tormented those who live on the earth.

But after the three and half days a breath of life from God entered them,
And they stood on their feet, and terror struck those who saw them.
Then they heard a loud voice from heaven saying to them,
'Come up here.' and they went up to heaven in a cloud,
While their enemies looked on.

At that very hour there was a severe earthquake and a tenth of the city collapsed.
Seven thousand people were killed in the earthquake,
And the survivors were terrified and gave glory to the God of heaven.

The second woe has passed; the third woe is coming soon. (Revelation 11:2-14)

God has two witnesses, two prophets, who He places in the street of Jerusalem
For the duration of The Great Tribulation.
These witnesses call down all the judgments of God during this time,
In full view of the whole world; in complete communication with Heaven.
The same way that Moses was God's instrument in bringing the plagues upon Egypt.

If anyone tries to stop them, fire comes out of their mouths and devours them.

The Time Of The END

You can be certain, in the three and one-half years of agony in the world,
Some tried.

When they have finished their assignment, at the end of The Great Tribulation,
The Beast who comes out of the Abyss is allowed to kill them.
This brings great joy to the people of the earth who think that the Tribulation is over,
And they gloat over the fate of the Prophets.
They even send each other gifts in celebration.
For three and one-half days the bodies of the Prophets lie in the street
And are not given burial.

However at the end of three and one-half days God breaths life back into them,
And in a loud voice says "Come up here."
The Prophets stand to their feet, and ascend to Heaven in a cloud,
In full view of the people of the world and Jerusalem.

As the people look on, a severe earthquake hits the city
And a tenth of the city collapses.
Seven thousand people are killed in the earthquake.
The survivors are terrified and give glory to the God of Heaven.
This is remarkable because most have cursed God during the Tribulation.

The SECOND WOE has now passed and the THIRD WOE is about to begin.

THE FIRST THROUGH THE SIXTH SEALS

The First Seal – Revelation 6:1-2

I watched as the lamb open the first of seven seals.
Then I heard one of the four living creatures say in a loud voice like thunder,
'Come!' I looked, and there before me was a white horse!
Its rider held a bow, and he was given a crown,
And he rode out as a conqueror bent on conquest. (Revelation 6:1-2)

Christ Jesus is the rider on the white horse
With a bow and a crown,
Riding out as a conqueror bent on conquest.
Christ Jesus said that the gates of hell will not prevail against His Church.
He came to destroy the work of the devil.
He has been gathering His people to Himself from the very beginning
In every generation.

However, after His resurrection
And the out pouring of the Holy Spirit upon all flesh,
This gathering has intensified.
This gathering will intensify even more for the last generation.

In the three and one-half period before The Great Tribulation
He reveals Himself in His fullness through His Bride.
This is the beginning of the final revival, the final move of God upon the earth.
Through His Bride, Christ Jesus is a conquer bent on conquest
To gather those who belong to Him.
This parallels Revelation 14:14-16, where the earth is harvested.

I looked and there before me was a white cloud,
And seated on the cloud was one "like a son of man"
With a crown of gold on his head
And a sharp sickle in his hand.
Then another angel came out of the temple and called in a loud voice
To him who was sitting on the cloud,
'Take your sickle and reap, because the time to reap has come,
For the harvest of the earth is ripe.'
So he that was seated on the cloud swung his sickle over the earth,
And the earth was harvested.

The Second Seal - Revelation 6:3-4

When the Lamb opened the second seal, I heard the second living creature say,
'Come!' Then another horse came out, a fiery red one.

Its rider was given power to take peace from the earth
And to make men slay each other.
To him was given a large sword.

The fiery red horse is given the power to take peace from the earth.
From the time of the resurrection of Christ the world has had little peace.
This lack of peace intensifies until the beginning of The Great Tribulation
When there is no peace at all.
Peace only comes with the second coming of the Prince of Peace.

The Third Seal – Revelation 6:5-6

When the Lamb opened the third seal,
I heard the third living creature say, "Come!"
I looked, and there before me was a black horse!
Its rider is holding a pair of scales in his hand.
Then I heard what sounded like a voice among the four living creatures, saying,

'A quart of wheat for a day's wages,
And three quarts of barley for a day's wages,
And do not damage the oil and the wine!' (Revelation 6:5-6)

From the beginning of The Great Tribulation there is famine.
There has often been famine on the earth
But this will be more pervasive than ever before.
The price for food rises dramatically.
A person will work all day for simply a quart of wheat or three quarts of barley.

The admonishment not to damage the oil and the wine,
I believe, refers to the Bride of Christ in the desert.

The Fourth Seal – Revelation 6:7-8

When the lamb opened the fourth seal,
I heard the voice of the fourth living creature say, "Come!"
I looked, and there before me was a pale horse!
Its rider was named Death, and Hades was following close behind him
They were given power over a fourth of the earth to kill by sword,
Famine and plague, and by the wild beasts of the earth. (Revelation 6:7-8)

With the Fourth Seal comes killing beyond what the earth has experienced before,
By famine, plague and wild beasts.

The Fifth Seal – Revelation 6:9-11

When he opened the fifth seal,
I saw under the altar the souls of those who had been slain

The Time Of The END

THE FIRST THROUGH THE SIXTH SEALS

Because of the word of God and the testimony they had maintained.
They called out in a loud voice,

'How long, Sovereign Lord, holy and true,
Until you judge the inhabitants of the earth and avenge our blood?'

Then each of them was given a white robe, and they were told to wait a little longer,
Until the number of their fellow servants and brothers
Who were to be killed as they had been was completed. (Revelation 6:9-11)

The Fifth Seal gives us a glimpse of the reality
Of what has gone on and is going on upon the earth.
The people of the earth through the deception of Satan, killing the people of God.
In this vision we see the people of God who have been slain,
Asking God how long will this continue until their blood is avenged.
They are told it will continue until the number of their fellow servants and brothers
Is completed according to the plan of God.

Related to this is the last chapter of the Book of Daniel which reads as follows:

Then I, Daniel, looked and there before me stood two others,
One on this bank of the river and one on the opposite bank.
One of them said to the man clothed in linen,
Who was above the waters of the river,
'How long will it be before these astonishing things are fulfilled?'

The man clothed in linen, who was above the waters of the river,
Lifted his right hand and his left hand toward heaven,
And I heard him swear by him who lives forever, saying,

'It will be for a time, times and half a time.
When the power of the holy people has been finally broken,
All these things will be completed.' (Daniel 12:5-7)

The Sixth Seal – 6:12-17

I watched as the Lamb opened the sixth seal.
There was a great earthquake.
The sun turned black like sackcloth made of goat hair,
The whole moon turned blood red, and the stars in the sky fell to earth,
As late figs drop from a fig tree when shaken by a strong wind.
The sky receded like a scroll, rolling up,
And every mountain and island was removed from its place.

Then kings of the earth, the princes, the generals, the rich, the mighty,
And every slave and every free man hid in caves

And among the rocks of the mountains.
They called to the mountains and the rocks,
'Fall on us and hide us from the face of him who sits on the throne
And from the wrath of the Lamb!
For the great day of their wrath has come, and who can stand?'
(Revelation 6:12-17)

The opening of the Sixth Seal gives the people of the earth
A great sign in the heavens.
The sun is blacked out, the moon turns blood red and stars fall from the sky.
The sky seems to "roll up."
Every mountain and island is moved from its present location.
The people of the earth from all walks of life try to hid from God's judgment
In caves and among mountain rocks,
Realizing that this is the judgment of God,
And they are unable to stand before Him.

THE SEVENTH SEAL AND THE GOLDEN SENSOR

Revelation 8:1-5

When he opened the seventh seal, there was silence in heaven
For about half an hour.

And I saw the seven angels who stand before God,
And to them were given seven trumpets.
Another angel, who had a golden censer, came and stood at the altar.
He was given much incense to offer, with the prayers of all the saints,
On the golden altar before the throne.
The smoke of the incense, together with the prayers of the saints,
Went up before God from the angel's hand.
Then the angel took the censer, filled it with fire from the altar,
And hurled it on the earth;
And there came peals of thunder, rumblings, flashes of lightning and an earthquake.
(Revelation 8:1-5)

The solemnity of this scene at the throne of God
Is marked by a half hour of silence.
This silence is unprecedented in Heaven.
God's final judgment on earth is about to begin.
The people of the earth have rejected Him and His Christ.
They have mistreated, persecuted and killed His saints.
Nevertheless, the magnitude and finality of what is about to begin is profound.
It is the heart of God that no person would have to experience His judgment.
However, His justice demands that it be so.
The angel hurls the fire from the altar to earth and The Great Tribulation continues.

THE TRUMPET JUDGMENTS

Revelation 8:6-21

Then the seven angels who had the seven trumpets prepared to sound them.

The first angel *sounded his trumpet,*
And there came hail and fire mixed with blood,
And it was hurled down upon the earth.
A third of the earth was burned up, a third of the trees were burned up,
And all the green grass was burned up.

The second angel *sounded his trumpet, and something like a huge mountain ,*
All ablaze, was thrown into the sea.
A third of the sea turned into blood, a third of the living creatures in the sea died,
And a third of the ships were destroyed.

The third angel *sounded his trumpet, and a great star, blazing like a torch,*
Fell from the sky on a third of the rivers and on the springs of water--
The name of the star is Wormwood.
A third of the waters turned bitter,
And many people died from the waters that had become bitter.

The fourth angel *sounded his trumpet, and a third of the sun was struck,*
A third of the moon, and a third of the stars, so that a third of them turned dark.
A third of the day was without light, a also a third of the night.

As I watched, I heard an eagle that was flying in mid air call out in a loud voice:
'Woe! Woe! Woe to the inhabitants of the earth, because of the trumpet blasts
About to be sounded by the other three angels!'

The fifth angel *sounded his trumpet,*
And I saw a star that had fallen from the sky to the earth.
The star was given the key to the shaft of the Abyss.
When he opened the Abyss,
Smoke rose from it like the smoke from a gigantic furnace.
The sun and sky were darkened by the smoke from the Abyss.
And out of the smoke locusts came down upon the earth
And were given power like that of scorpions of the earth.
They were told not to harm the grass of the earth or any plant or tree,
But only those people who did not have the seal of God on their foreheads.
The were not given power to kill them, but only to torture them for five months.
And the agony they suffered was like that of the sting of a scorpion
When it strikes a man.
During those days men will seek death, but will not find it;
They will long to die, but death will elude them.

The Time Of The END

The locusts looked like horses prepared for battle.
On their heads they wore something like crowns of gold,
And their faces resembled human faces.
Their hair was like women's hair, and their teeth were like lions' teeth.
They had breastplates like breastplates of iron,
And the sound of their wings was like the thundering of many horses
And chariots rushing into battle.
They had tails and stings like scorpions,
And in their tails they had power to torment people for five months.

They had as a king over them the angel of the Abyss,
Whose name in Hebrew is Abaddon,
And in Greek, Apollyon (Destroyer).
The first woe is past; two other woes are yet to come.

The sixth angel *blew his trumpet,*
And I heard a voice coming from the horns of the golden altar that is before God.
It said to the sixth angel who had the trumpet,
'Release the four angels who are bound at the river Euphrates.'
And the four angels who had been kept ready for this very hour
And day and month and year were released to kill a third of mankind.
The number of mounted troops was two hundred million.
I heard their number.

The horses and riders I saw in my vision looked like this:
Their breastplates were fiery red, dark blue, and yellow as sulfur.
The heads of the horses resembled the heads of lions,
And out of their mouths came fire, smoke and sulfur.
A third of mankind was killed by the three plagues of fire, smoke and sulfur
That came out of their mouths.
The power of the horses was in their mouths and in their tails;
For their tails were like snakes, having heads with which they inflict injury.

The rest of mankind that were not killed by these plagues
Still did not repent of the work of their hands;
They did not stop worshiping demons,
And idols of gold, silver, bronze, stone and wood--
Idols that cannot see or hear or walk.
Nor did they repent of their murders, their magic arts,
Their sexual immorality or their thefts.(Revelation 8, 9:1-21)

With the Trumpet Judgments
The ever increasing, devastation of earth and its people continue.
Nevertheless, the people who do not die will not turn to God in repentance.
They continue to worship demons and idols;
They continue their murders, magic arts, sexual immorality and stealing.

THE ANGEL AND THE LITTLE SCROLL

Revelation 10

Then I saw another mighty angel coming down from heaven.
He was robed in a cloud, with a rainbow above his head;
His face was like the sun, and his legs were like fiery pillars.
He was holding a little scroll, which lay open in his hand.
He planted his right foot on the sea and his left foot on the land,
And he gave a loud shout like the roar of a lion (the Lion of the Tribe of Judah).
When he shouted, the voices of the seven thunders spoke,
I was about to write; but I heard a voice from heaven say,

'Seal up what the seven thunders have said and do not write it down.'

Then the angel I had seen standing on the sea and on the land
Raised his right hand to heaven.
And he swore by him who lives for ever and ever, who created the heavens
And all that is in them, the earth and all that is in it,
And the sea and all that is in it, and said,

'There will be no more delay!
But in the days when the seventh angel is about to sound his trumpet,
The mystery of God will be accomplished,
Just as he announced to his servants the prophets.'

Then the voice that I had heard from heaven spoke to me once more:

'Go, take the scroll that lies open in the hand of the angel
Who is standing on the sea and on the land.'

So I went to the angel and asked him to give me the little scroll.
He said to me,

'Take it and eat it.
It will turn your stomach sour, but in your mouth it will be as sweet as honey.'

I took the little scroll from the angel's hand and ate it.
It tasted as sweet as honey in my mouth, but when I had eaten it,
My stomach turned sour.
Then I was told,
'You must prophesy again about many peoples, nations, languages and kings.'

The Time Of The END

The mighty angel is Christ Jesus.
The same One John saw at the beginning of the revelation.
The angel says that when the Seventh Trumpet is sounded,
The MYSTERY OF GOD will be accomplished,
Just as he announced to his servants the prophets.
Just as His Scriptures have foretold.

John is told to eat the scroll.
The angel tells him that it will be sweet in his mouth but will turn his stomach sour.
John eats the scroll as he is told and it is as the angel said;
It is sweet in his mouth but turns his stomach sour.

It is the same for all of us, the Church, the Bride.
We too, must eat the scroll figuratively, and digest what it speaks to us.
The promises and outcome of this revelation are sweet for those who believe.
Nevertheless, the understanding of what happens to those who do not
Is terrible to comprehend.

'Blessed is the one who reads the words of this prophecy,
And blessed are those who hear it and take to heart what is written in it,
Because the time is near.' (Revelation 1:3)

Christ Jesus says "Blessed" are those who read the words of His prophecy,
And "Blessed" are those who hear it; take it to heart,
And apply this understanding to their lives,
Because the time of His Second Coming is near.

THE LAST SEVEN PLAGUES

Revelation 15:1-8

I saw in heaven another great and marvelous sign:
Seven angels with the seven last plagues--
Last, because with them God's wrath is completed.
And I saw what looked like a sea of glass mixed with fire and,
Standing beside the sea, those who had been <u>victorious</u> over the beast
And his image and over the number of his name.
They held harps given them by God
And sang the song of Moses the servant of God and the song of the Lamb:

'Great and marvelous are your deeds Lord God Almighty.
Just and true are your ways, King of the ages.
Who will not fear you, O Lord,
And bring glory to your name?
For you alone are holy.
All nations will come and worship before you,
For your righteous acts have been revealed.'

After this I looked and in heaven the temple,
That is, the tabernacle of Testimony, was opened
Out of the temple came the seven angels with the seven plagues.
They were dressed in clean, shining linen
And wore golden sashes around their chests.
Then one of the four living creatures gave to the seven angels
Seven golden bowls filled with the wrath of God, who lives for ever and ever.
And the temple was filled with smoke from the glory of God and from his power,
And no one could enter the temple until the seven plagues
Of the seven angels were completed.

John sees standing by a sea of glass mixed with fire,
Those who have been victorious over the Beast
And his image and the number of his name
(The saints who have gone through The Great Tribulation
And have been beheaded by the Beast)
Holding harps given them by God.
They sing the song of Moses and the Lamb.

The saints declare that the deeds (judgments) of God Almighty
Are great and marvelous; that they are just and true.
Ultimately all the nations will fear God and bring glory to His name;
Acknowledging the righteousness of his acts of judgment,
Worshiping Him in His holiness.
He also sees the seven angels with the last seven plagues.
Dressed in clean shining linen, speaking of the holiness of Heaven;

THE LAST SEVEN PLAGUES

Gold sashes are around their chests speaking of the glory and majesty of God.
The temple is filled with smoke from the glory of God and His power.
No one can enter the temple of God until the last seven plagues are completed;
Speaking of the solemnity in Heaven because of God's judgment of the earth.

THE SEVEN BOWLS OF GOD'S WRATH

Revelation 16

Then I heard a loud voice from the temple saying to the seven angels,

'Go, pour out the seven bowls of God's wrath on the earth.'

The first angel *went and poured out his bowl on the land,*
And ugly and painful sores broke out on the people who had the mark of the beast
And worshiped his image.

The second angel *poured out his bowl on the sea,*
And it turned into blood
Like that of a dead man, and every living thing in the sea died.

The third angel *poured out his bowl on the rivers and springs of water,*
And they became blood.
Then I heard the angel in charge of the waters say:

'You are just in these judgments, you who are and who were, the Holy One,
Because you have so judged;
For they have shed the blood of your saints and prophets,
And you have given them blood to drink as they deserve.'

And I heard the altar respond:

'Yes, Lord God Almighty, true and just are your judgments.'

The fourth angel *poured out his bowl on the sun,*
And the sun was given the power to scorch people with fire.
They were seared by the intense heat and they cursed the name of God,
Who had control over these plagues, but they refused to repent and glorify him.

The fifth angel *poured out his bowl on the throne of the beast,*
And his kingdom was plunged into darkness.
Men gnawed their tongues in agony and cursed the God of heaven
Because of their pains and their sores,
But they refused to repent of what they had done.

The sixth angel *poured out his bowl on the great river Euphrates,*
And its water was dried up to prepare the way for the kings from the East.
Then I saw three evil spirits that looked like frogs;
They came out of the mouth of the beast and out of the mouth of the false prophet.

They are spirits of demons performing miraculous signs,
And they go out to the kings of the whole world,
To gather them for the battle on <u>the great day of God Almighty</u>.

'Behold, I come like a thief!'

'Blessed is he who stays awake and keeps his clothes with him,
So that he may not go naked and be shamefully exposed.'

Then they gathered the kings together to the place
That in Hebrew is called Armageddon.

The seventh angel *poured out his bowl into the air,*
And out of the temple came a loud voice from the throne, saying,

'It is done!'

Then there came flashes of lightning, rumblings, peals of thunder
And a severe earthquake.
No earthquake like it has ever occurred since man has been on earth,
So tremendous was the quake.

The great city split into three parts, and the cities of the nations collapsed.

God remembered Babylon the Great
And gave her the cup filled with the wine of the fury of his wrath.
Every island fled away and the mountains could not be found.
From the sky huge hailstones of about a hundred pounds each fell upon men.
And they cursed God on account of the plague of hail,
Because the plague was so terrible. (Revelation 16:1-21)

The angels pour out the last seven bowls of God's wrath.
Ugly, painful sores break out on the remaining people on earth
Who have received the "mark" of the Beast and worshiped his "image".
The sea turns into blood and every living thing in it dies.
The rivers and the springs of water turn to blood.
Those who shed the blood of God's prophets and saints are given blood to drink.
The sun is given the power to scorch people with fire;
They curse God and refuse to repent.

The Euphrates river is dried up so that the kings from the east can cross it.
Evil spirits come out of the mouth of the dragon and the Beast,
Performing miraculous signs to deceive the kings of the whole earth;
Gathering them to the battle against Christ Jesus.
Like puppets on strings the kings of the whole earth come to the battle,

The Time Of The END

The Great Day of God Almighty.
In the midst of the vision, Christ Jesus issues a warning
To those reading the prophecy, He says:
'Behold, I come like a thief!
Blessed is he who stays awake and keeps his clothes with him,
So that he may not go naked and be shamefully exposed.'

Christ Jesus warns that He will come at an unexpected time.
Blessed will be those dressed in the righteousness of Christ
And not be shamefully exposed.

The dragon and the Beast have gathered the kings of the earth
To the place called Armageddon,
Where they are destroyed by Christ Jesus,
With the breath of His mouth and the brightness of His appearing.

The seventh angel pours out his bowl into the air
And a voice from the throne declares, **"It is done!"**
The sorted history of a godless mankind is over.

The great city is split into three parts and the cities of the nations collapse.
God gives Babylon a cup filled with the wine of the fury of his wrath.
Every island flees away, the mountains cannot be found.
One hundred pound hailstones destroy everything that mankind has built.
The glory of mankind is pounded into dust.
And those still living continue to curse God because of the terrible plague.

God does not value anything produced by the hands of man.
Throughout the ages, mankind has been driven by the lust of the flesh,
The lust of what can be seen; that they have produced,
And their pride in all they see themselves as having obtained and accomplished.

In contrast, God values only what He sees in the heart of a man;
King David, for example, was a man after His own heart.
God is only concerned with those things that have eternal value,
And the only things of eternal value come from Christ Jesus,
Because He is the only Way, the only Truth and the only LIFE.

THE WOMAN ON THE BEAST

Revelation 17

One of the seven angels who had the seven bowls came and said to me,
'Come, I will show you the punishment of the great prostitute,
Who sits on many waters.
With her the kings of the earth committed adultery
And the inhabitants of the earth were intoxicated with the wine of her adulteries.'

Then the angel carried me away in the Spirit into a desert.
There I saw a woman sitting on a scarlet beast
That was covered with blasphemous names and had seven heads and ten horns.

The woman was dressed in purple and scarlet,
And was glittering with gold, precious stones and pearls.
She held a golden cup in her hand, filled with abominable things
And the filth of her adulteries.
This title was written on her forehead:

MYSTERY BABYLON THE GREAT
THE MOTHER OF PROSTITUTES
AND OF THE ABOMINATIONS OF THE EARTH.

I saw that the woman was drunk with the blood of the saints,
The blood of those who bore testimony to Jesus.

When I saw her, I was greatly astonished.
Then the angel said to me: 'Why are you astonished?
I will explain to you the mystery of the woman and of the beast she rides,
Which has the seven heads and ten horns.
The beast, which you saw, once was, now is not, and will come up out of the Abyss
And go to his destruction.
The inhabitants of the earth whose names have not been written in the book of life
From the creation of the world will be astonished when they see the beast,
Because he once was, now is not, and yet will come.

This calls for a mind with wisdom.
The seven heads are seven hills on which the woman sits.
They are also seven kings.
Five have fallen, one is, the other has not yet come;
But when he does come, he must remain for a little while.
The beast who once was and now is not, is an eighth king.
He belongs to the seven and is going to his destruction.
The ten horns you saw are ten kings who have not yet received a kingdom,
But who for one hour will receive authority as kings along with the beast.
They have one purpose and will give their power and authority to the beast.

They will make war against the Lamb, but the Lamb will overcome them
Because he is the Lord of Lords and the King of kings--
And with him will be his called, chosen and faithful followers.'

Then the angel said to me,
'The waters you saw, where the prostitute sits,
Are peoples, multitudes, nations and languages.
The beast and the ten horns you saw will hate the prostitute.
They will bring her to ruin and leave her naked;
They will eat her flesh and burn her with fire.
For God has put it into their hearts to accomplish his purpose
By agreeing to give the beast their power to rule, until God's words are fulfilled.

The woman you saw is the great city that rules over the kings of the earth.'

John is shown the Great Prostitute who seduces the world,
With her overabundance of everything mankind holds dear;
The lust of the flesh, the lust of the eyes and the pride of life;
The theology of Satan;
With whom the kings of the earth have committed adultery.
In other words this Prostitute has caused the kings of the earth
And the peoples of the earth to be unfaithful to God;
They are intoxicated with the wine of her adulteries.

This is the bride of Satan, the "church" of Satan.
The people sold out to his evil ways and plans; his theology.
The Prostitute personifies the deception of Satan.
As Satan's "church" on earth she masquerades as and angel of light.
Purporting to be interested in what is good for mankind but the truth is the opposite.
She is the primary entity through whom Satan works his evil plans.
The Prostitute sits on a Scarlet Beast, covered with blasphemous names
With seven heads and ten horns,
Representing the puppet nations she rules.
They are also sold out to Satan and ruled by him.
They are in the lineage of all the ungodly rulers from the beginning of time,
Until the present time, who Satan manipulates for his purposes.

She is dressed in purple and scarlet, glittering with gold, precious stones and pearls.
In her hand is a cup filled with abominable things and the filth of her adulteries.
She has a title written on her forehead:

MYSTERY BABYLON THE MOTHER OF PROSTITUTES
AND OF THE ABOMINATIONS OF THE EARTH.

The Prostitute is drunk with the blood of the saints,
Those who have maintained the testimony of Christ Jesus.

The Time Of The END

Christ Jesus and His followers are her only adversaries
And she kills all she can.
John is astonished at the sight of her.
The angel explains that the prostitute rides on a Beast with seven horns.
The Beast once was, now is not, and will come up out of the Abyss
And go to his destruction.
The inhabitants of the earth whose names have not been written in the Book of LIFE
Will be astonished when they see the Beast,
Because this Beast is recognizable as someone from the past,
Who was not present on earth at the time John is given the vision,
Yet will come again at The Time of The END.

Satan always copies what God does.
The Beast is a type of God's Christ, he is the evil anointed one.
Christ was present in the Old testament in supernatural visitations.
So the Beast was present in the past as a number of evil persons,
But was not present on earth at the time of John,
But is coming again at The Time of The END.

The angel tells John that this calls for a mind with wisdom.
He tells John that the woman sits on seven hills.
They are also seven kings.
Five have fallen, one is, The other has not yet come;
But when he does he must remain for a little while (possibly Hitler or Napoleon).
The Beast that John sees in his vision is the eighth of these kings.
He belongs to the seven (he is of the same spirit) who have preceded him,
And will be destroyed by Christ Jesus.

Here we gain insight from Chapter 7 of the Book of Daniel
And his vision of four beasts.

The first beast was like a lion, and it had the wings of an eagle.
This is most likely Babylonian Empire.

The second beast looked like a bear.
This is most likely the Medo-Persian Empire.

The third beast looked like a leopard.
This is most likely the Grecian Empire.

The fourth best, according to John was:
'Terrifying and frightening and very powerful.
It had large iron teeth; it crushed and devoured its victims
And trampled underfoot whatever was left.
It was different from all the former beasts, and it had ten horns.(Daniel 7:7)

The Time Of The END

This is the Roman Empire.

Then Daniel sees another horn, a little one, which comes up among the ten horns.
Three of the first horns are uprooted before it.
This horn had the eyes of a man and a mouth that spoke boastfully. (Daniel 7:8)

This is the Beast of the Book of Revelation, the final Beast, the Antichrist.
This final Beast arises from the Old Roman Empire:

'He will speak against the Most High and oppress his saints
And try to change the set times and the laws.
The saints will be handed over to him for a time, times and half a time.'
(Daniel 7:24-25)

According to Daniels vision:
'Out of one of them came another horn, which started small
But grew in power to the south and to the east and toward the Beautiful Land.
It grew until it reached the host of the heavens,
And it threw some of the starry host down to the earth and trampled on them.
It set itself up to be as great as the Prince of the host;
It took away the daily sacrifice from him,
And the place of his sanctuary was brought low.
Because of rebellion,
The host of the saints and the daily sacrifice were given over to it.
It prospered in everything it did, and truth was thrown to the ground.

Then I heard a holy one speaking, and another holy one said to him,

'How long will it take for the vision to be fulfilled--
The vision concerning the daily sacrifice, the rebellion that causes desolation,
And the surrender of the sanctuary
And of the host that will be trampled underfoot?'

He said to me, 'It will take 2,300 evenings and mornings;
Then the sanctuary will be reconsecrated.' (Daniel 8:9-14)

The Beast grows in power to the south and the east toward Israel.
By seduction, and deception the Beast throws some of the saints of God to the earth
And tramples on them.
He sets himself up to be as great as Christ Jesus,
He takes away the worship of the Living God
And the sanctuary of God (the Church of God) is brought low.
Because of the rebellion of the saints (a great apostasy),
Daily worship is given over to the Beast.
The saints of God will be trampled on
For the better part of The Great Tribulation, 1,150 days.

Then Christ Jesus then comes and puts an end to the Beast and his realm,
And the sanctuary of God is reconsecrated.

The Ten Horns and ten kings are those of the Book of Daniel,
Who have not received a kingdom at the time John is given his vision.
They will receive authority for a brief period of time, The Time of the END,
In subjugation to the Beast.

They have one purpose, to make war against the Lamb,
Because the Lamb and His saints are all that stand in the way
Of their total domination.

However, the Lamb overcomes them because He is the Lord of lords
And the King of kings;
And with Christ Jesus will be his chosen and faithful followers.

The Prostitute's Doom
The Beast and the ten kings in subjugation to him, come to hate the Prostitute.
For God puts it in their hearts to do so.
They completely destroy her with fire.
Babylon, the Prostitute, the greatest city on earth,
In the greatest nation on earth, as it has always been.
The city that rules over the kings of the earth is annihilated
By the Beast who created her and the kings he rules over.

THE FALL OF BABYLON

Revelation 18

After this I saw another angel coming down from heaven.
He had great authority, and the earth was illuminated by his splendor.
With a mighty voice he shouted:

'Fallen! Fallen is Babylon the Great!
She has become a home for demons
And a haunt for every evil spirit,
A haunt for every unclean and detestable bird.

For all the nations have drunk the maddening wine of her adulteries.
The kings of the earth committed adultery with her
And the merchants of the earth grew rich from her excessive luxuries.'

Then I heard another voice from heaven say:

'Come our of her, my people,
So that you will not share in her sins,
So that you will not receive any of her plagues;
For her sins are piled up to heaven,
And God has remembered her crimes.

Give back to her as she has given;
Pay back to her double for what she has done.
Mix her a double portion from her own cup.
Give her as much torture and grief
As the glory luxury she gave herself.'

In her heart she boasts,
'I sit as queen; I am not a widow,'
Therefore in one day her plagues will overtake her:
Death, mourning and famine.
She will be consumed by fire,
For mighty is the Lord God who judges her.

When the kings of the earth who committed adultery with her
And shared her luxury see the smoke of her burning
They will weep and mourn over her.
Terrified at her torment they will stand far off and cry:

'Woe! Woe, O great city,
O Babylon, city of power!
In one hour your doom has come!'

The Time Of The END

The merchants of the earth will weep and mourn over her
Because no one buys their cargoes any more--
Cargoes of gold, silver, precious stones and pearls;
Fine linen, purple, silk and scarlet cloth; every sort of citron wood,
And articles of every kind made of ivory, costly wood, bronze, iron and marble;
Cargoes of cinnamon and spice, of incense, myrrh and frankincense,
Of wine and olive oil, of fine flour and wheat, cattle and sheep;
Horses and carriages; and bodies and souls of men.

They will say,
'The fruit you longed for is gone from you.
All your riches and splendor have vanished, never to be recovered.'

The merchants who sold these things and gained their wealth from her
Will stand far off, terrified at her torment.
They will weep and mourn and cry out:

'Woe! Woe, O great city,
Dressed in fine linen, purple and scarlet,
And glittering with gold, precious stones and pearls!
In one hour such great wealth has been brought to ruin!'

Every sea captain, and all who travel by ship, the sailors,
And all who earn their living from the sea, will stand far off.
When they see the smoke of her burning, they will exclaim,

'Was there ever a city like this great city?'

They will throw dust on their heads, and with weeping and mourning cry out:

'Woe! Woe, O great city,
Where all who had ships on the sea
Became rich through her wealth!
In one hour she has been brought to ruin!'

Rejoice over her, O heaven!
Rejoice, saints and apostles and prophets!
God has judged her for the way she treated you.

Then a mighty angel picked up a boulder the size of a large mill stone
And threw it into the sea, and said:
'With such violence the great city of Babylon will be thrown down,
Never to be found again.
The music of harpists and musicians, flute players and trumpeters,
Will never be heard in you again.

No workman of any trade will ever be found in you again.

The sound of a millstone will never be heard in you again.

The light of a lamp will never shine in you again.

The voice of bridegroom and bride will never be heard in you again.

Your merchants were the world's great men.
By your magic spell <u>all the nations</u> were led astray.
In her was found the blood of prophets and of the saints,
And all who have been kill on the earth.'

A second angel announces the fall of Babylon.

A second angel followed and said, 'Fallen! Fallen is Babylon the great,
Which made <u>all the nations</u> drink the maddening wine of her adulteries.'
(Revelation 14:8)

The second angel announces the fall of Babylon the Great.
The city that personifies all human rebellion against God.
In her, every evil practice takes place; everything that God hates;
Everything that sentences man to hell, and is glorified by man.
Good is called evil and what is evil is called good.
Satan had gloated over his accomplishment, but not for long.

The kings of the earth were figuratively in bed with the Prostitute,
Committing adultery toward God with her.

The merchants of the earth had become wealthy
From her insatiable demand for ever increasing luxury.

Another voice from heaven issues a warning:
Telling the people of God to come out from the Prostitute,
The greatest city on earth, in the greatest nation on earth.
So that they can avoid the judgment of God that is about to fall upon her;
For the extent and grossness of her sins has risen to heaven.

In one day Babylon is destroyed, she is consumed by fire,
By the holy and mighty hand of God,
Through the instrument of the ten kings and the Beast.
God uses the Beast and the ten kings to accomplish His purposes.

The kings of the earth mourn over the destruction of the Prostitute.
These are not the ten kings who destroy her,
But the remaining rulers of the earth.

The Time Of The END

They also committed adultery with her, and are terrified at her fate.
She is utterly and completely destroyed.

The merchants of the earth mourn over her
Because she was the primary source of their wealth.
The greatness of the Prostitute was what every city in the world aspired to.
Never in the history of the world had such wealth been accumulated in one place.
Now, in one hour, it has all been brought to ruin.
The symbol of the greatness of mankind is brought to nothing in one hour.

The sea captains and the sailors mourn,
Those who had become rich through her,
And who had transported her wealth exclaim:

'Was there ever a city like this city?'
No, the truth is, that in the realm of men, there never was a city like this city.
In the natural, this city represented the ultimate accomplishment of mankind;
But what men call good, God calls evil.
This city is like the Tower of Babel; representing mankind exalting themselves,
Trying to become like God, just as Satan does.
Mankind, the puppets of Satan, pretending to be what they can never be
Just as the one who rules over them does.

Rejoice over her destruction!
The angel admonishes all of Heaven to rejoice over her downfall.
He admonishes the saints, apostles and prophets to rejoice over her downfall.
Because God has judged her for the way she treated them.
A mighty angel picks up a large millstone and throws it into the sea,
Symbolizing the violence involved with the fall of Babylon.
With such violence she will be destroyed never to be found again.

Her merchants were the worlds great men.
Her magic spell, that blinded men, by the power of Satan,
Led all the nations of the earth astray.
Babylon is responsible for the blood of all the prophets and all the saints,
And all who have been killed on the earth.
This Prostitute is the personification of wickedness,
The personification of all that exalts itself against the Way, the Truth and the LIFE.
All that exalts itself against God and His Christ.

Babylon The Great, the last of the great cities that personified the work of Satan
In this lost and fallen world he dominates.
She was preceded by all of the empires of old that lay in the dust,
Beginning with the Tower of Babel from which she derives her name.

THE RIDER ON THE WHITE HORSE

Revelation 19:11-21

I saw heaven standing open and there before me was a white horse,
Whose rider is called Faithful and True.
With justice he judges and makes war.
His eyes are like blazing fire, and on his head are many crowns.
He has a name written on him that no one but he himself knows.
He is dressed in a robe dipped in blood,
And his name is The Word of God.

The armies of heaven were following him,
Riding on white horses and dressed in fine linen, white and clean.

Out of his mouth comes a sharp sword with which to strike down the nations.

'He will rule them with an iron scepter.'

He treads the winepress of the fury of the wrath of God Almighty.
On his robe and on his thigh he has this name written:

KING OF KINGS AND LORD OF LORDS

And I saw an angel standing in the sun,
Who cried in a loud voice to all the birds flying in midair,

'Come, gather together for the great supper of God,
So you may eat the flesh of kings, generals, and mighty men,
Of horses and their riders, and the flesh of all people,
Free and slave, small and great.'

Then I saw the beast and the kings of the earth
And their armies gathered together
To make war against the rider on the horse and his army.
But the beast was captured, and with him the false prophet
Who had performed the miraculous signs on his behalf.

With these signs he had deluded those who had received the mark of the beast
And worshiped his image.
The two of them were thrown alive into the fiery lake of burning sulfur.
The rest of them were killed with the sword
That came out of the mouth of the rider on the horse,
And all the birds gorged themselves on their flesh.

Heaven opens, and there on a white horse stands Christ Jesus,
The Faithful and True One, the One who is Justice.

The Time Of The END

THE RIDER ON THE WHITE HORSE

His eyes are like blazing fire,
Because he sees all things, and no one can hide from the fire of His holiness.

On His head are many crowns; He is the King over all things.
He has a name written on Him that cannot be comprehended by anyone but Him.

He is dressed in a robe dipped in blood.
It took His own blood to bring about His plan and purpose on the earth.
And all those who oppose Him will pay with their blood.

His name is The Word of God.
His Word is not just words written on pages.
His Word embodies His Spirit, and He and His Word are ONE.

The armies of Heaven were following Him, riding on white horses
And dressed in fine linen, white and clean.
Everything and everyone in Heaven is holy, clean, good, and wonderful,
As is their Creator.

'Out of His mouth comes a sharp sword
With which to strike down the nations.'

The sharp sword is The Word of God, before which no one can stand.
Christ Jesus has sent his apostles, prophets, evangelists, pastors
And teachers to the nations, and they have been rejected.
Now the nations are struck down by the breath of His mouth, the TRUTH.

'He will rule them with an iron scepter.'

Now the nations, those few who remain alive,
Are ruled by Christ Jesus and His iron scepter.

'He treads the winepress of the fury of the wrath of God Almighty.'

At the battle of Armageddon all the nations of the earth come to fight Christ Jesus.
They are annihilated by Him and their blood rises as high as a horses bridle.

'On his robe and on his thigh he has this name written:

KING OF KINGS AND LORD OF LORDS.'

Christ Jesus is the King of kings and the Lord of lords.
He is JEHOVAH, The Self-Existent One, The Almighty One.
He is the Creator of all that exists.
He is LIFE itself.
Without Him (which is a contradiction in itself) there would be nothing.

The Time Of The END

He is the I AM, with no beginning and no end.
An angel standing in the sun, cries out in a loud voice,
And invites all the birds to come to the great supper of God.
To eat the flesh of the men and animals who have been killed by Christ Jesus
At the Battle of Armageddon.

The Beast and the kings of the earth had come to make war against Christ Jesus
And the armies of heaven.
The Beast and the False Prophet are captured and thrown into the Lake of Fire.
The rest of the Beast's army are killed and eaten by the birds.
Such is the ignoble, TIME OF THE END.

THE HARVEST OF THE EARTH

Revelation 14:14-19

I looked, and there before me was a white cloud,
And seated on the cloud was one 'like the son of man' (Christ Jesus)
With a crown of gold on his head and a sharp sickle in his hand.
Then another angel came out of the temple and called in a loud voice
To him who was sitting on the cloud, 'Take your sickle and reap,
Because the time to reap has come, for the harvest of the earth is ripe.'
So he that was seated on the cloud swung his sickle over the earth,
And the earth was harvested.

Here, we have the final harvest of those who are destined for heaven.
The saints who die for Christ in The Great Tribulation.

Another angel came out of the temple in heaven,
And he too had a sharp sickle.
Still another angel, who had charge of the fire,
Came from the altar and called in a loud voice to him who had the sharp sickle.

'Take your sharp sickle and gather the clusters of grapes from the earth's vine,
Because its grapes are ripe.'

The angel swung his sickle on the earth,
Gathered its grapes and threw them into the great winepress of God's wrath.
They were trampled in the winepress outside the city,
And the blood flowed out of the press, rising as high as the horses' bridles
For a distance of 1,600 stadia (about 180 miles).

Here, we are given a view of the what happens at The Battle of Armageddon.
The armies of the world are slaughtered as grapes in a winepress would be crushed.
The blood of the men and women in the armies flows out of the area of the battle
As high as a horses bridle for 180 miles.

THE SEVENTH TRUMPET

Revelation 11:15

The seventh angel sounded his trumpet,
And there were loud voices in heaven, which said:

'The kingdom of the world
Has become the kingdom of our Lord and of his Christ,
And he will reign for ever and ever.'

And the twenty-four elders, who were seated on their thrones before God,
Fell on their faces and worshiped God, saying:

'We give thanks to you, Lord God Almighty,
Who is and who was,
Because you have taken your great power and have begun to reign.
The nations were angry; and your wrath has come.
The time has come for judging the dead,
And for rewarding your servants the prophets
And your saints and those who reverence your name, both small and great--
And for destroying those who destroy the earth.'

Then God's temple in heaven was opened,
And within his temple was seen the ark of his covenant.
And there came flashes of lightning, rumblings, peals of thunder,
An earthquake and a great hailstorm. (Revelation 11:15-19)

Time Comes To An End

Christ Jesus wraps up "Time."
The devil is powerless and soon to be done away with.
Mankind has been given the opportunity to choose LIFE.
All those who received Christ Jesus found eternal LIFE.
All those who rejected Him found eternal death.

Christ Jesus personally spoke to every living person about His Kingdom,
Giving each one the opportunity to repent and enter into it.
Now all that remains is the judgment and the rewards,
Each according to the choice they made.

THE GREAT MULTITUDE IN WHITE ROBES

Revelation 7:9

After this I looked and there before me was a great multitude
That no one could count,
From every nation, tribe, people and language, standing before the throne
And in front of the Lamb.
They were wearing white robes and were holding palm branches in their hands.
And they cried out in a loud voice:

'Salvation belongs to our God, who sits on the throne, and to the Lamb.'

All the angels were standing around the throne and around the elders
And the four living creatures.
They fell down on their faces before the throne and worshiped God saying:

'Amen! Praise and glory and wisdom and thanks and honor and power and strength
Be to our God for ever and ever. Amen!

Then one of the elders asked me,
'These in white robes—who are they, and where did they come from?'

I answered, 'sir, you know.'
And he said, 'These are they who have come out of the great tribulation;
They have washed their robes and made them white in the blood of the Lamb.
Therefore, they are before the throne of God
And serve him day and night in his temple;
And he who sits on the throne will spread his tent over them.
Never again will they hunger; never again will they thirst.
The sun will not beat upon them, nor any scorching heat.
For the Lamb at the center of the throne will be their shepherd;
He will lead them to springs of living water.
And God will wipe away every tear from their eyes.' (Revelation 7:9-17)

These are the rest of the off-spring of the "Woman", the Bride of Christ,
That the dragon went off to make war against—who obey God's commandments
And hold to the testimony of Jesus in Revelation 12:17.
Jesus leads them to Springs of Living Water.
The Water of LIFE that they had not received until then.
He then immerses them in the Water of LIFE.
Their faith in the Word of God,
Enables them to resist receiving the "mark" of the Beast
And to die for Christ Jesus.

HALLELUJAH!
THE WEDDING SUPPER
OF THE LAMB

Revelation 19

After this I heard what sounded like the roar
Of a great multitude in heaven <u>shouting</u>:

'Hallelujah!
Salvation and glory and power belong to our God,
For true and just are his judgments.
He has condemned the great prostitute
Who corrupted the earth by her adulteries.
He has avenged on her the blood of his servants.'

'Hallelujah!
The smoke from her goes up for ever and ever.'

The twenty-four elders and the four living creatures fell down and worshiped God,
Who was seated on the throne. And they cried:

'Amen, Hallelujah!'

Then a voice came from the throne saying:
'Praise our God, all you his servants,
You who fear him, both small and great!'

Then I heard what sounded like a great multitude,
Like the roar of rushing waters and peals of thunder, <u>shouting</u>:

'Hallelujah!
For our Lord God Almighty reigns.
Let us rejoice and be glad and give him glory!

For the wedding of the Lamb has come,
And his bride has made herself ready.'

Fine linen, bright and clean, was given her to wear.
(Fine linen stands for the righteous acts of the saints)

Then the angel said to me,

120

THE WEDDING SUPPER OF THE LAMB

'Write: Blessed are those who are invited
To the wedding supper of the lamb!
These are the true words of God.'

At this I fell at his feet to worship him.
But he said to me,
'Do not do it!
I am a fellow servant with you
And with your brothers who hold to the testimony of Jesus.'

'For the testimony of Jesus is the spirit of prophecy.'

All of Heaven, a great multitude shout, HALLELUJAH!
The Prostitute, the primary instrument of Satan,
The perpetrator of every sort of evil and wickedness
Has been judged, never to rise again.
HALLELUJAH, for the Lord God Almighty reigns.

The voice from Heaven says:

'Let us rejoice and be glad and give Him glory!
For the wedding of the Lamb has come
And his bride has made herself ready.
Fine linen, bright and clean, was given her to wear.'
(Fine linen stands for the righteous acts of the saints)

Then the angel said to me, 'Write:
Blessed are those who are invited to the wedding supper of the Lamb!'
(Revelation19:7-9)

With the wedding of Christ Jesus and His Bride,
The plan and purpose of God on earth is complete.
Blessed are those who are invited to the wedding supper of the Lamb.
His Bride has made herself ready.
He has gathered to Himself a people with whom He will spend eternity.
No more sorrow, no more tears; Love, Peace and Joy will reign forever.

SATAN BOUND
FOR A THOUSAND YEARS

Revelation 20

And I saw an angel coming down out of heaven,
Having the key to the Abyss and holding in his hand a great chain.
He seized the dragon, that ancient serpent, who is the devil, or Satan,
And bound him for a thousand years.
He threw him into the Abyss, and locked and sealed it over him,
To keep him from deceiving the nations any more
Until the thousand years were ended.
After that, he must be set free for a short time.

An angel comes out of Heaven, takes hold of Satan, binds him with a chain
And throws him into the Abyss where he remains for a thousand years,
Unable to deceive mankind anymore.
This demonstrates the impotence of Satan before the Living God.
The only power Satan ever had was given to him by God,
And was always under the supervision of God.

CHRIST RULES AND REIGNS FOR A THOUSAND YEARS

Revelation 20:4-6

I saw thrones on which were seated those who had been given authority to judge.
And I saw the souls of those who had been beheaded
Because of their testimony for Jesus and because of the word of God.
They had not worshiped the beast or his image
And had not received his mark on their foreheads or their hands.
They came to life and reigned with Christ a thousand years.
(The rest of the dead did not come to life until the thousand years were ended.)
This is the first resurrection.

Blessed and holy are those who have part in the first resurrection.

The second death has no power over them,
But they will be priests of God and of Christ
And will reign with him for a thousand years.(Revelation 20:4-6)

John sees the saints of Christ Jesus, seated on thrones
And given the authority to judge.
He also sees the souls of those who were beheaded because of the Word of God;
Those who had not received the "mark" of the Beast on their forehead or hands;
Who had not worshiped the Beast or his "image";
These came to life and reigned with Christ for a thousand years.
This is the first resurrection.
These are the blessed and holy ones;
The second death has no power over them.
They are the priests of God and of Christ,
And will reign with him for a thousand years.
The rest of the dead remain dead until the end of the thousand years,
At which time they are judged and sentenced to eternal death
In the Lake of Fire with Satan, the Beast, the False Prophet
And all the fallen angels.

SATAN'S DOOM

Revelation 20:7

When the thousand years are over,
Satan will be released from his prison and will go out to deceive the nations
In the four corners of the earth—Gog and Magog—to gather them for battle.

In number they are like the sand on the seashore.
They marched across the breath of the earth
And surrounded the camp of God's people, the city he loves.
But fire came down from heaven and devoured them.
And the devil, who deceived them, was thrown into the lake of burning sulfur,
Where the beast and the false prophet had been thrown.
They will be tormented day and night for ever and ever.

One of the mysteries of the Book of Revelation
Is the release of Satan at the end of the thousand years of rest.
At this time, all of mankind, except for the Bride of Christ
Who were not killed in The Great Tribulation, and their off-spring,
Have lived in a sinless environment for a thousand years.
In perfect love, peace and joy.
Nevertheless, when Satan is released, is able to deceived these people
And lead them to march against God, His Christ, and the City of God.
However, they are devoured by God who sends fire from Heaven to destroy them.
Then they are all thrown into the Lake of Fire and eternal torment.

These people lived in Paradise, in the continual presence of God
Yet they were still able to be deceived.
Mankind, without Christ in them is unable to withstand the deception of Satan.
These people were in a similar situation as Adam and Eve.
They had a choice to obey God or not.
They chose not to, just as did Adam and Eve.

The only thing that enables any person to resist the deception of Satan
Is Christ in them, the anointing of the Anointed One.
It is Christ in us, our teacher who enables us to embrace the TRUTH,
And reject the LIE.

The LIE is that there is anything good outside of Christ.

Christ is the WAY, the TRUTH and the LIFE.
There is nothing good outside of Him.
Because He is LIFE itself.
When we receive and embrace Him we embrace LIFE.
When we reject Him we embrace DEATH.

THE DEAD ARE JUDGED

Revelation 20:11-15

Then I saw a great white throne and him who was seated on it.
Earth and sky fled from his presence, and there was no place for them.
And I saw the dead, great and small, standing before the throne,
And books were opened.
*Another book was opened, which is **the book of life**.*

The dead were judged according to what they had done as recorded in the books.
The sea gave up the dead that were in it,
And death and Hades gave up the dead that were in them,
And each person was judged according to what he had done.

Then death and hades were thrown into the lake of fire.
The lake of fire is the second death.
I anyone's name was not found written in the book of life,
He was thrown into the lake of fire. (Revelation 20:11-15)

The reality of the ultimate judgment of God on every living person
Is a fact that Satan keeps from people under the spell of his deception.
Under this spell, the fact of this judgment is ignored
Or people pretend that everyone goes to Heaven.
What a terrible awakening when they die and the TRUTH confronts them.

Christ Jesus came to dispel this LIE.

God's books in Heaven have recorded in them every detail of each of our lives.
All of our sin is written in red before a holy God.

The only hope of avoiding the judgment of God
Is to repent of our sin,
Which allows Christ to wash us clean in His blood;
Washing away all of our sin.
We must receive Christ Jesus as Savior, Lord and Anointing;
Allowing Him to baptize us, immerse us, in the Holy Spirit of God;
Then allowing Him to live in and through us.
It is Christ In us the hope of glory as the apostle Paul said.

Then we can live the WAY, the TRUTH and the LIFE,
And reject the LIE.
Then our name is written in the BOOK OF LIFE.

THE NEW JERUSALEM

Revelation 21

Then I saw a new heaven and a new earth,
For the first heaven and the first earth had passed away,
And there was no longer any sea.

I saw the Holy City, the new Jerusalem, coming down out of heaven from God,
Prepared as a bride beautifully dressed for her husband.
And I heard a loud voice from the throne saying,

'Now the dwelling of God is with men, and he will live with them.
They will be his people, and God himself will be with them and be their God.
He will wipe every tear from their eyes.
There will be no more death or mourning or crying or pain,
For the old order of things has passed away.'

He who was seated on the throne said,
'I am making everything new!'

Then he said,
'Write this down, for these words are trustworthy and true.'

He said to me:
'It is done.
I am the Alpha and the Omega, the Beginning and the End.
To him who is thirsty I will give to drink without cost
From the spring of the water of life.
*He who overcomes will inherit **all this,***
And I will be his God and he will be my son.'

'But the cowardly, the unbelieving, the vile, the murderers, the sexually immoral,
Those who practice magic arts, the idolaters and all liars—
Their place will be in the fiery lake of burning sulfur.
This is the second death.'

One of the seven angels
Who had the seven bowls full of the seven last plagues
Came and said to me,

'Come, I will show you the bride, the wife of the Lamb.'

And he carried me away in the Spirit to a mountain great and high,
And showed me the Holy City, Jerusalem,
Coming down out of heaven from God.
It shone with the glory of God,

THE NEW JERUSALEM

And its brilliance was like that of a very precious jewel, like jasper, clear as crystal.
It had a great high wall with twelve gates, and with twelve angels at the gates.
On the gates were written the names of the twelve tribes of Israel.
There were three gates on the east, three on the north, three on the south
And three on the west.
The wall of the city had twelve foundations,
And on them were the names of the twelve apostles of the Lamb.

The angel who talked with me had a measuring rod of gold to measure the city,
Is gates and its wall.
The city was laid out like a square, as long as it was wide.
He measured the city with the rod and found it to be 12,000 stadia in length
(about 1,400 miles),
And as wide and high as it is long.
He measured its wall and it was 144 cubits thick (about 200 feet),
By man's measurement, which the angel was using.

The wall was made of jasper, and the city of pure gold, as pure as glass.
The foundations of the city walls were decorated with every kind of precious stone.
The first foundation was jasper, the second sapphire, the third chalcedony,
The fourth emerald, the fifth sardonyx, the sixth carnelian, the seventh crysolite,
The eighth beryl, the ninth topaz, the tenth chrysoprase, the eleventh jacinth,
And the twelfth amethyst.
The twelve gates were twelve pearls, each made of a single pearl.
The street of the city was of pure gold, like transparent glass.

I did not see a temple in the city, because the Lord God Almighty
And the Lamb are its temple.
The city does not need the sun or the moon to shine on it,
For the glory of God gives it light, and the Lamb is its lamp.

The nations will walk by its light,
And the kings of the earth will bring their splendor into it.
On no day will its gates ever be shut, for there will be no night there.
The glory and honor of the nations will be brought into it.
Nothing impure will ever enter it,
Nor will anyone who does what is shameful or deceitful,
But only those whose names are written in the lamb's book of life.

John sees a new heaven and a new earth because the first earth has passed away.
The new earth has no sea.
Then the Holy City, the New Jerusalem comes down out of Heaven from God,
Like a Bride dressed beautifully for her husband.

A loud voice declares that,

The Time Of The END

"Now the dwelling of God is with men, and He will live in them."
God who is a Spirit will live in His people,
Just as He lives in those who receive Him today.
He will remove from them all sorrow
So that there are no more tears, crying, pain, mourning or death.
The former reality will be replaced with a new and glorious reality.

God Himself declares: "I am making everything new!"

The Lord says to John:

"It is done.
I am the Alpha and the Omega, the Beginning and the End.
To him who is thirsty I will give to drink without cost
From the Spring of the Water of LIFE.
He who overcomes will inherit all this,
And I will be his God and he will be my son."

"It is done." The history of mankind is over, its purpose completed.
The Holy Spirit has obtained a Bride for Christ Jesus,
And He is making everything new for their new state of being.
Those who were thirsty, drank, from the Spring of the Water of LIFE
And received and inherited **all this,** a new state of being in the Spirit of God.
They overcame the world by the blood of the Lamb
And the word of their testimony of Christ Jesus;
By Christ in them, who became the reality of their new state of glory.
Christ Jesus is their God and they are His sons and daughters.

Everyone else is destined for the Lake of Fire, the place of eternal torment.

One of the seven angels shows John the Bride the wife of the Lamb.
He is carried away in the Spirit and shown the Holy City, Jerusalem.
It is glorious beyond measure.
The City does not have a temple
Because the Lord God Almighty and the Lamb, who are ONE, are its temple.
The City does not need the sun or the moon for light
Because the glory of God gives off its supernatural light.
The nations now walk by the light of the City of God
And the kings of the earth bring their splendor to it.
The City's gates are never shut, because there is no night there.
The glory and honor of the nations will be brought into it.

"Nothing impure will ever enter it,
Nor will anyone who does what is shameful or deceitful,
Only those whose names are written in the Lambs Book of LIFE."

THE RIVER OF LIFE

Revelation 22

Then the angel showed me the river of the water of life, as clear as crystal,
Flowing from the throne of God and of the Lamb
Down the middle of the great street of the city.
On each side of the river stood the tree of life,
Bearing twelve crops of fruit yielding its fruit every month.
And the leaves of the tree are for the healing of the nations.
No longer will there be any curse.
The throne of God and of the Lamb will be in the city,
And his servants will serve him.
They will see his face, and his name will be on their foreheads.
They will not need the light of a lamp or the light of the sun,
For the Lord God will give them light.
And they will reign for ever and ever.

The angel said to me,

'These words are trustworthy and true.
The Lord, the God of the spirits of the prophets,
Sent his angel to show his servants the things that must soon take place.'

John is shown the River of the Water of LIFE, clear as crystal,
Flowing from the Throne of God.
The River from which all those in the Book of LIFE drank from;
Those who were thirsty and were baptized (immersed) in it.

The River of LIFE is the central feature of the City of God;
It is the Holy Spirit, the essence of God flowing continually;
Giving LIFE to the Tree of LIFE, which bears its fruit every month.
The leaves of which heal the nations, and remove the curse from them.
The throne of God and His Christ are in the City.
There his servants serve Him.
They see His face, and His name is on their foreheads
(They are permanently sealed with His holiness)
The light of God gives supernatural illumination to the City
And His Bride reigns with Him for ever.

The angel tells John that what he has seen will soon take place.

JESUS IS COMING SOON!

Revelation 22:7

'Behold, I am coming soon!
Blessed is he who keeps the words of the prophecy in this book.'

I, John am the one who heard and saw these things.
And when I had heard and seen them,
I fell down to worship at the feet of the angel
Who had been showing them to me.
But he said to me,

'Do not do it!
I am a fellow servant with you
And with your brothers the prophets
And of all who keep the words of this book.
Worship God!'

Then he told me ,

'Do not seal up the words of the prophecy of this book,
Because the time is near.'

'Let him who does wrong continue to do wrong;
Let him who is vile continue to be vile;
Let him who does right continue to do right;
And let him who is holy continue to be holy.'

'Behold, I am coming soon!
My reward is with me,
And I will give to everyone according to what he has done.
I am the Alpha and Omega, the First and the Last,
The beginning and the End.

Blessed are those who wash their robes,
That they may have the right to the tree of life
And may go through the gates into the city.

Outside are the dogs, those who practice magic arts,
The sexually immoral, the murderers, the idolaters
And everyone who loves and practices falsehood.

The Time Of The END

I Jesus, have sent my angel to give you this testimony for the churches.
I am the Root and the Offspring of David, and the bright and Morning Star.'

The Spirit and the bride say, 'Come!
And let him who hears say, 'Come!'
Whoever is thirsty, let him come;
And whoever wishes,
Let him take the free gift of the water of life.

I warn everyone who hears the words of the prophecy of this book;
If anyone adds anything to them,
God will add to him the plagues described in this book.
And if anyone takes words away from this book of prophecy,
God will take away from him his share in the tree of life and in the holy city,
Which are described in this book.

He who testifies to these things says,

'Yes, I am coming soon.'

Amen. Come, Lord Jesus.
The grace of the Lord Jesus be with God's people. Amen.

Christ Jesus makes His own declaration of the fact that He is coming soon.
That is, coming soon in God's timing.
When He will rest from His work with mankind,
And He will reign in love, peace and joy with His people for a thousand years.

Christ Jesus says that the one who KEEPS the words of the Book of Revelation
Will be blessed.
In other words, the book was not meant to be mysterious,
But understood and kept.

What are the words that Christ Jesus wants us to KEEP?
- We are to repent of what offends God.
- We are to keep our first love toward Christ Jesus.
- We are to have ears that hear what the Spirit says to the churches, and to each one of us individually.
- We are to overcome this world and it's ways by the blood of the Lamb and the word of our testimony and therefore have the right to the Tree of LIFE.
- We are to be faithful to the point of death.
- We are to suffer persecution when necessary.
- We are to hold on to what Christ Jesus has taught us.
- If we are spiritually dead, we are to wake up.

131

- We are to strengthen and hold on to what we have been given.
- We are to open the door of our heart to the knocking of Christ Jesus, and allow Him to come and eat with us; have intimate fellowship with us.
- We are to wash our robes and make them white in the blood of the Lamb.
- We must not worship the Beast or take his "mark."
- We must come out of the Harlot, Babylon.
- We must make ourselves ready to be the Bride of Christ.
- We are to be THIRSTY for the Water of LIFE.
- We are to TAKE the free gift the Water of LIFE.

Christ Jesus brings His REWARD with Him when He comes,
To give to everyone according to what he has done.
Those who wash their robes have the right to the Tree of LIFE,
And may go through the gates into the City of God.

Those who will not enter the City will be those who practice magic arts,
The sexually immoral, the murderers, the idolaters
And everyone who loves and practices falsehood.

Christ Jesus sent His angel to John to give this testimony to His Church
And to all mankind.
He is the Root and the Offspring of David, and the bright Morning Star;
In other words He is the Christ of God.

The Spirit and the Bride give the final invitation in the Word of God,

"Come!"

If anyone is THIRSTY, let him come to Christ Jesus
And receive the **FREE GIFT THE WATER OF LIFE.**

Christ Jesus warns everyone
Who hears the words of the prophecy of the Book of Revelation,
That if they add anything to them they will receive the plagues described in it.
If anyone takes away from the words in this book,
God will take away from him his share in the Tree of LIFE and the Holy City,
Which are described in this book.

Finally, Christ Jesus declares that He is coming SOON!

OTHER NEW TESTAMENT SCRIPTURES THAT SPEAK OF THE TIME OF THE END

The Day Of The Lord (2 Peter 3:1-13)
Dear friends, this is now my second letter to you.
I have written both of them as reminders to stimulate you to wholesome thinking.
I want you to recall the words spoken in the past by the holy prophets
And the command given by our Lord and Savior through your apostles.

First of all, you must understand that in the last days scoffers will come,
Scoffing and following their own evil desires.
They will say, 'Where is this coming' he promised?
Ever since our fathers died, everything goes on as it has
Since the beginning of creation.'

But they deliberately forget that long ago by God's word the heavens existed
And the earth was formed out of water and with water.
By water also the world of that time was deluged and destroyed.
By the same word the present heavens and earth are reserved for fire,
Being kept for the day of judgment and destruction of ungodly men.

But do not forget this one thing, dear friends:
With the Lord a day is like a thousand years, and a thousand years like a day.
The Lord is not slow in keeping his promise, as some understand slowness.
He is patient with you, not wanting anyone to perish,
But everyone to come to repentance.

But the day of the Lord will come like a thief.
The heavens will disappear with a roar;
The elements will be destroyed by fire,
And the earth and everything in it will be laid bare.

Since everything will be destroyed in this way, what kind of people ought you to be?
You ought to live holy and godly lives
As you look forward to the day of God and speed its coming.
That day will bring about the destruction of the heavens by fire,
And the elements will melt in the heat.
But in keeping with his promise we are looking forward to a new heaven
And a new earth, the home of the righteousness.

In The Last Times There Will Be Scoffers (Jude 17-18)
But, dear friends, remember what the apostles of our Lord Jesus Christ foretold.
They said to you,

'In the last times there will be scoffers
Who will follow their own ungodly desires.'

These are the men who divide you, who follow mere natural instincts
And do not have the Spirit.

[The entire Book of Jude is about the sin and doom of godless men]

The Coming Of The Lord (1 Thessalonians 4:13-18, 5:1-11))
Brothers, we do not want you to be ignorant about those who fall asleep,
Or to grieve like the rest of men, who have no hope.
We believe that Jesus died and rose again
And so we believe that God will bring with Jesus
Those who have fallen asleep in him.
According to the Lord's own word, we tell you that we who are still alive,
Who are left till the coming of the Lord,
Will certainly not precede those who have fallen asleep.

For the Lord himself will come down from heaven, with a loud command,
With the voice of the archangel and with the trumpet call of God,
And the dead in Christ will rise first.
After that, we who are still alive and are left
Will be caught up with them in the clouds to meet the Lord in the air.
And so we will be with the Lord forever,
Therefore encourage each other with these words.

[The Lord comes with a loud command and the trumpet call of God
At the end of The Great Tribulation an just before the Battle of Armageddon.
At that time the only saints left on earth alive are those in the desert
Who have been protected by God; the "Woman," the Bride of Christ.]

Now, brothers, about times and dates we do not need to write to you,
For you know very well that the day of the Lord
Will come like a thief in the night.
While people are saying, 'Peace and safety,'
Destruction will come on them suddenly, as labor pains on a pregnant woman,
And they will not escape.

But you, brothers, are not in darkness
So that this day should surprise you like a thief.

You are all sons of the light and sons of the day.
We do not belong to the night or to the darkness.
So then, let us not be like others, who are asleep,
But let us be alert and self-controlled.
For those who sleep, sleep at night, and those who get drunk, get drunk at night.
But since we belong to the day, let us be self-controlled, putting on faith
And love as a breastplate, and the hope of salvation as a helmet.

For God did not appoint us to suffer wrath
But to receive salvation through our Lord Jesus Christ.

He died for us so that, whether we are awake or asleep,
We may live together with him.
Therefore encourage one another and build each other up,
Just as in fact you are doing.

The Man Of Lawlessness (2 Thessalonians 2:1-12)
Concerning the coming of the Lord Jesus Christ
And our being gathered to him, we ask you brothers,
Not to become easily unsettled or alarmed by some prophecy, report or letter
Supposed to have come from us, saying that the day of the Lord has already come.

Don't let anyone deceive you in any way, for that day will not come,
*Until the rebellion occurs and **the man of lawlessness** is revealed,*
The man doomed to destruction.
He opposes and exalts himself over everything that is called God or is worshiped,
And even sets himself up in God's temple, proclaiming himself to be God.

Don't you remember that when I was with you I used to tell you these things?
And now you know what is holding him back,
So that he may be revealed at the proper time.
For the secret power of lawlessness is already at work;
But the one who now holds it back will continue to do so
Till he (the Holy Spirit) is taken out of the way.
*And then the **lawless one** will be revealed,*
Whom the Lord Jesus will over throw with the breath of his mouth
And destroy by the splendor of his coming.

*The coming of the **lawless one** will be in accordance with the work of Satan*
displayed in all kinds of counterfeit miracles, signs and wonders,
And every sort of evil that deceives those who are perishing.
They perish because they refused to love the truth and so be saved.

*For this reason God sends them **a powerful delusion***
*So that they will believe **the lie***

The Time Of The END

And so that all will be condemned who have not believed the truth
But have delighted in wickedness.

According to the apostle Paul,
The Great Day Of The Lord will not come until the man of lawlessness,
The Beast, the Antichrist is revealed.
At that time the Holy Spirit is taken out of the way
And Satan has complete rule over mankind.
Just prior to this, the rebellion within the Church occurs,
And the Beast sets up his "image" in the Church of God,
Claiming to be God and deceiving mankind
With counterfeit miracles, signs and wonders.
God allows this powerful delusion for those who have delighted in wickedness.

Godlessness In The Last Days (2 Timothy 3:1-7)
But mark this: There will be terrible times in the last days.
People will be lovers of themselves, lovers of money, boastful, proud, abusive,
Disobedient to their parents, ungrateful, unholy, without love, unforgiving,
Slanderous, without self-control, brutal, not lovers of the good,
Treacherous, rash, conceited.
Lovers of pleasure rather than lovers of God--
Having a form of godliness but denying its power.
Have nothing to do with them.

They are the kind who worm their way into homes
And gain control over weak-willed women, who are loaded down with sins
And are swayed by all kinds of evil desires,
Always learning but never able to acknowledge the truth.

[This description of Paul aptly describes the time we are living in.
This is what is seen on television every day,
Both in serial programs and on the news.
Churches claiming Christ, are defying The Word of God by their practices,
Which renders them powerless with God and in defiance of Him.]

Love, For The Day Is Near (Romans 13:8-14)
Let no debt remain outstanding, except the continuing debt to love one another,
For he who loves his fellow man has fulfilled the law.
The commandments, 'Do not commit adultery,' 'Do not murder,' 'Do not steal,'
'Do not covet,' and whatever other commandment there may be,
Are summed up in this one rule:

'Love your neighbor as yourself.'

The Time Of The END

Therefore love is the fulfillment of the law.
And do this, understanding the present time
The hour has come for you to wake up from your slumber,
Because our salvation is nearer now than when we first believed.

The night is nearly over; the day is almost here.
So let us put aside the deeds of darkness and put on the armor of light.
Let us behave decently, as in the daytime, not in orgies and drunkenness,
Not in sexual immorality and debauchery, not in dissension and jealousy.
Rather, clothe yourselves with the Lord Jesus Christ,
And do not think about how to gratify the desires of the sinful nature.

Because of These The Wrath of God Is Coming (Colossians 3:5-11)

Put to death, therefore, whatever belongs to your earthly nature:
Sexual immorality, impurity, lust, evil desires and greed, which are idolatry.
Because of these, the wrath of God is coming.
You used to walk in these ways, in the life you once lived.
But now you must rid yourselves of all such things as these:
Anger, rage, malice, slander, and filthy language from your lips.
Do not lie to each other, since you have taken off your old self with its practices
And have put on the new self, which is being renewed in knowledge
In the image of its Creator.
Here there is not Greek or Jew, circumcised or uncircumcised,
Barbarian, Scythian, Slave or free, **but Christ is all**, *and is in all.*

When The Lord Jesus Is Revealed From Heaven In Blazing Fire

(2 Thessalonians 1:4-10)
Therefore, among God's churches we boast about your perseverance and faith
In all the persecutions and trials you are enduring.

All this is evidence that God's judgment is right,
And as a result you will be counted worthy of the kingdom of God,
For which you are suffering.
God is just: He will pay back trouble to those who trouble you
And give relief to you who are troubled, and to us as well.
This will happen when the Lord Jesus is revealed from heaven in blazing fire
With his powerful angels.
He will punish those who do not know God
And do not obey the gospel of our Lord Jesus.
They will be punished with everlasting destruction
And shut out from the presence of the Lord and from the majesty of his power
On the day he comes *to be glorified in his holy people*
And to be marveled at among all those who have believed.
This includes you, because you believed our testimony to you.

God's Wrath Against Mankind; Men Are Without Excuse
(Romans 1:18-32)
The wrath of God is being revealed from heaven
Against all the godlessness and wickedness of men
Who suppress the truth by their wickedness,
Since what may be known about God is plain to them,
Because God has made it plain to them.
For since the creation of the world God's invisible qualities--
His eternal power and divine nature--
Have been clearly seen, being understood from what has been made,
So that men are without excuse.

For although they knew God, they neither glorified him as God
Nor gave thanks to him, but their thinking became futile
And their foolish hearts were darkened.
Although they claimed to be wise, they became fools
And exchanged the glory of the immortal God
For images made to look like mortal man and birds and animals and reptiles.

Therefore God gave them over in the sinful desires of their hearts to sexual impurity
For the degrading of their bodies with one another.
*They exchanged the truth of God for a **lie**,*
And worshiped and served created things rather than the Creator--
Who is forever praised. Amen.

Because of this, God gave them over to shameful lusts.
Even their women exchanged natural relations for unnatural ones.
In the same way the men also abandoned natural relations with women
And were inflamed with lust for one another.
Men committed indecent acts with other men,
And received in themselves the due penalty for their perversion.

Furthermore, since they did not think it worthwhile to retain the knowledge of God,
He gave them over to a depraved mind, to do what ought not to be done.
They have become filled with every kind of wickedness, evil, greed and depravity.
They are full of envy, murder, strife, deceit and malice.
They are gossips, slanderers, God-haters, insolent, arrogant and boastful;
They invent ways of doing evil;
They disobey their parents; they are senseless, faithless, heartless, ruthless.
Although they know God's righteous decree
That those who do such things deserve death,
They not only continue to do these very things
But also approve of those who practice them.

THE BRIDE OF CHRIST IN THE DESERT

[The following are examples in The Word of God
That describe the Bride of Christ in the desert as foretold in Revelation 12.]

God's Canopy For His Bride In The Desert (Isaiah 4:5-6)
Then the Lord will create over all of Mount Zion
And over those who assemble there a cloud of smoke by day
And a glow of flaming fire by night;
Over all the glory will be a canopy.
It will be a shelter and shade from the heat of the day,
And a refuge and hiding place from the storm and rain.

The Lord Has Established Zion (The Bride of Christ) (Isaiah 14:32)
'The Lord has established Zion, and in her his afflicted people will find refuge.'

[The Lord has established Zion, the City of God, from before the world began, and in her God's people will find refuge.]

Tribute Will Be Brought To The Daughter Of Zion (The Bride Of Christ) (Isaiah 16:1)
Send lambs as tribute to the ruler of the land (Christ),
From Sela, across the desert, to the mount of the Daughter of Zion.

The Bride Exalts Her God (Isaiah 24:14)
The Bride exalts her God while He lays waste the earth.
She is the only one on earth that is able to exalt God
While He devastates the earth during The Great Tribulation

They raise their voices, they shout for joy;
From the west they acclaim the Lord's majesty.
Therefore in the east give glory to the Lord;
Exalt the name of the Lord, the God of Israel, In the islands of the sea.
From the ends of the earth we hear singing;
'Glory to the Righteous One.'

But I said, 'I waste away, I waste away!
Woe to me!
The treacherous betray! With treachery the treacherous betray!'
Terror and pit and snare await you,
O people of the earth.

The Time Of The END

Whoever flees at the sound of terror will fall into a pit;
Whoever climbs out of the pit will be caught in a snare.
The floodgates of the heavens are opened,
The foundations of the earth shake.
The earth is broken up, the earth is split asunder,
The earth is thoroughly shaken.

The earth reals like a drunkard, it sways like a hut in the wind;
So heavy upon it is the guilt of its rebellion that it falls--
Never to rise again.

In that day the lord will punish the powers in the heavens above
And the kings on the earth below.
They will be herded together like prisoners bound in a dungeon;
The moon will be abashed, the sun ashamed;
For the Lord Almighty will reign on Mount Zion and in Jerusalem,
And before its elders, gloriously.

God's People Enter Their Rooms (Isaiah 26:20-21)
Go, my people, enter your rooms and shut the doors behind you;
Hide yourselves for a little while until his wrath has passed by.
See, the Lord is coming out of his dwelling
To punish the people of the earth for their sins.
The earth will disclose the blood shed upon her;
She will conceal her slain no longer.

[This is a picture of the Bride of Christ in the desert;
A place of protection from the wrath of God to be poured out upon the earth
Because of the blood the people of the earth have shed.]

In The Day Of Great Slaughter (Isaiah 30:25-33)
In the day of great slaughter, when the towers fall,
Streams of water will flow on every high mountain and every lofty hill.
The moon will shine like the sun,
And the sunlight will be seven times brighter,
Like the light of seven full days,
When the Lord binds up the bruises of his people and heals the wounds he inflicted.

See, the name of the Lord comes from afar,
With burning anger and dense clouds of smoke;
His lips are full of wrath, and his tongue is a consuming fire.
His breath is like a rushing torrent, rising to the neck.
He shakes the nations in the sieve of destruction.
He places in the jaws of the peoples a bit that leads them astray.

140

The Time Of The END

And you will sing as on the night you celebrate a holy festival;
Your hearts will rejoice as when people go up with flutes
To the mountain of the Lord to the Rock of Israel.
The Lord will cause men to hear his majestic voice
And will make them see his arm coming down with raging anger and consuming fire,
With cloudburst, thunderstorm and hail.

The voice of the Lord will shatter Assyria;
With his scepter he will strike them down.
Every stroke the Lord lays on them with his punishing rod
Will be to the music of tambourines and harps,
As he fights them in battle with the blows of his arm.

Topheth has been prepared; it has been made ready for the king (Satan).
Its fire has been made deep and wide,
With an abundance of fire and wood;
The breath of the Lord, like a stream of burning sulfur, sets it ablaze.

[As the Lord devastates the earth,
It is to the singing and music of the Bride of Christ in the desert,
Celebrating the destruction and defeat of the enemies of God.
The mention of Assyria here is both Assyria of old and a type of the world today.]

The Bride Of Christ In The Desert (Isaiah 32:14-20)
The fortress will be abandoned, the noisy city deserted;
Citadel and watchtower will become a wasteland forever,
The delight of donkeys, a pasture for flocks,
Till the Spirit is poured upon us from on high,
*And the **desert** becomes a fertile field,*
And the fertile field seems like a forest.

*Justice will dwell in the **desert** and righteousness live in the fertile field.*
The fruit of righteousness will be peace;
The effect of righteousness will be quietness and confidence forever.
My people will live in peaceful dwelling places, secure homes,
In undisturbed places of rest.

Though hail flattens the forest and the city is flattened completely,
How blessed you will be, sowing your seed by every stream,
And letting your oxen and donkeys range free.

[As the cities of the world are destroyed
The Lord makes a safe home for His Bride in the desert.]

The Bride Of Christ In The Desert (Isaiah 35)
The desert and the parched land will be glad;
The wilderness will rejoice and blossom.
Like the crocus, it will burst into bloom;
It will rejoice greatly and shout for joy.
The glory of Lebanon will be given to it,
The splendor of Carmel and Sharon;
They will see the glory of the Lord, the splendor of our God.

Strengthen the feeble hands, steady the knees that give way;
Say to those with fearful hearts,
'Be strong, do not fear; your God will come,
He will come with vengeance; with divine retribution
He will come to save you.'

Then will the eyes of the blind be opened and the ears of the deaf unstopped.
Then will the lame leap like a deer, and the tongue of the dumb shout for joy.

Water will gush forth in the wilderness and streams in the desert.
The burning sand will become a pool, the thirsty ground bubbling springs
In haunts where jackals once lay, grass and reeds and papyrus will grow.

And a highway will be there;
It will be called the Way of Holiness.
The unclean will not journey on it;
It will be for those who walk in that Way;
Wicked fools will not go about on it.
No lion will be there, nor will any ferocious beast get up on it;
They will not be found there.

The Bride Of Christ In The Desert (Isaiah 41:17-20)
The poor and needy search for water, but there is none;
Their tongues are parched with thirst.
But I the lord will answer them; I, the God of Israel, will not forsake them.
I will make rivers flow on barren heights, and springs within the valleys.
I will turn the desert into pools of water, and the parched ground into springs.
I will put in the desert the cedar and the acacia, the myrtle and the olive.
I will set pines in the wasteland, the fir and cypress together,
So that people may see and know, may consider and understand,
That the Holy One of Israel has created it.

God Is Doing A New Thing,
And Making A Way In The Desert (Isaiah 43:18-21)
'Forget the former things; do not dwell on the past.
See, I am doing a new thing!
Now it springs up; do you not perceive it?
I am making a way in the desert and streams in the wasteland.
The wild animals honor me, the jackals and the owls,
Because I provide water in the desert and streams in the wasteland,
To give drink to my people, my chosen,
The people I formed for myself
That they may proclaim my praise.

[What is the new thing that the Lord is doing?
He is raising up a Bride for His Son,
Who will minister in the fullness of Christ in the last days;
His chosen people, the people He formed to proclaim His praise.
And when her ministry is finished after three and one-half years,
He is making a place of safely for her in the desert.]

ISAIAH SPEAKS OF THE TIME OF THE END

In The Last Days (Isaiah 2:1-5)

This is what Isaiah son of Amoz saw concerning Judah and Jerusalem:

In the last days the mountain of the Lord's temple
Will be established as chief among the mountains;
It will be raised above the hills and all nations will stream to it.

Many peoples will come and say,
'Come, let us go to the mountain of the Lord, to the house of the God of Jacob.
He will teach us his ways, so that we may walk in his paths.'
The law will go out from Zion, the word of the Lord from Jerusalem.
He will judge between the nations and will settle disputes for many peoples.
They will beat their swords into plowshares
And their spears into pruning hooks.
Nation will not take up sword against nation,
Nor will they train for war anymore.

Come, O house of Jacob, let us walk in the light of the Lord.

The Day Of The Lord (Isaiah 2:6-22)

You have abandoned your people, the house of Jacob.
They are full of superstitions from the East;
They practice divination like the Philistines and clasp hands with pagans.
Their land is full of silver and gold;
There is no end to their treasures.
Their land is full of horses; there is no end to their chariots.
Their land is full of idols; they bow down to the work of their hands,
To what their fingers have made.

So man will be brought low and mankind humbled—do not forgive them.

Go into the rocks, hide in the ground from dread of the Lord
And the splendor of his majesty!
They eyes of the arrogant man will be humbled
And the pride of men brought low;
The Lord alone will be exalted in that day.

The Lord Almighty has a day in store for all the proud and lofty,
For all that is exalted (and they will be humbled),
For all the cedars of Lebanon, tall and lofty,
And all the oaks of Bashan,

The Time Of The END

For all the towering mountains and all the high hills,
For every lofty tower and every fortified wall,
For every trading ship and every stately vessel.

The arrogance of man will be brought low and the pride of men humbled.

The Lord alone will be exalted in that day,
And the idols will totally disappear.

Men will flee to caves in the rocks and to holes in the ground
From the dread of the Lord and the splendor of his majesty,
When he rises to shake the earth.

Stop trusting in man, who has but a breath in his nostrils.
Of what account is he?

[Isaiah often says "In that day." This often refers to something in the immediate future as well as "The Time of The END."]

Take Away Our Disgrace (Isaiah 4:1)
In that day seven women will take hold of one man and say,
'We will eat our own food and provide our own clothes;
Only let us be called by your name.
Take away our disgrace!'

The Branch Of The Lord (Isaiah 4:2-6)
In that day the Branch of the Lord will be beautiful and glorious,
And the fruit of the land will be the pride and glory of the survivors in Israel.
Those who are left in Zion, who remain in Jerusalem, will be called holy,
All who are recored among the living in Jerusalem.
The Lord will wash away the filth of the women of Zion;
He will cleanse the blood-stains from Jerusalem
By a Spirit of judgment and a Spirit of fire.

Then the lord will create over all of Mount Zion and over those who assemble there
A cloud of smoke by day and a glow of flaming fire by night;
Over all the glory will be a canopy.
It will he a shelter and shade from the heat of the day,
And a refuge and hiding place from the storm and rain.
[I believe that this speaks of the Bride of Christ in the desert.]

The Remnant Of Israel (Isaiah 10:20-23)
In that day the remnant of Israel, the survivors of the house of Jacob,
Will not longer rely on him who struck them down but will truly rely on the Lord,

The Time Of The END

The Holy One of Israel.
A remnant will return, a remnant of Jacob
Will return to the Mighty God.
Though your people, O Israel, be like the sand by the sea,
Only a remnant will return.
Destruction has been decreed, overwhelming and righteous.
The Lord, the Lord Almighty,
Will carry out the destruction decreed upon the whole land.

The Branch From Jesse (Isaiah 11:1-16)

A shoot will come up from the stump of Jesse (the father of king David);
From his roots a Branch (Christ) *will bear fruit.*
The Spirit of the Lord will rest on him--
The Spirit of wisdom and of understanding,
The Spirit of counsel and of power,
The Spirit of knowledge and of the fear of the Lord--
And he will delight in the fear of the Lord.

He will not judge by what he sees with his eyes,
Or decide by what he hears with his ears;
But with righteousness he will judge the needy,
With justice he will give decisions for the poor of the earth.

He will strike the earth with the rod of his mouth;
With the breath of his lips he will slay the wicked.
Righteousness will be his belt and faithfulness the sash around his waist.

The wolf will live with the lamb,
The leopard will lie down with the goat,
The calf and the lion and the yearling together;
And a little child will lead them.

The cow will feed with the bear,
Their young will lie down together,
And the lion will eat straw like the ox.
The infant will play near the hole of the cobra,
And the young child put his hand into the viper's nest.
They will neither harem nor destroy on all my holy mountain,
For the earth will be full of the knowledge of the Lord as the water covers the sea.

In that day the Root of Jesse (Christ) *will stand as a banner for the peoples;*
The nations will rally to him, and his place of rest will be glorious.
In that day the Lord will reach out his hand a second time
To reclaim the remnant that is left of his people from Assyria, from Lower Egypt,
From Upper Egypt, from Cush, from Elam, from Babylonia, from Hamath

The Time Of The END

And from the islands of the sea.

He will raise a banner for the nations and gather the exiles of Israel
(Both natural Israel and the Israel of God, which includes all end time believers);
He will assemble the scattered people of Judah from the four quarters of the earth.
Ephraim's jealousy will vanish, and Judah's enemies will be cut off;
Ephraim will not be jealous of Judah, nor Judah hostile toward Ephraim.
They will swoop down on the slopes of Philistia to the west;
Together they will plunder the people to the east.
They will lay hands on Edom and Moab,
And the Ammonites will be subject to them.

The Lord will dry up the gulf of the Egyptian sea;
With scorching wind he will sweep his hand over the Euphrates River.
He will break it up into seven streams
So men can cross over in sandals.
There will be a highway for the <u>remnant</u> *of his people that is left from Assyria,*
As there was for Israel when they came up from Egypt.

Songs Of Praise (Isaiah 12:1-6)
<u>*In that day*</u> *you will say:*

'I will praise you, O Lord.
Although you were angry with me,
Your anger has turned away and you have comforted me.
Surely God is my salvation; I will trust and not be afraid.
The Lord, the Lord, is my strength and my song;
 He has become my salvation.'

<u>*In that day*</u> *you will say:*

'Give thanks to the Lord, call on his name;
Make known among the nations what he has done,
And proclaim that his name is exalted.
Sing to the Lord, for he has done glorious things;
<u>*Let this be known to all the world.*</u>
Shout aloud and sing for joy, people of Zion (the Israel of God, the Church),
For great is the Holy One of Israel among you.'

A Prophecy Against Babylon (Isaiah 13)
(This is a prophesy of the final, end times Babylon)

An oracle concerning Babylon that Isaiah son of Amoz saw:

Raise a banner on a bare hilltop, shout to them; beckon to them

The Time Of The END

To enter the gates of the nobles.
I have commanded my holy ones;
I have summoned my warriors <u>to carry out my wrath</u>--
Those who rejoice in my triumph.

Listen, a noise on the mountains,
Like that of a great multitude!
Listen, an uproar among the kingdoms, <u>like nations massing together</u>!
The Lord almighty is mustering an army for war.

They come from faraway land, from the ends of the heavens--
The Lord and the weapons of his wrath--
<u>To destroy the whole country</u>.

Wail, for <u>the day of the Lord</u> is near;
It will come like destruction from the Almighty.
Because of this, all hands will go limp, every man's heart will melt.
Terror will seize them, pain and anguish will grip them;
They will writhe like a woman in labor.
They will look aghast at each other, their faces aflame.

See, <u>the day of the Lord is coming</u>—
A cruel day, with wrath and fierce anger--
To make the land desolate and destroy the sinners within it.

The stars of heaven and their constellations will not show their light.
The rising sun will be darkened and the moon will not give its light.

I will punish the world for its evil, the wicked for their sins.
I will put an end to the arrogance of the haughty
And will humble the pride of the ruthless.
I will make man scarcer than pure gold, more rare than the gold of Ophir.

Therefore, I will make the heavens tremble;
And the earth will shake from its place at the wrath of the Lord Almighty,
<u>In the day of his burning anger</u>.

Like hunted antelope, like sheep without a shepherd,
Each will return to his own people,
Each will flee to his native land.
Whoever is captured will be thrust through;
All who are caught will fall by the sword.
Their infants will be dashed to pieces before their eyes;
Their houses will be looted and their wives ravished.

Israel Brought Back to Its Own Land (Isaiah 14:1-27)
(A prophesy of the Jews being brought back to their own land
After having been dispersed to all the nations on earth.
This reality sets up The Time of The END.)

The Lord will have compassion on Jacob;
Once again he will choose Israel and will settle them in their own land.
Aliens will join them and unite with the house of Jacob.
Nations will take them and bring them to their own place.
And the house of Israel will possess the nations
As menservants and maidservants in the Lord's land.
They will make captives of their captors and rule over their oppressors.

[Ultimately there is one Israel of God which includes all believers,
Who rule and reign with Christ for a thousand years at Jerusalem.
The nations of the world, who once held the Jews captive
Are now captives of the Israel of God.]

On the day the Lord gives you relief from suffering and turmoil and cruel bondage,
You will take up this taunt against the king of Babylon (Satan):

How the oppressor (Satan) has come to an end!
How his fury has ended!
The Lord has broken the rod of the wicked,
The scepter of the rulers, which in anger struck down peoples with unceasing blows,
And in fury subdued nations with relentless aggression.
All the lands are at rest and at peace;

They break into singing.
Even the pine trees and the cedars of Lebanon exult over you and say,
'Now that you have been laid low, no woodsman comes to cut us down.'

The grave below is all astir to meet you (Satan) at your coming;
It rouses the spirits of the departed to greet you--
All those who were leaders in the world;
It makes them rise from their thrones--
All those who were kings over the nations.
They will respond, they will say to you,

'You also have become weak, as we are;
You have become like us.'

All your pomp has been brought down to the grave,
Along with the noise of your harps;
Maggots are spread out beneath you and worms cover you.

The Time Of The END

How you (Satan) have fallen from heaven, O morning star, son of the dawn!
You have been cast down to the earth,
You who once laid low the nations!

You said in your heart,
'I will ascend to heaven; I will raise my throne above the stars of God.
I will sit enthroned on the mount of assembly,
On the utmost heights of the sacred mountain.
I will ascend above the tops of the clouds;
I will make myself like the Most High.'

But you are brought down to the grave, to the depths of the pit.
Those who see you stare at you, they ponder your fate:

'Is this the man who shook the earth and made kingdoms tremble,
The man who made the world a desert,
Who overthrew its cities and would not let his captives go home?'

All the kings of the nations lie in state, each in his own tomb.
But you are cast out of your tomb like a rejected branch;
You are covered with the slain, with those pierced by the sword,
Those who descend to the stones of the pit.
Like a corpse trampled underfoot, you will not join them in burial.
For you have destroyed your land and killed your people.

The offspring of the wicked will never be mentioned again.
Prepare a place to slaughter his sons for the sins of their forefathers;
They are not to rise to inherit the land and cover the earth with their cities.

'I will rise up against them,' declares the Lord Almighty.
I will cut off from Babylon her name and survivors,
Her offspring and descendants,' declares the Lord.

'I will turn her into a place for owls and into swampland;
I will sweep her with the broom of destruction,' declares the Lord Almighty.

The Lord Almighty has sworn,
'Surely, as I have planned, so it will be,
And as I have purposed, so it will stand.
I will crush the Assyrian in my land;
(The Assyrian here is not only representative of Assyria
But all those who rebel against God)
On my mountains I will trample him down.
His yoke will be taken from my people,
And his burden removed from their shoulders.'

The Time Of The END

This is the plan determined for the whole world;
This is the hand stretched out over all the nations
For the Lord Almighty has purposed, and who can thwart him?
His hand is stretched out, and who can turn it back? (Isaiah 14:1-27)

The Oppressor Will Come To An End (Isaiah 15:4-5)
The oppressor will come to an end, and destruction will cease;
(At the end of The Great Tribulation, and The Battle of Armageddon)
The aggressor will vanish from the land.
In love a throne will be established; in faithfulness a man will sit on it--
One (Christ) *from the house of David--*
One who in judging seeks justice and speeds the cause of righteousness.

The Raging Of Many Nations (Isaiah 17:12-14)
Oh, the raging of many nations-
They rage like the raging sea!
Oh, the uproar of the peoples--
They roar like the roaring of great waters!
Although the peoples roar like the roar of surging waters,
When he (God) *rebukes them they flee far away,*
Driven before the wind like chaff on the hills,
Like tumbleweed before a gale.
In evening, sudden terror!
Before morning, they are gone!
This is the portion of those who loot us (the Israel of God),
The lot of those who plunder us.
[This is a picture of The Great Tribulation.]

All You People of the World (Isaiah 18:3)
All you people of the world, you who live on the earth,
When a banner is raised on the mountains, you will see it,
And when the trumpet sounds, you will hear it.
[This is God addressing the world. The banner is the banner of His Christ.]

An Altar To The Lord In The Heart Of Egypt (Isaiah19:16-22)
In that day the Egyptians will be like women.
They will shudder with fear at the uplifted hand
That the Lord Almighty raises against them.
And the land of Judah will bring terror to the Egyptians;
Everyone to whom Judah is mentioned will be terrified,
Because of what the Lord Almighty is planning against them.

In that day five cities in Egypt will speak the language of Canaan

The Time Of The END

And swear allegiance to the Lord Almighty.
One of them will be called the city of Destruction.
<u>In that day</u> there will be an altar to the Lord in the heart of Egypt,
And a monument to the Lord at its border.
It will be a sign and witness to the Lord Almighty in the land of Egypt.
When they cry out to the Lord because of their oppressors,
He will send them a savior and defender, and he will rescue them.

So the Lord will make himself known to the Egyptians,
And <u>in that day</u> they will acknowledge the Lord.
They will worship with sacrifices and grain offerings;
They will make vows to the Lord and keep them.
The Lord will strike Egypt with a plague;
He will strike them and heal them.
They will turn to the Lord,
And he will respond tho their pleas and heal them.

God Will Bless Assyria, Egypt and Israel In The Day Of The Lord
(Isaiah 19:23-25)
<u>In that day</u> there will be a highway from Egypt to Assyria.
The Assyrians will go to Egypt and the Egyptians to Assyria.
The Egyptians and Assyrians will worship together.
In that day Israel will be the third, along with Egypt and Assyria,
A blessing on the earth.
The Lord almighty will bless them, saying,
'Blessed be Egypt my people, Assyria my handiwork,
And Israel my inheritance.'

The Lord Plans To Humble All Who Are Renowned On The Earth
(Isaiah 23:9)
The Lord Almighty planned it, to bring low the pride of all glory
And to humble all who are renowned on the earth.

The Lord's Devastation Of The Earth (Isaiah 24)
See, the Lord is going to lay waste the earth and devastate it;
He will ruin its face and scatter its inhabitants--
It will be the same for priest as for people,
For master as for servant,
For mistress as for maid,
For seller as for buyer,
For borrower as for lender,
For debtor as for creditor.
The earth will be completely laid waste and totally plundered.
The Lord has spoken this word.

The Time Of The END

The world dries up and withers,
The world languishes and withers,
The exalted of the earth languish.
The earth is defiled by its people;
They have disobeyed the laws, violated the statutes
<u>*And broken the everlasting covenant*</u>*.*

Therefore a curse consumes the earth;
Its people must bear their guilt.
Therefore earth's inhabitants are burned up, and very few are left.
The new wine dries up and the vine withers;
All the merrymakers groan.
The gaiety of the tambourines is stilled,
The noise of the revelers has stopped,
The joyful harp is silent.
No longer do they drink wine with a song;
The beer is bitter to its drinkers.

The ruined city lies desolate;
The entrance to every house is barred.
In the streets they cry out for wine;
All joy turns to gloom, all gaiety is banished from the earth.
The city is left in ruins, its gate is battered to pieces.

So it will be on the earth and among the nations,
As when an olive tree is beaten,
Or as when gleanings are left after the grape harvest.

They raise their voices, they shout for joy;
From the west they acclaim the Lord's majesty.
Therefore in the east give glory to the Lord;
Exalt the name of the Lord, the God of Israel, In the islands of the sea.
From the ends of the earth we hear singing;
'Glory to the Righteous One.'
[This is the Bride of Christ, in the desert,
Rejoicing in the midst of The Great Tribulation.]

But I said, 'I waste away, I waste away!
Woe to me!
The treacherous betray! With treachery the treacherous betray!'
Terror and pit and snare await you,
O people of the earth.

Whoever flees at the sound of terror will fall into a pit;
Whoever climbs out of the pit will be caught in a snare.
The floodgates of the heavens are opened,

The Time Of The END

The foundations of the earth shake.
The earth is broken up, the earth is split asunder,
The earth is thoroughly shaken.
The earth reals like a drunkard, it sways like a hut in the wind;
So heavy upon it is the guilt of its rebellion that it falls--
Never to rise again.

In that day the lord will punish the powers in the heavens above
And the kings on the earth below.
They will be herded together like prisoners bound in a dungeon;
The moon will be abashed, the sun ashamed;
For the Lord almighty will reign on Mount Zion and in Jerusalem,
And before its elders, gloriously.

The People Of God, Praise The Lord At The Time Of The End
(Isaiah 25)
[This chapter speaks of the work of the Lord in The Time of The END.]

O Lord, you are my God:
I will exalt you and praise your name
For in perfect faithfulness you have done marvelous things,
Things planned long ago.
You have made the city a heap of rubble, the fortified town a ruin,
The foreigners' stronghold a city no more; it will never be rebuilt.
Therefore strong peoples will honor you.
You have been a refuge for the poor, a refuge for the needy in his distress,
A shelter from the storm and a shade from the heat.

For the breath of the ruthless is like a storm driving against a wall
And like the heat of the desert.
You silence the uproar of foreigners;
As heat is reduced by the shadow of a cloud,
So the song of the ruthless is stilled.

On this mountain the Lord Almighty will prepare a feast of rich food
For all peoples,
A banquet of aged wine—the best of meats and the finest of wines.

[This speaks of the wedding supper of the Lamb
That God is preparing for His elect, His chosen people, the Bride of Christ,
Who are represented by people from every nation on earth.]

On this mountain he will destroy the shroud that enfolds all peoples,
The sheet that covers all nations;
He will swallow up death forever.

154

The Time Of The END

[The shroud is the blindness that Satan places over all peoples and nations;
That is taken away only by faith in God and His Christ.
Then God Almighty swallows up death forever.]

The Sovereign Lord will wipe away the tears from all faces.
He will remove the disgrace of his people from all the earth.
The Lord has spoken.
In that day they will say,

'Surely this is our God; we trusted in him, and he saved us.
This is the Lord, we trusted in him;
Let us rejoice and be glad in his salvation.'

The People Of The World Learn Righteousness (Isaiah 26:9-11)
When your judgments come upon the earth,
The people of the world learn righteousness.
Though grace is shown to the wicked they do not learn righteousness.
Even in a land of uprightness they go on doing evil
And regard not the majesty of the Lord.
O Lord, your hand is lifted high, but they do not see it.
Let them see your zeal for your people and be put to shame;
Let the fire reserved for your enemies consume them.

[Today the hand of the Lord is lifted high, but the people of the world do not see it.
They do not understand the zeal that God has for the nation Israel
And the Israel of God, His people, His Bride.]

God's People Enter Their Rooms (Isaiah 26:20-21)
Go, my people, enter your rooms and shut the doors behind you;
Hide yourselves for a little while until his wrath has passed by.
See, the Lord is coming out of his dwelling
To punish the people of the earth for their sins.
The earth will disclose the blood shed upon her;
She will conceal her slain no longer.

[This is a picture of the Bride of Christ in the desert;
A place of protection from the wrath of God to be poured out upon the earth
Because of the blood the people of the earth have shed.]

God's Fruitful Vineyard, The Bride Of Christ (Isaiah 27:2)
In that day--
Sing about a fruitful vineyard; I the Lord watch over it;
I water it continually I guard it day and night
So that no one may harm it.

The Time Of The END

[This is a wonderful picture of God watching over a fruitful vineyard,
His Bride, the Israel of God.]

The Lord Almighty, A Glorious Crown, A Beautiful Wreath
(Isaiah 28:5-6)
In that day the Lord Almighty will be a glorious crown, a beautiful wreath
For the remnant of his people.
He will be a spirit of justice to him who sits in judgment,
A source of strength to those who turn back the battle at the gate.

[In the last days the Lord Almighty will be a glorious crown, a beautiful wreath
For the remnant of His people, His Bride,
Who in the strength of her God will hold back the battle at the gate.]

The Hordes Of All The Nations Will Fight Against Ariel
(Isaiah 29:7-8)
Then the hordes of all the nations that fight against Ariel,
That attack her and her fortress and besiege her,
Will be as it is with a dream, with a vision in the night--
That he is eating, but he awakens, and his hunger remains;
As when a thirsty man dreams that he is drinking, but he awakens faint,
With his thirst unquenched.
So it will be with the hordes of all the nations that fight against Mount Zion.

[All the nations of the world come against God and His Christ, against Israel,
In a stupor of deception, perpetrated by Satan.]

A Warning To The People Of God (Isaiah 29:13-14)
The Lord says:
'These people come near to me with their mouth
And honor me with their lips,
But their hearts are far from me.
Their worship of me is made up only of rules taught by men.
Therefore once more I will astound these people with wonder upon wonder;
The wisdom of the wise will perish,
The intelligence of the intelligent will vanish.'

[I believe that here, God is speaking of the last days.
Many Christians will come near to God with their mouths
But will not have a heart to heart relationship with Him.
They, then will be astounded by what He will do in the last days.
All their intelligence will count for nothing at that time.]

The Time Of The END

In The Day Of Great Slaughter (Isaiah 30:25-33)
In the day of great slaughter, when the towers fall,
Streams of water will flow on every high mountain and every lofty hill.
The moon will shine like the sun,
And the sunlight will be seven times brighter,
Like the light of seven full days,
When the Lord binds up the bruises of his people and heals the wounds he inflicted.

See, the name of the Lord comes from afar,
With burning anger and dense clouds of smoke;
His lips are full of wrath, and his tongue is a consuming fire.
His breath is like a rushing torrent, rising to the neck.
He shakes the nations in the sieve of destruction.
He places in the jaws of the peoples a bit that leads them astray.

And you will sing as on the night you celebrate a holy festival;
Your hearts will rejoice as when people go up with flutes
To the mountain of the Lord to the Rock of Israel.
The Lord will cause men to hear his majestic voice
And will make them see his arm coming down with raging anger and consuming fire,
With cloudburst, thunderstorm and hail.

The voice of the Lord will shatter Assyria;
With his scepter he will strike them down.
Every stroke the Lord lays on them with his punishing rod
Will be to the music of tambourines and harps,
As he fights them in battle with the blows of his arm.

Topheth has been prepared; it has been made ready for the king (Satan).
Is fire has been made deep and wide,
With an abundance of fire and wood;
The breath of the Lord, like a stream of burning sulfur, sets it ablaze.

[As the Lord devastates the earth,
It is to the singing and music of the Bride of Christ in the desert,
Celebrating the destruction and defeat of the enemies of God.
The mention of Assyria here is both Assyria of old and a type of the world today.]

The Lord Comes To Do Battle (Isaiah 31:4-5)
This is what the Lord says to me:
'As the lion growls, a great lion over his prey--
And though a whole band of shepherds is called together against him,
He is not frightened by their shouts
Or disturbed by their clamor--
So the Lord Almighty will come down to do battle on Mount Zion and on its heights.

157

The Time Of The END

Like birds hovering overhead, the Lord Almighty will shield Jerusalem;
He will shield it and deliver it,
He will 'pass over' it and will rescue it.'

[This is a picture of the Lord coming to do battle against the nations of the world.
It is also a picture of the Lord protecting Jerusalem.]

The Bride Of Christ In The Desert (Isaiah 32:14-20)
The fortress will be abandoned, the noisy city deserted;
Citadel and watchtower will become a wasteland forever,
The delight of donkeys, a pasture for flocks,
Till the Spirit is poured upon us from on high,
And the **desert** *becomes a fertile field,*
And the fertile field seems like a forest.

Justice will dwell in the **desert** *and righteousness live in the fertile field.*
The fruit of righteousness will be peace;
The effect of righteousness will be quietness and confidence forever.
My people will live in peaceful dwelling places, secure homes,
In undisturbed places of rest.

Though hail flattens the forest and the city is flattened completely,
How blessed you will be, sowing your seed by every stream,
And letting your oxen and donkeys range free.

[As the cities of the world are destroyed
The Lord makes a safe home for His Bride in the desert.]

The Lord Arises In The Last Days (Isaiah 33)
Woe to you, O destroyer (Satan), *you who have not been destroyed!*
Woe to you, O traitor, you who have not been betrayed!
When you stop destroying, you will be destroyed;
When you stop betraying, you will be betrayed.

O Lord, be gracious to us; we long for you.
Be our salvation in time of distress.
At the thunder of your voice, the peoples flee;
When you rise up, the nations scatter.

Your plunder, O nations is harvested as by young locusts;
Like a swarm of locusts men pounce on it.

The Lord is exalted, for he dwells on high;
He will fill Zion with justice and righteousness.
He will be the sure foundation for your times,

The Time Of The END

A rich store of salvation and wisdom and knowledge;
The fear of the Lord is the key to this treasure.

Look, their brave men cry aloud in the streets; the envoys of peace weep bitterly.
The highways are deserted, no travelers are on the roads.
The treaty is broken, its witnesses are despised, no one is respected.
The land mourns and wastes away, Lebanon is ashamed and withers;
Sharon is like the Arabah, and Bashan and Carmel drop their leaves.

'Now will I arise,' says the Lord.
'Now will I be exalted; now will I be lifted up.
You conceive chaff, you give birth to straw;
Your breath is a fire that consumes you.
<u>The peoples will be burned as if to lime;</u>
Like cut thornbushes they will be set ablaze.'

You who are far away, hear what I have done;
Acknowledge my power!
<u>The sinners in Zion are terrified; trembling grips the godless;</u>

'Who of us can dwell with the consuming fire?
Who of us can dwell with everlasting burning?'

He who walks righteously and speaks what is right,
Who rejects gain from extortion
And keeps his hand from accepting bribes,
Who stops his ears against plots of murder
And shuts his eyes against contemplating evil--
This is the man who will dwell on the heights,
Whose refuge will be the mountain fortress.
His bread will be supplied and water will not fail him.

Your eyes will see the king in his beauty
And view a land that stretches afar.
In your thoughts you will ponder the former terror:
'Where is that chief officer?
Where is the one who took the revenue?
Where is the officer in charge of the towers?'

<u>You will see those arrogant people no more</u>,
Those people of an obscure speech,
With their strange, incomprehensible tongue.

Look upon Zion, the city of our festivals; your eyes will see Jerusalem,
A peaceful abode, a tent that will not be moved;
Its stakes will never be pulled up, nor any of its ropes broken.

The Time Of The END

There the Lord will be our Mighty One.
It will be like a place of broad rivers and streams.
No mighty ship will sail them.
For the Lord is our judge, the Lord is our lawgiver, the Lord is our king;
It is he who will save us.

Your rigging hangs loose:
The mast is not held secure, the sail is not spread.
Then an abundance of spoils will be divided
And even the lame will carry off plunder.

No one living in Zion will say, 'I am ill';
And the sins of those who dwell there will be forgiven.

Judgment Against The Nations (Isaiah 34)
Come near, you nations, and listen; pay attention , you peoples!
Let the earth hear, and all that is in it,
The world, and all that comes out of it!

The Lord is angry with all nations; his wrath is upon all their armies.
He will totally destroy them, he will give them over to slaughter.
Their slain will be thrown out, their dead bodies will send up a stench;
The mountains will be soaked with their blood.
All the stars of the heavens will be dissolved and the sky rolled up like a scroll;
All the starry host will fall like withered leaves from the vine,
Like shriveled figs from the fig tree.

My sword has drunk its fill in the heavens;
See, it descends in judgment on Edom (Edom here represents the ungodly),
The people I have totally destroyed.
The sword of the Lord is bathed in blood, it is covered with fat--
The blood of lambs and goats, fat from the kidneys of rams.
For the Lord has a sacrifice in Bozrah and a slaughter in Edom.
And the wild oxen will fall with them, the bull calves and the great bulls.
Their land will be drenched with blood, and the dust will be soaked with fat.
For the Lord has a day of vengeance,
A year of retribution, to uphold Zion's cause.
Edom's streams will be turned into pitch, her dust into burning sulfur;
Her land will become blazing pitch!
It will not be quenched night and day;
Its smoke will rise forever.
From generation to generation it will lie desolate;
No one will ever pass through it again.

The desert owl and screech owl will possess it;

The Time Of The END

The great owl and the raven will nest there.
God will stretch out over Edom the measuring line of chaos
And the plumb line of desolation.

Her nobles will have nothing there to be called a kingdom,
All her princes will vanish away.
Thorns will overrun her citadels, nettles and brambles her strongholds.
She will become a haunt for jackals,
Desert creatures will meet with hyenas, and wild goats will bleat to each other;
There the night creatures will also repose and find for themselves places of rest.
The owl will nest there and lay eggs,
She will hatch them, and care for her young under the shadow of her wings;
There also the falcons will gather, each with its mate.

Look in the scroll of the Lord and read:
None of these will be missing, not one will lack her mate.
For it is his mouth that has given the order,
And his Spirit will gather them together.
He allots their portions; his hand distributes them by measure.
They will possess it forever and dwell there from generation to generation.

The Bride Of Christ In The Desert (Isaiah 35)

The desert and the parched land will be glad;
The wilderness will rejoice and blossom.
Like the crocus, it will burst into bloom;
It will rejoice greatly and shout for joy.
The glory of Lebanon will be given to it,
The splendor of Carmel and Sharon;
They will see the glory of the Lord, the splendor of our God.

Strengthen the feeble hands, steady the knees that give way;
Say to those with fearful hearts,
'Be strong, do not fear; your God will come,
He will come with vengeance; with divine retribution
He will come to save you.'

Then will the eyes of the blind be opened and the ears of the deaf unstopped.
Then will the lame leap like a deer, and the tongue of the dumb shout for joy.

Water will gush forth in the wilderness and streams in the desert.
The burning sand will become a pool, the thirsty ground bubbling springs
In haunts where jackals once lay, grass and reeds and papyrus will grow.

And a highway will be there;
It will be called the Way of Holiness.

161

The Time Of The END

The unclean will not journey on it;
It will be for those who walk in that Way;
Wicked fools will not go about on it.
No lion will be there, nor will any ferocious beast get up on it;
They will not be found there.

But only the redeemed will walk there,
And the ransomed of the Lord will return.
They will enter Zion with singing;
Everlasting joy will crown their heads.
Gladness and joy will overtake them,
And sorrow and sighing will flee away.

The Remnant (Isaiah 37:32)
Once more a remnant of the house of Judah
Will take root below and bear fruit above.
For out of Jerusalem will come a remnant,
And out of Mount Zion a band of survivors.
The zeal of the Lord Almighty will accomplish this.

[God has maintained a remnant in every generation.
The remnant always comes out of Judah, the house of praise.
The last generation will be no different.
The "Woman" of Revelation 12 will take root below and bear fruit above.]

The Nations Are A Drop In A Bucket (Isaiah 40:15-17)
Surely the nations are like a drop in a bucket;
They are regarded as dust on the scales;
He weighs the islands as though they were fine dust.
Lebanon is not sufficient for altar fires,
Nor its animals enough for burnt offerings.

Before him all the nations are as nothing;
They are regarded by him as worthless and less than nothing.

[The nations are regarded as less than nothing because they are godless
And therefore have no eternal value.
Nevertheless, God takes a people for Himself out of every nation on earth.
A remnant who love and serve Him.]

He Reduces The Rulers Of The World To Nothing (Isaiah 40:21-24)
Do you not know?
Have you not heard?
Has it not been told you from the beginning?
Have you not understood since the earth was founded?

The Time Of The END

He sits enthroned above the circle of the earth, and its people are like grasshoppers.
He stretches out the heavens like a canopy,
And spreads them out like a tent to live in.
He brings princes to naught and reduces the rulers of this world to nothing.
No sooner are they planted, no sooner are they sown,
No sooner do they take root in the ground,
Than he blows on them and they wither,
And a whirlwind sweeps them away like chaff.

[All of human history is a vivid illustration of this fact,
And it will be true of The Time of The END as well.]

God Almighty Will Vindicate Israel In The Last Days (Isaiah 41:8-16)

But you, O Israel, my servant, Jacob, whom I have chosen,
You descendants of Abraham my friend,
I took you from the ends of the earth, from its farthest corners I called you.
So do not fear, for I am with you; do not be dismayed, for I am your God.
I will strengthen you and help you;
I will uphold you with my righteous right hand.

'All who rage against you will surely be ashamed and disgraced;
Those who oppose you will be as nothing and perish.
Though you search for your enemies, you will not find them.
Those who wage war against you will be as nothing at all.
For I am the Lord, your God, who takes hold of your right hand
And says to you, Do not fear; I will help you.
Do not be afraid, O worm Jacob, O little Israel,
For I myself will help you,' declares the Lord, your Redeemer,
The Holy One of Israel.
'See, I will make you into a threshing sledge,
New and sharp, with many teeth.
You will thresh the mountains and crush them,
And reduce the hills to chaff.
You will winnow them, the wind will pick them up
And a gale will blow them away.
But you will rejoice in the Lord and glory in the Holy One of Israel.'

The Bride Of Christ In The Desert (Isaiah 41:17-20)

The poor and needy search for water, but there is none;
Their tongues are parched with thirst.
But I the lord will answer them; I, the God of Israel, will not forsake them.
I will make rivers flow on barren heights, and springs within the valleys.
I will turn the desert into pools of water, and the parched ground into springs.
I will put in the desert the cedar and the acacia, the myrtle and the olive.
I will set pines in the wasteland, the fir and cypress together,

163

The Time Of The END

So that people may see and know, may consider and understand,
That the Holy One of Israel has created it.

In The Last Days The Lord Will Be A Mighty Warrior (Isaiah 42:13-15)
The Lord will march out like a mighty man,
Like a warrior he will stir up his zeal;
With a shout he will raise the battle cry and will triumph over his enemies.

For a long time I have kept silent,
I have been quiet and held myself back.
But now, like a woman in childbirth,
I cry out, I gasp and pant.
I will lay waste the mountains and hills
And dry up all their vegetation:
I will turn rivers into islands and dry up the pools.

Israel Is Gathered From The Ends Of The Earth (Isaiah 43:4-7)
Since you are precious and honored in my sight, and because I love you,
I will give men in exchange for you, and people in exchange for your life.
Do not be afraid, for I am with you;
I will bring your children from the east and gather you from the west.
I will say to the north, 'Give them up!'
And to the south, 'Do not hold them back.'
Bring my sons from afar and my daughters from the ends of the earth--
Everyone who is called by my name,
Whom I created for my glory,
Whom I formed and made.
[I believe that this scripture is true of the natural nation Israel
And the Israel of God, the Bride of Christ.]

God Is Doing A New Thing,
Making A Way In The Desert For The Bride Of Christ
(Isaiah 43:18-21)
Forget the former things; do not dwell on the past.
See, I am doing a new thing!
Now it springs up; do you not perceive it?
I am making a way <u>in the desert</u> and streams in the wasteland.
The wild animals honor me, the jackals and the owls,
Because I provide water <u>in the desert</u> and streams in the wasteland,
To give drink to my people, my chosen,
The people I formed for myself
That they may proclaim my praise.

The Time Of The END

[What is the new thing that the Lord is doing?
He is raising up a Bride for His Son,
Who will minister in the fullness of Christ in the last days;
His chosen people, the people He formed to proclaim His praise.
And when her ministry is finished after three and one-half years,
He is making a place of safety for her in the desert.]

I Will Pour Out My Spirit (Isaiah 44:1-5)
But now listen, O Jacob my servant,
Israel, whom I have chosen.
This is what the Lord says—he who made you,
Who formed you in the womb, and who will help you;
Do not be afraid, o Jacob, my servant, Jeshurun, whom I have chosen

For I will pour water on the thirsty land, and streams on the dry ground;
I will pour out my Spirit on your offspring, and my blessing on your descendants.

They will spring up like grass in a meadow,
Like poplar trees by flowing streams.
One will say, 'I belong to the Lord';
Another will call himself by the name of Jacob;
Still another will write on his hand, 'The Lord's,'
And will take the name Israel.

[This passage has application to The Day of Pentecost.
It also will be true of the out pouring of God's Spirit at The Time of The END,
During the ministry of the Bride of Christ, before The Great Tribulation begins.
This end time outpouring will have a mighty effect on the nation Israel.]

God's Appeal To All Peoples To Be Saved (Isaiah 45:22-25)
Turn to me and be saved, all you ends of the earth;
For I am God, and there is no other.
By myself I have sworn, my mouth has uttered in all integrity
A word that will not be revoked:
Before me every knee will bow;
By me every tongue will swear.
They will say of me,
'In the Lord alone are righteousness and strength.'
All who have raged against him will come to him and be put to shame.
But in the Lord all the descendants of Israel will be found righteous and will exult.

[All of the Israel of God, the true believers, the faithful, will be saved.
This will include peoples form every nation on the face of the earth.
All of the godless will bow before the Christ of God
And swear that in Him alone are righteousness and strength.]

Depart, Depart From Babylon (Isaiah 52:10-12)
The Lord will lay bare his holy arm in the sight of all the nations,
And all the ends of the earth will see the salvation of our God.

Depart, depart, go out from there!
Touch no unclean thing!
Come out from it and be pure, you who carry the vessels of the Lord.
But you will not leave in haste or go in flight;
For the Lord will go before you,
The God of Israel will be your rear guard.

[During The Great Tribulation God bares His Holy arm in the sight of all the nations.
As He does in the Book of Revelation, he tells His people to come out of Babylon;
Babylon being the world system, in every aspect, including economics, social life,
Political life, false religion and godlessness.
Before the Tribulation begins the God takes His Bride into the desert,
To the place He has prepared for her.
They will not leave in haste or go in a hurry;
Rather it will be an orderly exodus from their normal lives.
The Lord will go before His Bride and He will be her rear guard.
This is the time when one will be taken and one will remain or be left behind.
The Bride will be taken on the wings of an eagle to a place safety.]

The State Of The World
And The Rebellious Church Before The Great Tribulation (Isaiah 59)
Surely the arm of the Lord is not too short to save, nor his ear too dull to hear.
But your iniquities have separated you from your God;
Your sins have hidden his face from you, so that he will not hear.
For your hands are stained with blood, your fingers with guilt.
Your lips have spoken lies, and your tongue mutters wicked things.
No one calls for justice; no one pleads his case with integrity.
They rely on empty arguments and speak lies;
They conceive trouble and give birth to evil.
They hatch the eggs of vipers and spin a spiders web.
Whoever eats their eggs will die,
And when one is broken, and adder is hatched.
Their cobwebs are useless for clothing;
They cannot cover themselves with what they make.
Their deeds are evil deeds, and acts of violence are in their hands.
Their feet rush into sin; they are swift to shed innocent blood.
Their thoughts are evil thoughts; ruin and destruction mark their ways.
The way of peace they do not know; there is no justice in their paths.
They have turned them into crooked roads;
No one who walks in them will know peace.

The Time Of The END

So justice is far from us, and righteousness does not reach us.
We look for light, but all is darkness;
Like the blind we grope along the wall,
Feeling our way like men without eyes.
At midday we stumble as if it were twilight;
Among the strong, we are like the dead.
We all growl like bears; we moan mournfully like doves.
We look for justice, but find none;
For deliverance, but it is far away.

For our offenses are many in your sight, and our sins testify against us.
Our offenses are ever with us and we acknowledge our iniquities:
Rebellion and treachery against the Lord,
Turning our backs on our God,
Fomenting oppression and revolt,
Uttering lies our hearts have conceived.

So justice and righteousness stands at a distance;
Truth has stumbled in the streets, honesty cannot enter.
Truth is nowhere to be found, and whoever shuns evil becomes a prey.

The Lord looked and was displeased that there was no justice.
He saw that there was no one,
He was appalled that there was no one to intercede;
So his own arm worked salvation for him,
And his own righteousness sustained him.

He put on righteousness as his breastplate,
And the helmet of salvation on his head;
He put on garments of vengeance and wrapped himself in zeal as in a cloak.
According to what they have done,
So will he repay wrath to his enemies and retribution to his foes;
He will repay the islands their due.

From the west, men will fear the name of the Lord,
And from the rising of the sun, they will revere his glory.
For he will come like a pent-up flood
That the breath of the Lord drives along.
'The Redeemer will come to Zion,
To those in Jacob who repent of their sins,' declares the Lord.

'As for me, this is my covenant with them,' says the Lord.
'My Spirit, who is on you, and my words that I have put in your mouth
Will not depart from your mouth, or from the mouths of your children,
Or from the mouths of their descendants from this time on and forever,'
Says the Lord.

The Time Of The END

[In spite of the condition of the world and the rebellious Church,
Zion, the Bride of Christ remains true to God,
And God will redeem Zion, the Israel of God, the Bride of Christ;
Those who have repented of their sins.
God made a covenant with Zion;
His Spirit is on them and He has put His words in their mouth
And those words will never depart from them,
Their children and their descendants, forever.]

The Glory of Zion, The Bride Of Christ, The City Of God (Isaiah 60)

Arise, sine, for your light has come, and the glory of the Lord rises upon you.
See, darkness covers the earth and thick darkness is over the peoples,
But the Lord rises upon you and his glory appears over you.
Nations will come to your light, and kings to the brightness of your dawn.

Lift up your eyes and look about you:
All assemble and come to you;
Your sons come from afar, and your daughters are carried on the arm.
Then you will look and be radiant, your heart will throb and swell with joy;
The wealth on the seas will be brought to you,
To you the riches of the nations will come.

Herds of camels will cover your land, young camels of Midian and Ephah.
And all from Sheba will come, bearing gold and incense
And proclaiming the praise of the Lord.
All Kedar's flocks will be gathered to you,
The rams of Nebaioth will serve you;
They will be accepted as offerings on my altar,
And I will adorn my glorious temple *(the Bride of Christ).*

Who are these that fly along like clouds, like doves to their nests?
Surely the islands look to me; in the lead are the ships of Tarshish,
Bringing your sons from afar, with their silver and gold,
To the honor of the Lord your God, the Holy One of Israel,
For he has endowed you with splendor.

Foreigners will rebuild your walls, and their kings will serve you.
Though in anger I struck you, in favor I will show you compassion.
Your gates will always stand open, they will never be shut, day or night,
So that men may bring you the wealth of the nations--
Their kings led in triumphal procession.
For the nation or kingdom that will not serve you will perish;
It will be utterly ruined.

The glory of Lebanon will come to you, the pine, the fir and the cypress together,

The Time Of The END

To adorn the place of my sanctuary;
And I will glorify the place of my feet.
The sons of your oppressors will come bowing before you;
All who despise you will bow down at your feet
*And will call you **The City of the Lord,***
***Zion** of the Holy One of Israel.*
Although you have been forsaken and hated, with no one traveling through,
I will make you the everlasting pride and the joy of all generations.
You will drink the milk of nations and be nursed at royal breasts.
Then you will know that I, the Lord, am your Savior,
Your Redeemer, the Mighty One of Jacob.

Instead of bronze I will bring you gold,
Instead of wood I will bring you bronze, and iron in place of stones.
I will make peace your governor and righteousness your ruler.
No longer will violence be heard in your land,
Nor ruin or destruction within your borders,
But you will call your walls Salvation and your gates Praise.

The sun will no more be your light by day,
Nor will the brightness of the moon shine on you,
For the Lord will be your everlasting light,
And your God will be your glory.

Your sun will never set again
And your moon will wane no more;
The Lord will be your everlasting light, and your days of sorrow will end.

Then will all your people be righteous and they will possess the land forever.
They are the shoot I have planted, the work of my hands,
For the display of my splendor.
The least of you will become a thousand,
The smallest a mighty nation.
I am the Lord; in its time I will do this swiftly.

[**Zion**, The City of God, The Bride of Christ, the Israel of God, will be glorious;
God will be Her everlasting light.
Her gates will always stand open,
And the nations will bring their wealth to Her.
Her walls will be Salvation and Her gates Praise.
God Almighty will bring this about swiftly, in a moment of time,
And this will be the everlasting condition of His Bride.]

The Year Of The Lord's Favor,
The Day Of Vengeance Of Our God
And The Destiny Of His Bride (Isaiah 61)

The Spirit of the Sovereign Lord is on me,
Because the Lord has anointed me to preach good news to the poor.
He has sent me to bind up the brokenhearted,
To proclaim freedom for the captives and release for the prisoners,
To proclaim the year of the Lord's favor
And the day of vengeance of our God.

To comfort all who mourn and provide for those who grieve in Zion--
To bestow on them a crown of beauty instead of ashes,
The oil of gladness instead of mourning,
And a garment of praise instead of a spirit of despair.
They will be called oaks of righteousness, a planting of the Lord
For the display of his splendor.

They will rebuild the ancient ruins and restore the places long devastated;
They will renew the ruined cities that have been devastated for generations.
Aliens will shepherd your flocks;
Foreigners will work your fields and vineyards.
And you will be called priests of the Lord,
You will be named ministers of our God.
You will feed on the wealth of nations, and in their riches you will boast.

Instead of their shame my people will receive a double portion,
And instead of disgrace they will rejoice in their inheritance;
And so they will inherit a double portion in their land
And everlasting joy will be theirs.

For I, the Lord, love justice; I hate robbery and iniquity.
In my faithfulness I will reward them
And make an everlasting covenant with them.
Their descendants will be known among the nations
And their offspring among the peoples.
All who see them will acknowledge that they are a people the Lord has blessed.

I delight greatly in the Lord; my soul rejoices in my God.
For he has clothed me with garments of salvation
And arrayed me in a robe of righteousness,
As a bridegroom adorns his head like a priest,
And as a bride adorns herself with her jewels.

For as the soil makes the sprout come up

ISAIAH SPEAKS

And a garden causes seeds to grow,
So the Sovereign Lord
Will make righteousness and praise spring up before all nations.

[Isaiah sees the ministry of Christ Jesus; the year of the Lord's favor
And the day of vengeance of God.
He sees the Bride of Christ, her ministry and her destiny.]

The Lord's Passion For Zion, The Bride Of Christ And His Reward For Her (Isaiah 62)

For Zion's sake I will not keep silent,
For Jerusalem's sake I will not remain quiet,
Till her righteousness shines out like the dawn,
Her salvation like a blazing torch.
The nations will see your righteousness, and all kings your glory;
You will be called by a new name
That the mouth of the Lord will bestow.
You will be a crown of splendor in the Lord's hand,
A royal diadem in the hand of your God.
No longer will they call you Deserted, or your land Desolate.
But you will be called Hephzibah, and your land Beulah,
For the Lord will take delight in you,
And your land will be married.

As a young man marries a maiden, so will your sons marry you;
As a bridegroom rejoices over his bride,
So will your God rejoice over you.

I have posted watchmen on your walls, O Jerusalem;
They will never be silent day or night.
You who call on the Lord, give yourselves no rest,
And give him no rest till he establishes Jerusalem
And makes her the praise of the earth.

The Lord has sworn by his right hand and by his mighty arm:
'Never again will I give your grain as food for your enemies,
And never again will foreigners drink the new wine for which you have toiled;
But those who harvest it will eat it and praise the Lord,
And those who gather the grapes will drink it in the courts of my sanctuary.'

Pass through, pass through the gates!
Prepare the way for the people.
Build up, build up the highway!
Remove the stones.
Raise a banner for the nations.

The Time Of The END

The Lord has made proclamation to the ends of the earth:
Say to the daughter of Zion, 'See your Savior comes!
See, his reward is with him, and his recompense accompanies him.'

They will be called The Holy People, The Redeemed of the Lord;
And you will be called Sought After,
The City No Longer Deserted.

[**For Zion's sake**, for the sake of the Israel of God, for the sake of His Bride,
The Lord promises He will never remain quiet
Until Her righteousness shines out like the dawn,
Her salvation like a blazing torch.

All the nations of the world will see the righteousness and glory
Of The Bride of Christ.
She will be given a new name by the Lord,
No longer Deserted but My Delight and Married.
God will rejoice over His Bride.

The Lord declares that He has placed watchmen
On the walls of His Church, who will never be silent day or night.
The people of God are to give themselves no rest and to give God no rest,
Until the Lord makes Jerusalem, the Israel of God, the Church, the Bride of Christ,
The praise of the earth.

Never again will the people of God be mistreated;
God is preparing a way for them.
His reward is with Him.
The people of God will be called The Holy People,
The Redeemed of the Lord, Sought After, The City No Longer Deserted.]

God's Day Of Vengeance, The Battle Of Armageddon
(Isaiah 63:1-6)
Who is this coming from Edom, from Bozrah, with his garments stained crimson?
Who is this, robed in splendor, striding forward in the greatness of his strength?
'It is I, speaking in righteousness, mighty to save.'
Why are your garments red, like those of one treading the winepress?

'I have trodden the winepress alone;
From the nations no one was with me.
I trampled them in my anger and trod them down in my wrath;
Their blood spattered my garments,
And I stained all my clothing.
For the day of vengeance was in my heart,
And the year of my redemption has come.

The Time Of The END

I looked, but there was no one to help,
I was appalled that no one gave support;
So my own arm worked salvation for me,
And my own wrath sustained me.

I trampled the nations in my anger;
In my wrath I made them drunk
And poured their blood on the ground.'

[Here, the nations have all gathered to fight against the Christ of God.
He defeats them by the breath of His mouth and the brightness of His appearing.
Their blood rises as high as a horses bridle, covering the ground.
No nation comes to His side; they are all wicked.
Such is The Day of the Vengeance of God.]

Judgment And Salvation (Isaiah 65)
This chapter has application in Isaiah's time and The Time of The END.

I revealed myself to those who did not ask for me;
I was found by those who did not call on my name,
I said, 'Here am I, here am I.'
(This speaks of the Gentiles who come to Christ)

All day long I have held out my hands to an obstinate people,
(This speaks of natural Israel who forsook their God
And the rebellious Church in The Time of the End.)
Who walk in ways not good, pursuing their own imaginations--
People who continually provoke me to my very face.,
Offering sacrifices in gardens and burning incense on altars of brick;
Who sit among the graves and spend their nights keeping secret vigil;
Who eat the flesh of pigs, and whose pots hold broth of unclean meat;
Who say, 'Keep away; don't come near me,
For I am too sacred for you!'
Such people are smoke in my nostrils, a fire that keeps burning all day.

'See, it stands written before me:
I will not keep silent but will pay back in full;
I will pay it back into their laps--
Both your sins and the sins of your fathers,' says the Lord.

'Because they burned sacrifices on the mountains and defied me on the hills,
I will measure into their laps the full payment for their former deeds.'

This is what the Lord says:
'As when juice is still found in a cluster of grapes

<u>The Time Of The END</u>

And men say, 'Don't destroy it, there is yet some good in it,'
So will I do in behalf of my servants;
I will not destroy them all.
I will bring forth descendants from Jacob,
And from Judah those who will possess my mountains;
<u>My chosen people will inherit them,</u>
And there will my servants live.
Sharon will become a pasture for flocks,
And the Valley of Achor a resting place for my people who seek me.

But as for you who forsake the Lord and forget my holy mountain,
Who spread a table for Fortune and fill bowls of mixed wine for Destiny,
I will destine you for the sword, and you will all bend down for the slaughter;
For I called but you did not answer,
I spoke but you did not listen.
You did evil in my sight and chose what displeases me.'

Therefore this is what the Sovereign Lord says:

'My servants will eat, but you will go hungry;
My servants will drink, but you will go thirsty;
My servants will rejoice, but you will be put to shame.
My servants will sing out of the joy of their hearts,
But you will cry out from anguish of heart
And wail in brokenness of spirit.

You will leave your name to my chosen ones as a curse;
The Sovereign Lord will put you to death,
But to his servants he will give another name.

Whoever invokes a blessing in the land will do so by the God of truth;
He who takes an oath in the land will swear by the God of truth.
For the past troubles will be forgotten
And hidden from my eyes.

Behold, I will create new heavens and a new earth.
The former things will not be remembered,
Nor will they come to mind.
But be glad and rejoice forever in what I will create
For I will create Jerusalem to be a delight and its people a joy.
I will rejoice over Jerusalem and take delight in my people;
The sound of weeping and of crying will be heard in it no more.
Never again will there be in it an infant that lives but a few days,
Or an old man who does not live out his years;
He who dies at a hundred will be thought a mere youth;

The Time Of The END

He who fails to reach a hundred will be considered accursed.
They will build houses and dwell in them;
They will plant vineyards and eat their fruit.
No longer will they build houses and others live in them,
Or plant and others eat.

For as the days of a tree, so will be the days of my people;
My chosen ones will long enjoy the works of their hands.
They will not toil in vain or bear children doomed to misfortune;
For they will be a people blessed by the Lord,
They and their descendants with them.
Before they call I will answer;
While they are still speaking I will hear.

The wolf and the lamb will feed together,
And the lion will eat straw like the ox,
But dust will be the serpent's food.
They will neither harm nor destroy in all my holy mountain,'
Says the Lord.

The Lord Addresses All People In All Times
Concerning His Judgment
And The Hope For His Chosen Ones
(Isaiah 66) – The final chapter in the Book of Isaiah.

This is what the Lord says:
'Heaven is my throne and the earth is my footstool.
Where is the house you will build for me?
Where will my resting place be?
Has not my hand made all these things,
And so they came into being?' declares the Lord.

'This is the one I esteem:
He who is humble and contrite in spirit,
And trembles at my word.

But whoever sacrifices a bull is like one who kills a man,
And whoever offers a lamb, like one who breaks a dog's neck;
Whoever makes a grain offering is like one who presents pig's blood
And whoever burns memorial incense, like one who worships an idol.

They have chosen their own ways,
And their souls delight in their abominations;
So I also will choose harsh treatment for them
And will bring upon them what they dread.

The Time Of The END

For when I called, no one answered,
When I spoke, no one listened.
They did evil in my sight and chose what displeases me.'

Hear the word of the Lord,
You who tremble at his word:
Your brothers who hate you,
And exclude you because of my name, have said:

'Let the Lord be glorified, that we may see your joy!'
Yet they will be put to shame.

Hear that uproar from the city, hear that noise from the temple!
It is the sound of the Lord repaying his enemies all they deserve.

Before she goes into labor, she gives birth;
Before the pains come upon her, she delivers a son.
Who has ever heard of such a thing?
Who has ever seen such things?
Can a country be born in a day
Or a nation be brought forth in a moment?
Yet no sooner is Zion in labor than she gave birth to her children.

[This is a description of the "male child" being born to the "Woman",
The Bride of Christ, the 144,000 sealed to God and snatched up to Heaven.]

'Do I bring to the moment of birth and not give delivery?' says the Lord.
'Do I close up the womb when I bring to delivery?' says your God.

Rejoice with Jerusalem and be glad for her,
All you who love her; rejoice greatly with her,
All you who mourn over her.
For you will nurse and be satisfied at her comforting breasts;
You will drink deeply and delight in her overflowing abundance.

For this is what the Lord says:
'I will extend peace to her like a river,
And the wealth of nations like a flooding stream;
You will nurse and be carried on her arm
And dandled on her knees.
As a mother comforts her child, so will I comfort you;
And you will be comforted over Jerusalem.'

When you see this, your heart will rejoice
And you will flourish like grass;
The hand of the Lord will be made known to his servants,

The Time Of The END

But his fury will be shown to his foes.
See, the Lord is coming with fire,
And his chariots are like a whirlwind;
He will bring down his anger with fury,
And his rebuke with flames of fire.
For with fire and with his sword
The Lord will execute judgment upon all men,
And many will be those slain by the Lord.

Those who consecrate and purify themselves to go into the gardens,
Following the one in the midst of those who eat the flesh of pigs and rats
And other abominable things--
They will meet their end together,' declares the Lord.

'And I, because of their actions and their imaginations,
Am about to come and gather all nations and tongues,
And they will come and see my glory.
I will set a sign among them,
And I will send some of those who survive to the nations--
To Tarshish, to the Libyans and Lydians (famous as archers),
To Tubal and Greece, and to the distant islands
That have not heard of my fame or seen my glory.
They will proclaim my glory among the nations.
And they will bring all your brothers, from all the nations,
To my holy mountain in Jerusalem as an offering to the Lord--
On horses, in chariots and wagons, and on mules and camels,' says the Lord.
'They will bring them, as the Israelites bring their grain offerings,
To the temple of the Lord in ceremonially clean vessels.
And I will select some of them also to be priests and Levites,' says the Lord.

'As the new heavens and the new earth
That I make will endure before me,' declares the Lord,
'So will your name and descendants endure.
From one New Moon to another and from one Sabbath to another,
All mankind will come and bow down before me,' says the Lord.
'And they will go out and look upon the dead bodies
Of those who rebelled against me;

Their worm will not die, nor will their fire be quenched,
And they will be loathsome to all mankind.'

[The Lord says that the "worm" of the wicked will not die,
That is, in death they are still consumed with their desire for their evil lusts.]

JEREMIAH SPEAKS OF THE TIME OF THE END

I Will Punish All Who Are Circumcised Only In The Flesh
(Jeremiah 11:25-26)
'The days are coming,' declares the Lord,
*'When I will punish **all** who are circumcised only in the flesh--*
Egypt, Judah, Edom, Ammon, Moab and all who live in the desert in distant places.
For all these nations are really uncircumcised,
And even the whole house of Israel is uncircimcised in heart.'

Judgment Against All Who Live On The Earth (Jeremiah 25:30-38)
This is what the Lord, the God of Israel, said to me:
'Take from my hand this cup filled with the wine of my wrath
And make all the nations to whom I send you drink it.
When they drink it, they will stagger and go mad
Because of the sword I will send among them.'

So I took the cup from the Lord's hand
And made all the nations to whom he sent me drink it:
Jerusalem and the towns of Judah, its kings and officials,
To make them a ruin and an object of horror
And scorn and cursing, as they are today;

Pharaoh king of Egypt, his attendants, his officials and all his people,
And all the foreign people there;

All the kings of Uz; all the kings of the Philistines
(Those of Ashkelon, Gaza, Ekron, and the people left at Ashdod);
Edom, Moab and Ammon;
All the kings of Tyre and Sidon;
The kings of the coastlands across the sea;
Dedan, Tema, Buz and all who are in distant places;
All the kings of Arabia and all the kings of the foreign people who live in the desert;
All the kings of Zimri, Elam and Media;
And all the kings of the north, near and far, one after the other--
All the kingdoms on the face of the earth.
And after all of them, the king (Satan) of Sheshach (Babylon) will drink it too.

Then tell them,
This is what the Lord Almighty, the God of Israel, says:
'Drink, get drunk and vomit, and fall to rise no more
Because of the sword I will send among you.'

The Time Of The END

But if they refuse to take the cup from your hand and drink,
Tell them, This is what the Lord Almighty says:
'You must drink it!
See, I am beginning to bring disaster on the city that bears my Name,
And will you indeed go unpunished?
You will not go unpunished,
For I am calling down a sword upon all who live on the earth,'
Declares the Lord almighty.

Now prophesy all these words against them and say to to them:
'The Lord will roar from on high;
He will lift his voice from his holy dwelling and roar mightily against his land.
He will shout like those who tread the grapes,
Shout against all who live on the earth.
The tumult will resound to the ends of the earth,
For the Lord will bring charges against the nations;
He will bring judgment on all mankind
And put the wicked to the sword,' declares the Lord.

This is what the Lord Almighty says:
'Look! Disaster is spreading from nation to nation;
A mighty storm is rising from the ends of the earth.

At that time those slain by the Lord will be everywhere--
From one end of the earth to the other.
They will not be mourned or gathered up or buried,
But will be like refuse lying on the ground.

Weep and wail, you shepherds;
Roll in the dust, you leaders of the flock.
For your time to be slaughtered has come;
You will fall and be shattered like fine pottery.
The shepherds will have nowhere to flee,
The leaders of the flock no place to escape.
Hear the cry of the shepherds,
The wailing of the leaders of the flock,
For the Lord is destroying their pasture.

The peaceful meadows will be laid waste
Because of the fierce anger of the Lord.
Like a lion he will leave his lair,
And their land will become desolate
Because of the sword of the oppressor
And because of the Lord's fierce anger.' (Jeremiah 25:30-38)

Restoration Of Israel (Jeremiah 30)

This is the word that came to Jeremiah from the Lord:
This is what the Lord, the God of Israel, says:
'Write in a book all the words I have spoken to you.
The days are coming,' declares the Lord,
'When I will bring my people Israel and Judah back from captivity
And restore them to the land I gave their forefathers to possess,' says the Lord.

These are the words the Lord spoke concerning Israel and Judah:
This is what the Lord says:
'Cries of fear are heard terror, not peace.
Ask and see:
Can a man bear children?
Then why do I see every strong man
With his hands on his stomach like a woman in labor,
Every face turned deathly pale?
How awful that day will be !
None will be like it.
It will be a time of trouble for Jacob,
But he will be saved out of it.'

'In that day,' declares the Lord Almighty,
'I will break off the yoke off their necks
And will tear off their bonds,
No longer will foreigners enslave them.
Instead, they will serve the Lord their God and David their king.
Whom I will raise up for them.

So do not fear, O Jacob my servant;
Do not be dismayed, O Israel,' declares the Lord.
'I will surely save you out of a distant place,
Your descendants from the land of their exile.
Jacob will again have peace and security,
And no one will make him afraid.

I am with you and will save you,' declares the Lord.
'Though I completely destroy all the nations among which I scatter you,
I will not completely destroy you.
I will discipline you but only with justice;
I will not let you go entirely unpunished.'

This is what the Lord says:
'Your wound is incurable, your injury beyond healing.
There is no one to plead your cause, no remedy for your sore, no healing for you.
All your allies have forgotten you:

180

The Time Of The END

They care nothing for you.
I have struck you as an enemy would and punished you as would the cruel,
Because your guilt is so great and your sins so many.
Why do you cry out over your wound, your pain has no cure?
Because of your great guilt and many sins I have done these things to you.

But all who devour you will be devoured;
All your enemies will go into exile.
Those who plunder you will be plundered;
All who make spoil of you I will despoil.
But I will restore you to health and heal your wounds,' declares the Lord,
'Because you are called an outcast, Zion for whom no one cares.'

This is what the Lord says:
'I will restore the fortunes of Jacob's tents and have compassion on his dwellings;
The city will be rebuilt on her ruins, and the palace will stand in its proper place.
From them will come songs of thanksgiving and the sound of rejoicing.
I will add to their numbers, and they will not be decreased;
I will bring them honor, and they will not be disdained.
Their children will be as in days of old,
And their community will be established before me;
I will punish all who oppress them.
Their leader will be one of their own;
Their ruler will arise from among them.
I will bring him near and he will come close to me,
For who is he who will devote himself to be close to me?' *declares the Lord.*
'So you will be my people, and I will be your God.

See, the storm of the Lord will burst out in wrath,
A driving wind swirling down on the heads of the wicked.
The fierce anger of the Lord will not turn back
Until he fully accomplishes the purposes of his heart.
In days to come you will understand this.'

The Distant Future, The Remnant To Be Saved,
And The New Covenant (Jeremiah 31)
'At that time' (a time in the distant future), *declares the Lord,*
'I will be the God of all the clans of Israel, and they will be my people.'
This is what the lord says:

'The people who survive the sword <u>will find favor in the desert</u>;
I will come to give rest to Israel.'

[God is looking forward to the "Woman" of Revelation 12, the Israel of God,
Being taken into the desert on the wings of an eagle.]

181

The Time Of The END

The Lord appeared to us in the past, saying:
'I have loved you with an everlasting love;
I have drawn you with loving-kindness.
I will build you up again and you will rebuild, O Virgin Israel,
Again you will take up your tambourines and go out to dance with the joyful.
Again you will plant vineyards on the hills of Samaria;
The farmers will plant them and enjoy their fruit.
There will be a day when watchmen cry out on the hills of Ephraim,
'Come, let us go up to Zion, to the Lord our God.'

This is what the Lord says:
'Sing with joy for Jacob;
Shout for the greatest of the nations.
Make your praises heard, and say,
O Lord, save your people , <u>the remnant of Israel</u>.

See, I will bring them from the land of the north
And gather them from the ends of the earth.
Among them will be the blind and the lame,
Expectant mothers and women in labor;
A great throng will return.
They will come with weeping;
They will pray as I bring them back.
I will lead them beside streams of water
On a level path where they will not stumble,
Because I am Israel's father, and Ephraim is my firstborn son.'

[This is a picture of Israel being restored as a nation in 1948,
An unheard of event in the history of the world.]

'Hear the word of the Lord, O nations;
Proclaim it in distant coastlands:
He who scattered Israel will gather them
And will watch over his flock like a shepherd.
For the Lord will ransom Jacob
And redeem them from the hand of those stronger than they.

They will come and shout for joy on the heights of Zion;
They will rejoice in the bounty of the Lord--
The grain, the new wine and the oil, the young of the flocks and herds.
They will be like a well-watered garden, <u>and they will sorrow no more</u>.

[In saying that Israel will sorrow no more, God jumps to The Time of The END,
To the Israel of God, because Israel will suffer in The Great Tribulation.
However, at the end of the Tribulation the Israel of God, Zion, the Bride of Christ
Will have no more enemies, they will all be done away with.]

The Time Of The END

Then maidens will dance and be glad, young men and old as well.
I will turn their mourning into gladness;
I will give them comfort and joy instead of sorrow.
I will satisfy the priests with abundance,
And my people will be filled with my bounty,' declares the Lord.

This is what the Lord says:
'A voice is heard in Ramah, mourning and great weeping,
Rachel weeping for her children and refusing to be comforted,
Because her children are no more.'

[This is a reference to the time when king Herod
Killed all the children two years of age and under
In an attempt to kill Christ Jesus as a baby.]

This is what the Lord says:
'Restrain your voice from weeping and your eyes from tears,
For your work will be rewarded,' declares the lord.
'They will return from the land of the enemy.
So there is hope for your future,' declares the Lord.
'Your children will return to their own land.'

'I have surely heard Ephraim's moaning:
You disciplined me like a unruly calf, and I have been disciplined.
Restore me, and I will return, because you are the Lord my God.
After I strayed, I repented;
After I came to understand, I beat my breast.
I was ashamed and humiliated because I bore the disgrace of my youth.

Is not Ephraim my dear son, the child in whom I delight?
Though I often speak against him, I still remember him.
Therefore my heart yearns for him;' declares the Lord.

'Set up road signs; put up guideposts.
Take note of the highway, the road that you take.
Return, O Virgin Israel, return to your towns.
How long will you wander, O unfaithful daughter?

The Lord will create a new thing on earth--
A woman will surround a man.'

[The Bride of Christ will surround the "male child" in Revelation 12.]

This is what the Lord Almighty, the God of Israel, says:
'When I bring them back from captivity,
The people in the land of Judah and in its towns will once again use these words:

183

The Time Of The END

JEREMIAH SPEAKS

'The Lord bless you O righteous dwelling, O sacred mountain (Zion).'

People will live together in Judah and all its towns—
Farmers and those who move about with their flocks.
I will refresh the weary and satisfy the faint.'

At this I awoke and looked around.
My sleep had been pleasant to me.

'The days are coming,' declares the Lord, 'when I will plant the house of Israel
And the house of Judah with the offspring of men and of animals.
Just as I watched over them to uproot and tear down,
And to overthrow, destroy and bring disaster,
So I will watch over them to build and to plant,' declares the Lord.

In those days people will no longer say,
'The fathers have eaten sour grapes, and the children's teeth are set on edge.'
Instead, everyone will die for his own sin;
Whoever eats sour grapes—his own teeth will be set on edge.

'The time is coming,' declares the Lord,
'When I will make a new covenant with the house of Israel
And with the house of Judah.
It will not be like the covenant I made with their forefathers
When I took them by the hand to lead them out of Egypt,
Because they broke my covenant,
Though I was a husband to them,' declares the Lord.

'This is the covenant I will make with the house of Israel after that time,'
Declares the Lord.
'I will put my law in their minds and write it on their hearts.
I will be their God and they will be my people.
No longer will a man teach his neighbor, or a man his brother, saying,
'Know the Lord,'
Because they will all know me, from the least of them to the greatest,'
Declares the Lord.
'For I will forgive their wickedness and will remember their sins no more.'

[Here, God is talking about the New Covenant
That Christ Jesus would bring into effect by His shed blood on the cross of Calvary
And the out pouring of the Holy Spirit on the day of Pentecost.
In the New Covenant the Holy Spirit puts God's law in the mind of the believer
And writes it upon their heart and becomes their teacher.]

This is what the Lord says,
He who appoints the sun to shine by day,

The Time Of The END

Who decrees the moon and stars to shine by night,
Who stirs up the sea so that its waves roar--
The Almighty is his name:

'Only if these decrees vanish from my sight,' declares the Lord,
'Will the descendants of Israel ever cease to be a nation before me.'

This is what the Lord says:
'Only if the heavens above can be measured
And the foundations of the earth below be searched out
Will I reject all the descendants of Israel because of all they have done,'
Declares the Lord.

'The days are coming,' declares the Lord,
'When this city will be rebuilt for me
From the Tower of Hananel to the corner Gate.
The measuring line will stretch from their straight to the hill of Gareb
And then turn to Goah.
The whole valley where dead bodies and ashes are thrown,
And all the terraces out to the Kidron Valley on the east
As far as the corner of the Horse Gate,
Will be holy to the Lord.
The city will never again be uprooted or demolished.'

God Makes An Everlasting Covenant With Israel
(Jeremiah 32:36-41)
You are saying about this city,
By the sword, famine and plague it will be handed over to the king of Babylon';
But this is what the Lord, the God of Israel, says:
'I will surely gather them from all the lands where I banish them
In my furious anger and great wrath;
I will bring them back to this place and let them live in safety.
They will be my people and I will be their God.
I will give them singleness of heart and action,
So that they will always fear me for their own good
And the good of their children after them.

I will make an everlasting covenant with them:
I will never stop doing good to them,
And I will inspire them to fear me,
So that they will never turn away from me.
I will rejoice in doing them good
And will assuredly plant them in this land with all my heart and soul.'

The Time Of The END

Flee From Babylon! (Jeremiah 51:6)
'Flee from Babylon!
Run for you lives!
Do not be destroyed because of her sins.
It is time for the Lord's vengeance;
He will pay her what she deserves.
Babylon was a gold cup in the Lord's hand;
She made the whole earth drunk.
The nations drank her wine;
Therefore they have now gone mad.
Babylon will suddenly fall and be broken.
Wail over her!
Get balm for her pain; perhaps she can be healed.

We would have healed Babylon, but she cannot be healed;
Let us leave her and each go to his own land,
For her judgment reaches to the skies,
It rises as high as the clouds.'

The Lord has vindicated us;
'Come, let us tell in Zion what the Lord our God has done.'

[This is a picture of the end times Babylon,
Spoken of in the Book of Revelation
And God' admonishment to His people to flee from her.]

EZEKIEL SPEAKS OF THE TIME OF THE END

The Lord Makes An Everlasting Covenant With Israel (Ezekiel 37:26)

I (the Lord) *will make a covenant of peace with them* (the Israel of God);
It will be an everlasting covenant.
I will establish them and increase their numbers,
And I will put my sanctuary among them <u>forever</u>.
My dwelling place will be with them;
I will be their God, and they will be my people.
Then the nations will know that I the Lord make Israel holy,
When my sanctuary is among them <u>forever</u>.'

A Prophecy Against Gog
God Fights For Israel, Against Gog

(Ezekiel 38-39)
The word of the Lord came to me:
'Son of man, set your face against Gog, of the land of Magog,
The chief prince of Meshech and Tubal;'
Prophesy against him and say;
'This is what the sovereign Lord says:
I am against you, O Gog, chief prince of Meschech and Tubal.
I will turn you around, put hooks in your jaws
And bring you out with your whole army--
Your horses, your horsemen full armed,
And a great horde with large and small shields,
All of them brandishing their swords.
Persia, Cush and Put will be with them,
All with shields and helmets, also Gomer with all its troops,
And Beth Togarmah from the far north with all its troops--
The many nations with you.'

'Get ready;
Be prepared, you and all the hordes gathered about you,
And take command of them.
After many days you will be called to arms.
In the future years you will invade a land that has recovered from war,
<u>*Whose people were gathered from many nations to the mountains of Israel,*</u>
Which had long been desolate.
They had been brought out from the nations,
And now all of them live in safety.
You and all your troops and the many nations with you will go up,
Advancing like a storm;
You will be like a cloud covering the land.'

187

The Time Of The END

This is what the Sovereign Lord says:
'On that day thoughts will come into your mind and you will devise an evil scheme.
You will say,
'I will invade a land of unwalled villages;
I will attack a peaceful and unsuspecting people--
All of them living without walls and without gates and bars.
I will plunder and loot and turn my hand against the resettled ruins
And the people gathered from the nations,
Rich in livestock and goods, living at the center of the land.'

Sheba and Dedan and the merchants of Tarshish and all her villages will say to you,
'Have you come to plunder?
Have you gathered your hordes to loot,
To carry off silver and gold, to take away livestock and goods
And to seize much plunder?'

Therefore, son of man, prophesy and say to Gog:
This is what the Sovereign Lord says:
'In that day, when my people Israel are living in safety,
Will you not take notice of it?
You will come from your place in the far north,
You and many nations with you,
All of them riding on horses, a great horde, a mighty army.
You will advance against my people Israel like a cloud that covers the land.
In days to come, O Gog, I will bring you against my land,
So that the nations may know me
When I show myself holy through you before their eyes.

This is what the sovereign Lord says:
'Are you not the one I spoke of
In former days by my servants the prophets of Israel?
At that time they prophesied for years that I would bring you against them.
This is what will happen in that day;
When Gog attacks the land of Israel,
My hot anger will be aroused,' declares the Sovereign Lord.
'In my zeal and fiery wrath I declare that at that time
There shall be a great earthquake in the land of Israel.
The fish of the sea, the birds of the air, and the beasts of the field,
Every creature that moves along the ground
And all the people on the face of the earth will tremble at my presence.
The mountains will be overturned, the cliffs will crumble
And every wall will fall to the ground.
I will summon a sword against Gog on all my mountains,'
Declares the Sovereign Lord.
'Every man's sword will be against his brother.
I will execute judgment upon him with plague and bloodshed;

The Time Of The END

I will pour down torrents of rain, hailstones and burning sulfur
On him and on his troops and on the many nations with him.
And so I will show my greatness and my holiness,
And I will make myself known in the sight of many nations.
Then they will know that I am the Lord.'

Son of man, prophesy against Gog and say:
'This is what the Sovereign Lord says:
I am against you, O Gog, chief prince of Meshech and Tubal.
I will turn you around and drag you along.
I will bring you from the far north
And send you against the mountains of Israel.
Then I will strike your bow from your left hand
And make your arrows drop from your right hand.
On the mountains of Israel you will fall,
You and all your troops and the nations with you.
I will give you as food to all kinds of carrion birds and to the wild animals.
You will fall in the open field, for I have spoken,' declares the Sovereign Lord.
'I will send fire on Magog and on those who live in safety in the coastlands,
And they will know that I am the Lord.

I will make known my holy name among my people Israel.
I will no longer let my holy name be profaned,
And the nations will know that I the Lord am the Holy One in Israel.
It is coming!
It will surely take place,' declares the sovereign Lord.
<u>'This is the day I have spoken of.</u>

Those who live in the towns of Israel will go out
And use the weapons for fuel and burn them up--
The small and large shields, the bows and arrows, the war clubs and spears.
For seven years they will use them for fuel.
They will not need to gather wood from the fields or cut it from the forests,
Because they will use the weapons for fuel.
And they will plunder those who plundered them
And loot those who looted them,' declares the Sovereign Lord.

'On that day I will give Gog a burial place in Israel,
In the valley of those who travel east toward the Sea (the Dead Sea).
It will block the way of travelers,
Because Gog and all his hordes will be buried there.
So it will be called the Valley of Hamon Gog.

For seven months the house of Israel will be burying them
In order to cleanse the land.
All the people of the land will bury them,

The Time Of The END

And the day I am glorified will be a memorable day for them,'
Declares the Sovereign Lord.

'Men will be regularly employed to cleanse the land.
Some will go throughout the land and, in addition to them,
Others will bury those that remain on the ground.
At the end of the seven months they will begin their search.
As they go through the land and one of them sees a human bone,
He will set up a marker beside it until the gravediggers have buried it
In the Valley of Hamon Gog.
(Also a town call Hamonah will be there.)
And so they will cleanse the land.'

Son of man, this is what the Sovereign Lord says:
'Call out to every kind of bird and all the wild animals:
Assemble and come together from all around
To the sacrifice I am preparing for you,
The great sacrifice on the mountains of Israel.
There you will eat flesh and drink blood.
You will eat the flesh of mighty men
And drink the blood of the princes of the earth
As if they were rams and lambs, goats and bulls--
All of them fattened animals from Bashan.
At the sacrifice I am preparing for you, you will eat fat till you are glutted
And drink blood till you are drunk.
At my table you will eat your fill of horses and riders,
Mighty men and soldiers of every kind,' declares the Sovereign Lord.

'I will display my glory among the nations,
And all the nations will see the punishment I inflict
And the hand I lay upon them.
From that day forward the house of Israel will know
That I am the Lord their God.
And the nations will know that the people of Israel went into exile for their sin,
Because they were unfaithful to me.
So I hid my face from them and handed them over to their enemies,
And they all fell by the sword.
I dealt with them according to their uncleanness
And their offenses, and I hid my face from them.'

Therefore this is what the Sovereign Lord says:
'I will now bring Jacob back from captivity
And will have compassion on all the people of Israel,
And I will be zealous for my holy name.
They will forget their shame and all the unfaithfulness they showed toward me
When they lived in safety in their land with no one to make them afraid.

The Time Of The END

When I have brought them back from the nations
And have gathered them from the countries of their enemies,
I will show myself holy through them in the sight of many nations.
Then they will know that I am the Lord their God,
For though I sent them into exile among the nations,
I will gather them to their own land, not leaving any behind.
I will no longer hid my face from them,
For I will pour out my Spirit on the house of Israel,' declares the Sovereign Lord.
(The house of Israel spoken of here is the nation Israel).

DANIEL SPEAKS
OF THE TIME OF THE END

Daniel's Dream Of Four Beasts (Daniel 7:1-14)

In the first year of Belshazzar king of Babylon, Daniel had a dream,
And visions passed through his mind as he was lying on his bed.
He wrote down the substance of his dream.

Daniel said:
'In my vision at night I looked,
And there before me were the four winds of heaven
Churning up the great sea.
(Bringing to the nations of the world, social, economic and political unrest).
Four great beasts, each different from the others, came up out of the sea.

The first (the Babylonian empire under Nebuchadnezzar), *was like a lion*
And it had the wings of and eagle.
I watched until its wings were torn off
And it was lifted from the ground so that it stood on two feet like a man,
And the heart of a man was given to it.

And there before me was a second beast (the Media-Persia empire),
Which looked like a bear.
It was raised up on one of its sides (one part of the empire),
And it had three ribs in its mouth between its teeth.
It was told, 'Get up and eat your fill of flesh!'

'After that, I looked, and there before me was another beast
(the Grecian Empire of Alexander the Great),
One that looked like a leopard.
And on its back it had four wings like those of a bird.
This beast had four heads (Alexander's four generals, his successors),
And it was given authority to rule.

After that, in my vision at night I looked, and there before me was a fourth beast--
Terrifying and frightening and very powerful.
It had large iron teeth;
It crushed and devoured its victims and trampled underfoot what ever was left.
*It was different from all the former beasts, and it had **ten** horns*
(symbolizing ten kings).

While I was thinking about the horns, there before me was another horn,
A little one, which came up among them;
And three of the first horns were uprooted before it.

The Time Of The END

This horn *had eyes like the eyes of a man and a mouth that spoke boastfully.*

As I looked, thrones were set in place *(for the Court of God),*
And the Ancient of Days *(God, the Father Almighty)* *took his seat.*
His clothing was as white as snow;
The hair of his head was white like wool.
His throne was flaming with fire,
And its wheels were all ablaze.
Thousands upon thousands attended him;
Ten thousand times then thousand stood before him.
The court was seated, and the books were opened.

Then I continued to watch because of the boastful words *the horn* *was speaking.*
I kept looking until *the beast* *was slain*
And its body destroyed and thrown into the blazing fire.
*(**The other beasts** had been stripped of their authority,*
But were allowed to live for a period of time.)

In my vision at night I looked, and there before me was one like a son of man,
Coming with the clouds of heaven.
He (Christ) approached the Ancient of days and was led into his presence.
He was given authority, glory and sovereign power;
All peoples, nations and men of every language worshiped him.
His dominion is an everlasting dominion that will not pass away,
And his kingdom is one that will never be destroyed.'

The Interpretation Of The Dream Of Four Beasts (Daniel 7:15-28)
I Daniel, was troubled in spirit,
And the visions that passed through my mind disturbed me.
I approached one of those standing there
And asked him the true meaning of all this.

So he told me and gave me the interpretation of these things:
'The four great beasts are four kingdoms that will rise from the earth.
But the saints of the Most High will receive the kingdom
And will possess it forever--yes, for ever and ever.'

Then I wanted to know the true meaning of the fourth beast,
Which was different from all the others and most terrifying,
With its iron teeth and bronze claws—
The beast that crushed and devoured its victims
And trampled underfoot what ever was left.
I also wanted to know about the ten horns on its head
And about *the other horn* *that came up, before which three of them fell—*
The horn *that looked more imposing than the others*

And that had eyes and a mouth that spoke boastfully.
*As I watched, **this horn** was waging war against the saints and defeating them,*
Until the Ancient of days came and pronounced judgment
In favor of the saints of the Most High,
And the time came when they possessed the kingdom.

He gave me this explanation:
'The fourth beast is a fourth kingdom that will appear on earth.
It will be different from all the other kingdoms
And will devour the whole earth, trampling it down and crushing it.
The ten horns are ten kings who will come from this kingdom.
After them another king will arise, different from the earlier ones;
He (the Antichrist) will subdue three kings.
He will speak against the Most high and oppress his saints
*And **try** to change the set times (of sacred feasts and holy days) and the laws.*
The saints will be handed over to him for a time, times and half a time.
(The three and one half years of The Great Tribulation).

But the court will sit, and his (the Antichrist's) power will be taken away
And completely destroyed forever.
Then the sovereignty, power and greatness of the kingdoms
Under the whole heaven Will be handed over to the saints,
The people of the Most High.
His kingdom will be an everlasting kingdom,
And all rulers will worship and obey him.

This is the end of the matter.'
I Daniel, was deeply troubled by my thoughts, and my face turned pale,
But I kept the matter to myself.

Daniel's Vision Of A Ram And A Goat (Daniel 8:1-14)

In the third year of King Belshazzar's reign, I, Daniel, had a vision,
After the one that had already appeared to me.
In my vision I saw myself in the citadel of Susa (the capital of Persia)
In the province of Elam;
In the vision I was beside the Ulai Canal.
I looked up, and there before me was a ram with two horns
(Representing two kings of Media-Persia, Darius the Mede, then Cyrus),
Standing beside the canal, and the horns were long.
One of the horns was longer than the other but grew up later.
I watched the ram (Media-Persia) as he charged toward the west
And the north and the south.
No animal could stand against him, and none could rescue from his power.
He did as he pleased and became great.

The Time Of The END

DANIEL SPEAKS

As I was thinking about this,
Suddenly a goat (the king of Greece) *with a prominent horn between his eyes*
Came from the west, crossing the whole earth without touching the ground.
He came toward the two-horned ram I had seen standing beside the canal
And charged at him in great rage.
I saw him attack the ram (the Media-Persian Empire) *furiously,*
Striking the ram and shattering his two horns.
The ram was powerless to stand against him;
The goat (Alexander) *knocked him to the ground and trampled on him,*
And none could rescue the ram from his power.
The goat became very great,
But at the height of his power his large horn was broken off,
And in its place **four** *prominent horns grew up toward the four winds of heaven.*

Out of **one** *of them came* **another horn** (the Antichrist),
Which started small but grew in power
To the south and to the east and toward the Beautiful Land.
It grew until it reached the host of the heavens,
And it threw some to the starry host down to the earth and trampled on them.
It set itself up to be as great as the Prince of the host;
It took away the daily sacrifice from him,
And the place of his sanctuary was brought low.
Because of rebellion, the host of the saints
And the daily sacrifice were given over to it.
It prospered in everything it did, <u>and truth was thrown to the ground</u>.

[The Antichrist grows in power to the south and to the east
And toward the Beautiful Land, Israel.
He throws some of the starry host (saints of God) to the ground
And tramples on them.
He sets himself up to be as great as the Prince of the host, Christ Jesus.
Because of rebellion in the Church of God
The Antichrist is allowed to take away the daily sacrifice, the worship of God.
He prospers in everything he does (at this time) and truth is thrown to the ground.]

Then I heard a holy one speaking, and another holy one said to him,
'How long will it take for the vision to be fulfilled--
The vision concerning the daily sacrifice,
The rebellion that causes desolation,
And the surrender of the sanctuary
And of the host that will be trampled underfoot?'

He said to me, 'It will take 2,300 evenings and mornings;
Then the sanctuary will be reconsecrated.'

DANIEL SPEAKS

[The angel tells Daniel it will be 1,150 days or approximately
Three and one-half years before the sanctuary is reconsecrated.]

Interpretation Of The Vision Of A Ram And A Goat (Daniel 8:15-27)

While I, Daniel, was watching the vision and trying to understand it,
There before me stood one who looked like a man.
And I heard a man's voice from the Ulai calling,
'Gabriel, tell this man the meaning of the vision.'

As he came near the place where I was standing, I was terrified and fell prostrate.
'Son of man,' he said to me,
'Understand that the vision concerns <u>the time of the end</u>.'

While he was speaking to me, I was in a deep sleep, with my face to the ground.
Then he touched me and raised me to my feet.

He said: 'I am going to tell you what will happen later <u>in the time of wrath</u>,
Because the vision concerns <u>the appointed time of the end</u>.
The two-horned ram that you saw represents the kings of Media and Persia.
The shaggy goat is the king of Greece,
And the large horn between his eyes is the first king.
The four horns that replaced the one that was broken off
Represent four kingdoms that will emerge from his nation
But will not have the same power.

In the latter part of their reign,
When rebels(within the Church of God) **have become completely wicked,**
A stern-faced king, a master of intrigue, will arise.
He will become very strong, <u>but not by his own power</u>.
<u>He will cause astounding devastation</u>
And will succeed in what ever he does.
He will <u>destroy</u> the mighty men <u>and the holy people</u>
And he will consider himself superior.
When they feel secure,
He will destroy many and take a stand against the Prince of princes.
Yet he will be destroyed <u>but not by human power</u>.

[In the latter part of the reign of the kingdoms
That emerge from Alexander's kingdom,
When those who have rebelled against God and His Christ
Have become completely wicked,
A stern-faced king, a master of intrigue, will arise.
This is the Beast, the Antichrist of The Time of The END.
He will destroy prominent men and the saints of God.
He will consider himself superior to all men.

196

DANIEL SPEAKS

(Because he is possessed by Satan and has Satan's supernatural abilities)
When the rebels feel secure, the Antichrist will destroy many of them,
And take his stand against the Princes of princes, Christ Jesus.
Yet he will be destroyed by the power of God and His Christ.]

The vision of the evenings and mornings that has been given you is true,
But seal up the vision, for its concerns the <u>distant future</u>.'

I, Daniel, was exhausted and lay ill for several days.
Then I got up and went about the king's business.
I was appalled by the vision; it was beyond understanding.

The Seventy Sevens (Daniel 9:20-27)
While I was speaking and praying, confessing my sin and the sin of my people Israel
And making my request to the Lord my God for his holy hill--
While I was still in prayer, Gabriel, the man I had seen in the earlier vision,
Came to me in swift flight about the time of the evening sacrifice.
He instructed me and said to me,
'Daniel, I have now come to give you insight and understanding.
As soon as you began to pray, and answer was given,
Which I have come to tell you, for you are highly esteemed.
Therefore, consider the message and understand the vision:

Seventy 'sevens' (490 years) are decreed for your people and your holy city
To finish transgression, to put and end to sin, to atone for wickedness
To bring everlasting righteousness, to seal up vision and prophecy
And to anoint the most holy.

Know and understand his:
From the issuing of the decree to restore and rebuild Jerusalem
Until the Anointed One, the ruler, comes,
There will be seven 'sevens,' and sixty-two 'sevens.'
It will be rebuilt with streets and a trench, but in times of trouble.
After the sixty-two 'sevens,' the Anointed One will be cut off and will have nothing.

The people of the ruler who will come will destroy the city and the sanctuary.
The end will come like a flood:
War will continue until the end, and desolations have been decreed.

He** (the Anointed One) **will confirm a covenant with many for one 'seven,'
(7 years)
But in the middle of that 'seven' he will put an end to sacrifice and offering.
*And **one** (the, Beast, the Antichrist) who causes desolation*
Will place abominations <u>on a wing of the temple</u>
Until the end that is decreed is poured out on him.'

The Time Of The END

[Christ Jesus, the Anointed One, confirms a covenant with many
(The "Woman" of Revelation 12, the Bride of Christ), for seven years.
The three and one-half years preceding The Great Tribulation,
The time of the ministry of the "woman," the Bride of Christ
And the three and one-half years of The Great Tribulation.
In the middle of that seven years, the beginning of The Great Tribulation,
Because of apostasy and rebellion within His Church,
Christ Jesus puts and end to worship and offering to Himself.
At the same time the Beast, the Antichrist,
Sets up his "image," "the abomination that causes desolation,"
In the Church of Christ Jesus,
Until the end takes place at The Battle of Armageddon,
Where the Beast, the Antichrist, is defeated and sent to the Lake of Fire.]

The Daily Sacrifice Is Abolished (Daniel 11:30-35)

[Daniel 11:30-35 Seems To Describe The Events Related To Antiochus Epiphanes, An
Archtype Of The Antichrist,
However, They Are Also A Description Of End Time Events
Related To The Antichrist, The Beast.]

Then he (the Antichrist) *will turn back and vent his fury against the holy covenant.*

[When the Dragon cannot kill the "Woman" of Revelation 12,
He turns to make war against the rest of he off-spring—*'those who obey God 's
commandments and hold to the testimony of Jesus.'*]

He will return and show favor to those who forsake the holy covenant.

[The dragon, through his emissary the Beast, shows favor to those
Who claim the name of Christ but are apostates,
And have rebelled against Christ Jesus.]

*His armed forces will rise up to desecrate the temple fortress
And will abolish the daily sacrifice.
Then they will set up the abomination that causes desolation.
With flattery he will corrupt those who have violated the covenant,
But the people who know their God will firmly resist him.*

[The Beast by force of arms, will forbid the people of God to worship God
And will set up the "image" of the Beast in the Church of God
And require worship of the "image."
Those who claim the name of Christ Jesus,
Who are apostates and have rebelled against Christ Jesus
Will be flattered and corrupted by the Beast,

198

The Time Of The END

But those who "know" their God will firmly resist the Beast.]

'Those who are wise will instruct many,
Though for a time they will fall by the sword or be burned or captured or plundered.
When they fall, they will receive little help,
And many who are insincere will join them.
Some of the wise will stumble,
So that they may be refined, purified and made spotless
Until the time of the end,
For it will still come at the appointed time.'

[This speaks of the time of The Great Tribulation,
Where the Beast requires worship of his "image."
Those who name the name of Christ, who are wise,
Who know and believe the Word of God will instruct many.
For three and one-half years they will be killed.
They will receive little help.
Many who are insincere will pretend to join them
To try to get them to worship the Beast and live.
Some of the wise will stumble or loose their bearing temporarily;
Through this, God refines and purifies them and makes them spotless.]

The King Who Exalts Himself, The Beast (Daniel 11:36-45)
*The **king** (the Beast) will do as he pleases.*
He will exalt and magnify himself above every god
And will say unheard-of things against the God of gods.
He will be successful until the time of wrath is completed,
For what has been determined must take place.
He will show no regard for the gods of his fathers or for the one desired by women,
Nor will he regard any god, but will exalt himself above them all.
Instead of them, he will honor a god of fortress;
A god unknown to his fathers he will honor with gold and silver,
With precious stones and costly gifts.

He will attack the mightiest fortresses with the help of a foreign god
And greatly honor those who acknowledge him.
He will make them rulers over many people and will distribute the land at a price.

At the time of the end the king of the South will engage him in battle,
And the king of the North will storm out against him
With chariots and cavalry and a great fleet of ships.
He will invade many countries and sweep through them like a flood.
He will also invade the Beautiful Land.
Many countries will fall,
But Edom, Moab and the leaders of Ammon will be delivered from his hand.

The Time Of The END

He will extend his power over many countries;
Egypt will not escape.
He will gain control of the treasures of gold and silver
And all the riches of Egypt, with Libyans and Nubians in submission.
But reports from the east and the north will alarm him,
And he will set out in a great rage to destroy and annihilate many.
He will pitch his royal tents between the seas at the beautiful holy mountain.
Yet he will come to his end, and no one will help him.

The Time Of The End (Daniel 12:1-13)

'At that time Michael, the great prince who protects your people, will arise.
There will be a time of distress such as has not happened
From the beginning of nations until then.
But at that time your people—
Everyone whose name is found written in the book—will be delivered.
Multitudes who sleep in the dust of the earth will awake:
Some to everlasting life, others to shame and everlasting contempt.
Those who are wise will shine like the brightness of the heavens,
And those who lead many to righteousness, like the stars for ever and ever.
But you, Daniel, close up and seal the words of the scroll until the time of the end.
Many will go here and there to increase knowledge.'

Then I, Daniel, looked and there before me stood two others,
One on this bank of the river and one on the opposite bank.
One of them said to the man clothed in linen,
Who was above the waters of the river,
'How long will it be before these astonishing things are fulfilled?'

The man clothed in linen, who was above the water of the river,
Lifted his right hand and his left hand toward heaven,
And I heard him swear by him who lives forever, saying,

'It will be for a time, times and half a time. (Three and one-half years)
When the power of the holy people has been finally broken,
All these things will be completed.'

[Time will end with the killing of the last of the saints by the Beast
At the end of The Great Tribulation
And Christ Jesus defeating the Beast at The Battle of Armageddon.]

I heard, but I did not understand.
So I asked, 'My lord, what will the outcome of all this be?

He replied, 'Go your way, Daniel,
Because the words are closed up and sealed until the time of the end.

The Time Of The END

DANIEL SPEAKS

Many will be purified, made spotless and refined,
But the wicked will continue to be wicked.
None of the wicked will understand, but those who are wise will understand.

Form the time that the daily sacrifice is abolished
And the abomination that causes desolation is set up,
There will be 1,290 days.
Blessed is the one who waits for and reaches the end of the 1,335 days.'

[From the time the abomination that causes desolation, the "image" of the Beast,
Is set up in the Church of Christ Jesus, to the end of the Tribulation
There will be 1,290 days, approximately three and one-half years.]

'As for you, go your way till the end.
You will rest, and then at the end of the days
You will rise to receive your allotted inheritance.'

HOSEA SPEAKS
OF THE TIME OF THE END

You Will Call Me My Husband (Hosea 2:14-23)
[Hosea prophesies about the Bride of Christ in the desert
And the fact that God is going to make her His wife, forever.]

'Bow and sword and battle I will abolish from the land,
So that all may lie down in safety.
Therefore I am now going to allure her;
I will lead her into the desert and speak tenderly to her.
There I will give her back her vineyards,
And will make the Valley of Achor a door of hope.
There she will sing as in the days of her youth,
As in the day she came up out of Egypt.'

In that day, declares the Lord, 'you will call me 'my husband';
You will no longer call me 'my master.'
I will remove the names of the Baals from her lips;
No longer will their names be invoked.
In that day I will make a covenant for them
With the beasts of the field and the birds of the air
And the creatures that move along the ground.

Bow and sword and battle I will abolish from the land,
So that all may lie down in safety.

I will betroth you to me forever;
I will betroth you in righteousness and justice, in love and compassion.
I will betroth you in faithfulness, and you will acknowledge the Lord.'

'In that day I will respond,' declares the Lord--
'I will respond to the skies, and they will respond to the earth;
And the earth will respond to the grain, the new wine and oil,
And they will respond to Jezreel.
I will plant her for myself in the land;
I will show my love to the one I called 'Not my loved one.'
I will say to those called 'Not my people,' 'You are my people';
And they will say, 'You are my God.'

[God says that He will lead His Bride into the desert and speak tenderly to her.
He will give Her back Her vineyards.
The Bride, the Israel of God will call God Her Husband and no longer Her master.
God declares He will marry Her forever.

The Time Of The END

HOSEA SPEAKS

He will plant Her for Himself in the land;
He will show love to the One who was not His loved one;
He will call those who were not His people, His people.
In other words, God will call the Gentiles, who have come to Him in faith,
As well as the Jews who have come to Him in faith, His people.
They will all, Gentile and Jew, declare that Christ Jesus is their God.]

In The Last Days Israel Will Come Trembling To The Lord
(Hosea 3:4-5)
For the Israelites will live many days without king or prince,
Without sacrifice or sacred stones, without ephod or idol.
Afterward the Israelites will return and seek the Lord their God and David their king.
They will come trembling to the Lord and to his blessings in the last days.

Israel Revived and Restored (Hosea 6:2)
After two days he will revive us;
On the third day he will restore us,
That we may live in his presence.

Let us acknowledge the Lord; let us press on to acknowledge him.
As surely as the sun rises, he will appear;
He will come to us like the winter rains,
Like the spring rains that water the earth.'

[After two days, two thousand years after the birth of Christ,
God is going to revive Israel.
On the third day, the thousand year Millennial reign of Christ,
God restores Israel so that they may live in His presence.]

When He Roars Like A Lion,
His Children Will Come Trembling (Hosea 11:8-11)
[God will roar like a lion in the last days
And His children will come trembling to Him.]

'My heart is changed within me; all my compassion is aroused.
I will not carry out my fierce anger, nor devastate Ephraim again.
For I am God, and not man—the Holy One among you.
They will follow the Lord; he will roar like a lion.
When he roars, his children will come trembling from the west.
They will come trembling like birds from Egypt, like doves from Assyria.
I will settle them in their homes.' declares the Lord.

[God's children will include people from Egypt and Assyria.]

JOEL SPEAKS OF THE TIME OF THE END

An Invasion of Locusts (Joel 1:1-20)

The word of the Lord that came to Joel son of Pethuel.
Hear this, you elders; listen, all who lie in the land.
Has anything like this ever happened in your days
Or in the days of your forefathers?
Tell it to your children, and let your children tell it to their children,
And their children to the next generation.

What the locust swarm has left the great locusts have eaten;
What the great locusts have left the young locusts have eaten;
What the young locusts have left other locusts have eaten.

Wake up, you drunkards, and weep!
Wail, all you drinkers of wine; wail because of the wine,
For it has been snatched from your lips.
A nation has invaded my land, powerful and without number;
It has the teeth of a lion, the fangs of a lioness.
It has laid waste my vines and ruined my fig trees.
It has stripped off their bark and thrown it away, leaving their branches white.

Mourn like a virgin in sackcloth grieving for the husband of her youth.
Grain offerings and drink offerings are cut off from the house of the Lord.
The priests are in mourning those who minister before the Lord.
The fields are ruined, the ground is dried up;
The grain is destroyed the new wine is dried up, the oil fails.

Despair, you farmers, wail, you vine growers;
Grieve for the wheat and the barley,
Because the harvest of the field is destroyed.
The vine is dried up and the fig tree is withered;
The pomegranate, the palm and the apple tree--
All the trees of the field—are dried up.
Surely the joy of mankind is withered away.

[This is a picture of The Time of The END and its devastation.]

Call To Repentance (Joel 1:13-20)

Put on sackcloth, O priests, and mourn; wail, you who minister before the altar.
Come, spend the night in sackcloth, you who minister before my God;
For the grain offerings and drink offerings
Are withheld from the house of your God.

The Time Of The END

JOEL SPEAKS

Declare a holy fast; call a sacred assembly.
Summon the elders
And all who live in the land to the house of the Lord your God,
<u>And cry out to the Lord</u>.

What a dreadful day! For the day of the Lord is near;
It will come like destruction from the Almighty.

Has not the food been cut off before our very eyes—
Joy and gladness from the house of our God?
The seeds are shriveled beneath the clods.
The storehouses are in ruins, the granaries have been broken down,
For the grain has dried up.
How the cattle moan! The herds mill about because they have no pasture;
Even the flocks of sheep are suffering.

To you, O Lord, I call, for fire has devoured the open pastures
And flames have burned up all the trees of the field.
Even the wild animals pant for you; the streams of water have dried up
And fire has devoured the open pastures.

[This is another picture of the devastation that precedes the Battle of Armageddon.]

Blow The Trumpet In Zion, An Army Of Locusts Is Coming (Joel 2)

Blow the trumpet in Zion; sound the alarm on my holy hill.
Let all who live in the land tremble, <u>for the day of the Lord is coming</u>.
It is close at hand—a day of darkness and gloom, a day of clouds and blackness.
Like dawn spreading across the mountains a large and mighty army comes,
Such as never was of old nor ever will be in ages to come.

Before them fire devours, behind them a flame blazes.
Before them the land is like the garden of Eden,
Behind them, a desert waste—nothing escapes them.
They have the appearance of horses; they gallop along like cavalry.
With a noise like that of chariots they leap over the mountaintops,
Like a crackling fire consuming stubble, like a mighty army drawn up for battle.

At the sight of them, nations are in anguish; every face turns pale.
They charge like warriors; they scale walls like soldiers.
They all march in line, not swerving from their course.
They do not jostle each other; each marches straight ahead.
They plunge through defenses without breaking ranks.
They rush upon the city; the run along the wall.
They climb into the houses; like thieves they enter through the windows.

The Time Of The END

Before them the earth shakes, the sky trembles,
The sun and moon are darkened, and the stars no longer shine.
<u>The Lord thunders at the head of his army</u>; his forces are beyond number,
And mighty are those who obey his command.
The day of the Lord is great, it is dreadful. Who can endure it?

Rend Your Heart, Return To The Lord (Joel 2:12-17)

'Even now,' declares the Lord, 'return to me with all your heart,
With fasting and weeping and mourning.'
Rend your hearts and not your garments.
Return to the Lord your God, for he is gracious and compassionate,
Slow to anger and abounding in love, and he relents from sending calamity.
Who knows? He may turn and have pity and leave behind a blessing--
Grain offerings and drink offerings for the Lord your God.

Blow the trumpet in Zion, declare a holy fast, call a sacred assembly.
Gather the people, consecrate the assembly; bring together the elders,
Gather the children, those nursing at the breast.
Let the bridegroom leave his room and the bride her chamber.
Let the priests, who minister before the Lord,
Weep between the temple porch and the altar.
Let them say, 'Spare your people, O Lord.
Do not make your inheritance an object of scorn,
A byword among the nations.
Why should they say among the peoples, '<u>Where is their God</u>.'

The Lord's Answer (Joel 2:18-27)

Then the Lord will be jealous for his land and take pity on his people
The Lord will reply to them:
'I am sending you grain, new wine and oil, enough to satisfy you fully;
Never again will I make you an object of scorn to the nations.

I will drive the northern army far from you,
Pushing it into a parched and barren land,
With its front columns going into the eastern sea
And those in the rear into the western sea.
And its stench will go up; its smell will rise.'
(This speaks of Gog and Magog and The Battle of Armageddon.)

Surely he has done great things.
Be not afraid, O land; be glad and rejoice.
Surely the Lord has done great things.
Be not afraid, O wild animals, for the open pastures are becoming green.
The trees are bearing their fruit; the fig tree and the vine yield their riches.
Be glad, O people of Zion, rejoice in the Lord your God,

The Time Of The END

For he has given you a <u>teacher</u> for righteousness (Christ).
He sends you abundant showers, both autumn and spring rains, as before.
The threshing floors will be filled with grain;
The vats will overflow with new wine and oil.

I will repay you for the years the locusts have eaten—
The great locust and the young locust,
The other locusts and the locust swarm—my great army that I sent among you.
You will have plenty to eat, until you are full,
And you will praise the name of the Lord your God,
Who has worked wonders for you;
Never again will my people be shamed.
Then you will know that I am in Israel, that I am the Lord your God.
And that there is no other;
Never again will my people be shamed.

I Will Pour Out My Spirit (Joel 2:28-29)
'Afterward, I will pour out my Spirit on all people.
Your sons and daughters will prophesy,
Your old men will dream dreams, your young men will see visions.
Even on my servants, both men and women,
I will pour out my Spirit in those days.

[This is the passage that the apostle Peter quoted,
Describing the out pouring of the Spirit by Christ Jesus on The Day of Pentecost.]

The Day Of The Lord (Joel 2:30-32)
I will show wonders in the heavens and on the earth,
Blood and fire and billows of smoke.
The sun will be turned to darkness and the moon to blood
Before the coming of the great and dreadful <u>day of the Lord</u>.
And everyone who calls on the name of the Lord will be saved;
For on Mount Zion and in Jerusalem there will be deliverance, as the Lord has said,
Among the survivors who the Lord calls.

[This passage parallels passages from Acts 2:20 and Revelation 6:12]

The Nations Judged (Joel 3:1-3)
In those days and at that time, when I restore the fortunes of Judah and Jerusalem,
I will gather all nations and bring them down to the Valley of Jehoshaphat.
There I will enter into judgment against them concerning my inheritance,
My people Israel, for they scattered my people among the nations
And divided up my land.
They cast lots for my people and traded boys for prostitutes;
They sold girls for wine that they might drink.

Proclaim This Among The Nations (Joel 3:9-16)

Proclaim this among the nations:
Prepare for war! Rouse the warriors!
Let all the fighting men draw near and attack.
Beat your plowshares into swords and your pruning hooks into spears.
Let the weakling say, 'I am strong!'
Come quickly, all you nations from every side, and assemble there.
Bring down your warriors, O Lord!

Let the nations be roused; let them advance into the Valley of Jehoshaphat,
For there I will sit to judge all the nations on every side.
Swing the sickle, for the harvest is ripe.
Come, trample the grapes, for the winepress is full and the vats overflow--
So great is their wickedness!

Multitudes, multitudes in the valley of decision!
For the day of the Lord is near in the valley of decision.
The sun and moon will be darkened,
And the stars no longer shine.
The Lord will roar from Zion and thunder from Jerusalem;
The earth and the sky will tremble.
But the Lord will be a refuge for his people, a stronghold for the people of Israel.

Blessings For God's People (Joel 3:17-21)

'Then you will know that I, the Lord your God, dwell in Zion, my holy hill.
Never again will foreigners invade her.'

'In that day the mountains will drip new wine, and hills will flow with milk;
All the ravines of Judah will run with water.
A fountain will flow out of the Lord's house and will water the valley of acacias.
But Egypt will be desolate, Edom a desert waste,
Because of violence done to the people of Judah,
In whose land they shed innocent blood.
Judah will be inhabited forever and Jerusalem through all generations.
Their blood guilt, which I have not pardoned, I will pardon.'

The Lord dwells in Zion.

AMOS SPEAKS
OF THE TIME OF THE END

The Lord Does Nothing Without Revealing It To His Prophets
(Amos 3:6-8)

When disaster comes to a city, has not the Lord caused it?
Surely the Sovereign Lord does nothing without revealing his plan
To his servants the prophets.

The lion has roared—who will not fear?
The Sovereign Lord has spoken—who can but prophesy?

[The Word of God declares that the Lord reveals his wrath every day.
He is sovereign over all His creation; He is in total and complete control;
Even in His giving Satan control, under His supervision, at the present time.
Satan can do nothing without the permission of God.

The Lord has revealed through His prophets His plan and purpose for mankind.
It is made clear in His Word, His gift to them.
It is His desire that all men be saved by repenting of their sin
And allowing the shed blood of Christ Jesus to wash them clean;
Allowing Christ to live in and through them.

All those who read the Word of God, with understanding,
And have heard the roar of the Lion of the tribe of Judah,
Will fear and love God.
When you hear what He has spoken, you are compelled to prophesy.]

MICAH SPEAKS OF THE TIME OF THE END

Hear, O Peoples Of The Earth (Micah 1:1-4)
[Micah is speaking to Samaria, Jerusalem and all mankind.
He is looking forward to the The Time of the End.]

Hear, O peoples, all of you listen, O earth and all who are in it,
That the Sovereign Lord may witness against you,
The Lord from his holy temple.

Look! The Lord is coming from his dwelling place;
He comes down and treads the high places of the earth
The mountains melt beneath him.
And the Valleys split apart, like wax before the fire,
Like water rushing down a slope.

Man's Plans Versus God's Plans (Micah 2:1-5)
Woe to those who plan iniquity, to those who plot evil on their beds!
At morning's light they carry it out because it is in their power to do it.
They covet fields and seize them, and houses, and take them.
They defraud a man of his home, a fellow man of his inheritance.

Therefore, the Lord says:
'I am planning disaster against this people,
From which you cannot save yourselves.
You will no longer walk proudly, for it will be a time of calamity.
In that day men will ridicule you;
They will taunt you with this mournful song:
'We are utterly ruined; my people's possession is divided up.
He takes it from me! He assigns our fields to traitors.'

Therefore you will have no one in the assembly of the Lord
To divide the land by lot.'

[All those who steal, and defraud will be brought to ruin.]

False Prophets (Micah 2:6-11)
'Do not prophesy,' their prophets say (the false church prophets).
'Do not prophesy about these things; disgrace will not overtake us.'
Should it be said, O house of Jacob (the false church):
Is the Spirit of the Lord angry? Does he do such things?

The Time Of The END

Do not my words do good to him whose ways are upright?
Lately my people (the false church) *have risen up like an enemy.*
You strip off the rich robe from those who pass by without a care,
Like men returning from battle.
You drive the women of my people (the Bride of Christ)
From their pleasant homes.
You take away my blessing from their children forever.
Get up, go away!
For this is not your resting place, because it is defiled,
It is ruined, beyond all remedy.
[At The Time of The END the iniquity of the false church and the world will be full,
To the point of no return.]

If a liar and deceiver comes and says,
'I will prophesy for you plenty of wine and beer,'
He would be just the prophet for this people!

Deliverance Promised For A Remnant (Micah 2:12-13)
I will surely gather all of you O Jacob;
I will surely bring together the remnant of Israel
I will bring them together like sheep in a pen,
Like a flock in its pasture;
The place will throng with people
One (Christ Jesus) *who breaks open the way will go up before them;*
They will break through the gate and go out.
Their king (Christ Jesus) *will pass through before them,*
The Lord at their head.

[God always reserves for Himself a remnant, lead by Christ Jesus.
In The Time of The END this remnant is The Bride of Christ.]

Leaders And Prophets Rebuked By The Lord (Micah 3)
Then I said,
'Listen you leaders of Jacob (the false church), *you rulers of the house of Israel.*
Should you not know justice, you who hate good and love evil;
Who tear the skin from my people (those who belong to Christ)
And the flesh from their bones;
Who eat my people's flesh, strip off their skin
And break their bones in pieces;
Who chop them up like meat for the pan, like flesh for the pot?'

Then they (false church rulers) *will cry out to the Lord, but he will not answer them.*
At that time he will hide his face from them
Because of the evil they have done.

The Time Of The END

This is what the Lord says;
'As for the prophets (all those predicting the future from their own intellect).
Who lead my people astray (as well as the people of the whole world)*,*
If one feeds them, they proclaim 'peace';
If he does not, they prepare to wage war against him.
(If you feed the false prophets, they tell you what you want to hear,
But if you do not they become your enemy.)
Therefore night will come over you, without visions,
And darkness , without divination.
The sun will set for the prophets (the false prophets)*,*
And the day will go dark for them.
The seers will be ashamed and the diviners disgraced.
They will all cover their faces because there is no answer form God.'

But as for me, I am filled with power,
With the Spirit of the Lord, and with justice and might,
To declare to Jacob his transgression, to Israel his sin.

[In these last days the Bride of Christ will arise
To declare to the false church and the world their transgression against God.]

Here this, you leaders of Jacob (leaders of the false church)*,*
You rulers of the house of Israel (in Micah's day)*,*
Who despise justice and distort all that is right;
Who build Zion (the false church) *with bloodshed,*
And Jerusalem (the false church) *with wickedness.*
Her leaders judge for a bribe, her priests teach for a price,
And her prophets tell fortunes for money.
Yet they lean upon the Lord and say,
'Is not the Lord among us?
No disaster will come upon us.'

Therefore because of you (the false church)*, Zion* (the false church)
Will be plowed like a field, Jerusalem (the false church)
Will become a heap of rubble, the temple mound overgrown with thickets.

[Israel and Jerusalem in Micah's day were unfaithful to God
And suffered the consequences,
As will the false church in The Time of The END.]

In The Last Days, The Mountain of The Lord Will Be Established

(Micah 4:1-5)
In the last days the mountain of the Lord's temple will be established
As chief among the mountains;
It will be raised above the hills, and peoples will stream to it.

The Time Of The END

Many nations will come and say,
'Come, let us go up to the mountain of the Lord,
To the house of the God of Jacob.
He will teach us his ways, so that we may walk in his paths.'

The law will go out from Zion (the Bride of Christ, the City of God),
The word of the Lord from Jerusalem.
He will judge between may peoples
And will settle disputes for strong nations far and wide.
They will beat their swords into plowshares
And their spears into pruning hooks.
Nation will not take up sword against nation,
Nor will they train for war anymore.
Every man will sit under his own vine and his own fig tree,
And no one will make them afraid,
For the Lord Almighty has spoken.
All nations may walk in the name of their gods;
We will walk in the name of the Lord our God for ever and ever.

The Lord's Plan (Micah 4:6-13)

*'**In that day**,' declares the Lord,*
'I will gather the lame;
I will assemble the exiles and those I have brought to grief.
I will make the lame a remnant, those driven away a strong nation.
The Lord will rule over them in Mount Zion from that day and forever.

As for you, O watchtower of the flock,
O stronghold of the Daughter of Zion,
The former dominion will be restored to you;
Kingship will come to the Daughter of Jerusalem.'

Why do you now cry aloud-- have you no king?
Has your counselor perished,
That pain seizes you like that of a woman in labor?
Writhe in agony, O Daughter of Zion, like a woman in labor,
For now you must leave the city.
To camp in the open field.
You will go to Babylon; there you will be rescued.
There the Lord will redeem you out of the hand of your enemies.

[This was God's judgment on Jerusalem in the days of Micah.]

But now may nations are gathered against you.
They say, 'Let her be defiled, let our eyes gloat over Zion!'
But they do not know the thoughts of the Lord;

The Time Of The END

They do not understand his plan,
He who gathers them like sheaves to the threshing floor.

'Rise and thresh, O Daughter of Zion,
For I will give you horns of iron;
I will give you hoofs of bronze and you will break to pieces many nations.
You will devote their ill-gotten gains to the Lord,
Their wealth to the Lord of all the earth.'

[In the last days, God will use the nation Israel, to subdue the nations,
Because God Himself will fight for Israel,
And the wealth of the nations will be devoted to the Lord.]

The Promised Ruler From Bethlehem, Christ Jesus (Micah 5:1-5)
Marshal your troops, O city of troops, for a siege is laid against us.
They will strike Israel's ruler on the cheek with a rod.

But you, Bethlehem Ephrathah,
Though you are small among the clans of Judah,
Out of you will come for me one who will be ruler over Israel,
Whose origins are from of old, from ancient times.

Therefore Israel will be abandoned
Until the time when she (the Bride) *who is in labor gives birth* (to the "male child")
And the rest of his brothers return to join the Israelites.

He (Christ) will stand and shepherd his flock in the strength of the Lord,
In the majesty of the name of the Lord his God.
And they will live securely,
For then his greatness will reach to the ends of the earth.
And he will be their peace. (This speaks of The Time of the End.)

The Remnant of Jacob Will be Like A Lion Among The Nations
(Micah 5:7-15)
[This is speaking of the last days
When the Lord will use Israel to subdue **all** the nations of the earth.]

The remnant of Jacob will be in the midst of many peoples
Like dew from the Lord, like showers on the grass,
Which do not wait for man or linger for mankind.
The remnant of Jacob will be among the nations,
In the midst of many peoples like a lion among the beasts of the forest,
Like a young lion among flocks of sheep,
Which mauls and mangles as it goes, and no one can rescue.
Your hand will be lifted up in triumph over your enemies,

214

The Time Of The END

And <u>all</u> your foes will be destroyed.

'In that day,' *declares the Lord,*(speaking of all the nations on earth)
'I will destroy your horses from among you and demolish your chariots.
I will destroy the cities of your land and tear down all your strongholds.
I will destroy your witchcraft and you will no longer cast spells.
I will destroy your carved images and your sacred stones from among you;
You will no longer bow down to the work of your hands.
I will uproot from among you your Asherah poles and demolish your cities.
I will take vengeance in anger and wrath
Upon the nations that have disobeyed me.'

He Has Shown You O Man What Is Good (Micah 6-8)
With what shall I come before the Lord and bow before the exalted God.
Shall I come before him with burnt offerings, with calves a year old?
Will the Lord be pleased with thousands of rams,
With ten thousand rivers of oil?
Shall I offer my firstborn for my transgression,
The fruit of my body for the sin of my soul?
He has shown you, O man, what is good.
What does the Lord require of you?
To act justly and to love mercy
And to walk humbly with your God.

The Guilt And Punishment of Israel In The Time O Micah And All The Nations In The Time Of The End (Micah 6:9-16)
Listen! The Lord is calling to the city—and to fear your name is wisdom--
Heed the rod and the One who appointed it.
Am I still to forget, O wicked house,
Your ill-gotten treasures and short ephah, which is accursed?
Shall I acquit a man with dishonest scales, with a bag of false weights?
Her rich men are violent; her people are liars and their tongues speak deceitfully.

Therefore, I have begun to destroy you, to ruin you because of your sins.

You will eat but not be satisfied; your stomach will still be empty.
You will store up but save nothing,
Because what you save I will give to the sword.
You will plant but not harvest;
You will press olives but not use the oil on yourselves.
You will crush grapes but not drink the wine.
You have observed the statutes of Omri and all the practices of Ahab's house,
And you have followed their traditions.
Therefore I will give you over to ruin and your people to derision;
You will bear the scorn of the nations.

Israel's Misery In The Time Of Micah
And All The Nations In The Time Of The End (Micah 7:1-7)
What misery is mine!
I am like one who gathers summer fruit at the gleaning of the vineyard;
There is no cluster of grapes to eat,
None of the early figs that I crave.

The godly have been swept from the land;
Not one upright man remains.

All men lie in wait to shed blood;
Each hunts his brother with a net.
Both hands are skilled in doing evil;
The ruler demands gifts, the judge accepts bribes,
The powerful dictate what they desire--
They all conspire together.
The best of them is like a brier,
The most upright worse than a thorn hedge.
The day of your watchmen has come,
The day God visits you.
Now is the time of their confusion.
Do not trust a neighbor;
Even with her who lies in your embrace, be careful of your words.
For a son dishonors his father,
A daughter rises up against her mother,
A daughter-in-law against her mother-in-law--
A man's enemies are the members of his own household.

But as for me, I watch in hope for the Lord,
I wait for God my Savior;
My God will hear me.

Israel Will Rise In The Time Of The End (Micah 7:8-13)
Do not gloat over me, my enemy!
Though I have fallen, I will rise.
Though I sit in darkness, the Lord will be my light.
Because I have sinned against him,
I will bear the Lord's wrath,
Until he pleads my case and establishes my right.
He will bring me out into the light;
I will see his justice.
Then my enemy will see it and will be covered with shame,
She (Satan's Harlot) who said to me,
'Where is the Lord your God?'

The Time Of The END

My eyes will see her downfall;
Even now she will be trampled underfoot like mire in the streets.

The day for building your wall will come,
The day for extending your boundaries.
In that day people will come to you from Assyria and the cities of Egypt,
Even from Egypt to the Euphrates and from sea to sea
And from mountain to mountain.
The earth will become desolate because of its inhabitants,
As a result of their deeds.

God Will Show The Nations His Wonders (Micah 7:14-20)

Shepherd your people with your staff, (speaking of Christ Jesus)
The flock of your inheritance,
Which lives by itself in a forest, in fertile pasture lands.
Let them feed in Bashan and Gilead as in days long ago.

'As in the days when you came out of Egypt,
I will show them my wonders.'

[This speaks of God taking the "woman" of Revelation 12, the Bride of Christ, into the desert, where she is protected during The Great Tribulation.]

Nations will see and be ashamed, deprived of all their power.
They will lay their hands on their mouths and their ears will become deaf.
They will lick dust like a snake, like creatures that crawl on the ground.
They will come trembling out of their dens;
They will turn in fear to the Lord our God and will be afraid of you.

Who is a God like you,
Who pardons sin and forgives the transgression of the remnant of his inheritance?
You do not stay angry forever but delight to show mercy.
You will again have compassion on us;
You will tread our sins underfoot
And hurl all our iniquities into the depths of the sea.
You will be true to Jacob,and show mercy to Abraham,
As you pledged on oath to our fathers in days long ago.

NAHUM SPEAKS OF THE TIME OF THE END

[What Nahum speaks about Nineveh is also true of Babylon in the Book of Revelation. Therefore, Nahum is also speaking of The Time of The END]

The Lord's Anger Against Nineveh And Against All His Enemies, Including Those At The Time Of The End (Nahum 1:1-15)

An oracle concerning Nineveh.
The book of the vision of Nahum the Elkoshite.
The Lord is a jealous and avenging God;
The Lord takes vengeance and is filled with wrath.
The Lord takes vengeance on his foes
And maintains his wrath against his enemies.

The Lord is slow to anger and great in power;
The Lord will not leave the guilty unpunished.
His way is in the whirlwind and the storm,
And the clouds are the dust of his feet.
He rebukes the sea and dries it up;
He makes all the rivers run dry.
Bashan and Carmel wither and the blossoms of Lebanon fade.
The mountains quake before him and the hills melt away.
The earth trembles at his presence,
The world and all who live in it.

Who can withstand his indignation?
Who can endure his fierce anger?
His wrath is poured out like fire;
The rocks are shattered before him.

The Lord is good, and a refuge in times of trouble.
He cares for those who trust in him,
But with an overwhelming flood he will make an end of Nineveh (Babylon);
He will pursue his foes into darkness.
Whatever they plot against the Lord he will bring to an end;
Trouble will not come a second time.
They will be consumed like dry stubble.
From you, O Nineveh (Babylon),
Has one come forth who plots evil against the Lord and counsels wickedness.

This is what the Lord says:
'Although they are unscathed and numerous,
They will be cut down and pass away.
Although I have afflicted you, O Judah, I will afflict you no more.

218

The Time Of The END

Now I will break their yoke from your neck
And tear your shackles away.'

The Lord has given a command concerning you, Nineveh (Babylon):
'You will have no descendants to bear your name.
I will destroy the carved images and cast idols that are in the temple of your gods.
I will prepare your grave, for you are vile.'

Look, there on the mountains the feet of one who brings good news,
Who proclaims peace!
Celebrate your festivals, O Judah, and fulfill your vows.
No more will the wicked invade you;
They will be completely destroyed.

Nineveh (Babylon) To Fall (Nahum 2)
An attacker advances against you, Nineveh, Guard the fortress,
Watch the road, brace yourselves, marshal all your strength!

The Lord will restore the splendor of Jacob like the splendor of Israel,
Though destroyers have laid them waste and have ruined their vines.

The shields of his soldiers are red;
The warriors are clad in scarlet.
The metal on the chariots flashes on the day they are made ready;
The spears of pine are brandished.
The chariots storm through the streets
Rushing back and forth through the squares.
They look like flaming torches;
They dart about like lightning.

He summons his picked troops, yet they stumble on their way.
They dash to the city wall; the protective shield is put in place.
The river gates are thrown open and the palace collapses.
It is decreed that the city be exiled and carried away.
Its slave girls moan like doves and beat upon their breasts.
Nineveh (Babylon) is like a pool, and its water is draining away.

'Stop! Stop!' they cry, but no one turns back.
Plunder the silver! Plunder the gold!
The supply is endless, the wealth from all its treasures!
She is pillaged, plundered, stripped!
Hearts melt, knees give way, bodies tremble, every face grows pale.

Where now is the lions' den, the place where they fed their young,
Where the lion and lioness went,

The Time Of The END

NAHUM SPEAKS

And the cubs, with nothing to fear?
The lion killed enough for his cubs and strangled the prey for his mate,
Filling the lairs with the kill and his dens with the prey.
'I am against you,' declares the Lord Almighty.
'I will burn up your chariots in smoke,
And the sword will devour your young lions.
I will leave you no prey on the earth.
The voices of your messengers will not longer be heard.'

Woe To Nineveh (Babylon) (Nahum 3)

Woe to the city of blood full of lies,
Full of plunder, never without victims!
The crack of whips, the clatter of wheels,
Galloping horses and jolting chariots!
Charging cavalry, flashing swords and glittering spears!
Many casualties, piles of dead, bodies without number,
People stumbling over the corpses--

All because of the wanton lust of a harlot,
Alluring, the mistress of sorceries,
Who enslaved nations by her prostitution
And her peoples by her witchcraft.

'I am against you,' declares the Lord Almighty.
'I will lift your skirts over your face.
I will show the nations your nakedness and kingdoms your shame.
I will pelt you with filth, I will treat you with contempt
And make you a spectacle.
All who see you will flee from you and say,
'Nineveh (Babylon) *is in ruins--*
Who will mourn for her?'
Where can I find anyone to comfort you?'

Are you better than Thebes, situated on the Nile, with water around her?
The river was her defense, the waters her wall.
Cush and Egypt were her boundless strength;
Put and Libya were among her allies.
Yet she was taken captive and went into exile.
Her infants were dashed to pieces at the head of every street.
Lots were cast for her nobles, and all her great men were put in chains.
You too will become drunk; you will go into hiding
And seek refuge from the enemy.

All your fortresses are like fig trees with their first ripe fruit;
When they are shaken, the figs fall into the mouth of the eater.

The Time Of The END

NAHUM SPEAKS

Look at your troops-- they are all women!
The gates of your land are wide open to your enemies;
Fire has consumed their bars.
Draw water for the siege, strengthen your defenses!
Work the clay, tread the mortar, repair the brickwork!
There the fire will devour you; the sword will cut you down
And, like grasshoppers, consume you.
Multiply like grasshoppers, multiply like locusts!
You have increased the number of your merchants
Till they are more than the stars of the sky,
But like locusts they strip the land and then fly away.
Your guards are like locusts, your officials like swarms of locusts
That settle in the walls on a cold day--
But when the sun appears the fly away, and no one knows where.

O king of Assyria (Babylon), your shepherds slumber;
Your nobles lie down to rest.
Your people are scattered on the mountains with no one to gather them.
Nothing can heal your wound; your injury is fatal.
Everyone who hears the news about you claps his hands at your fall.
For who has not felt your endless cruelty?

HABAKKUK SPEAKS OF THE TIME OF THE END

The Nations Exhaust Themselves For Nothing (Habakkuk 2:13-14)

Has not the Lord Almighty determined that the people's labor is for fuel for the fire,
That the nations exhaust themselves for nothing?
For the earth will be filled with the knowledge of the glory of the Lord,
As the waters cover the sea.

[This passages speaks of the Millennium, the thousand years of rest,
When the knowledge of the glory of the Lord will cover the earth
As the waters cover the sea.
At that time all the labor of the nations will have come to nothing.
All labor of each person not done in the light of God and His Covenant
Will have been done for nothing; it will come to nothing.]

God Comes To Deliver His People (Habakkuk 3:3-19)

[Habakkuk is given a vision of God coming in The Time of The END
To deliver His people.]

God came from Teman, the Holy One from Mount Paran.
His glory covered the heavens and his praise filled the earth.
His splendor was like the sunrise; rays flashed from his hand,
Where his power was hidden.
Plague went before him; pestilence followed his steps.
He stood, and shook the earth;
He looked, and made the nations tremble.
The ancient mountains crumbled and the age-old hills collapsed.
His ways are eternal.
I saw the tents of Cushan in distress, the dwellings of Midian in anguish.

Were you angry with the rivers, O Lord?
Was your wrath against the streams?
Did you rage against the sea when you rode with your horses
And your victorious chariots?
You uncovered your bow, you called for many arrows.

You split the earth with rivers; the mountains saw you and writhed.
Torrents of water swept by; the deep roared and lifted its waves on high.

Sun and moon stood still in the heavens at the glint of your flying arrows,
At the lightning of your flashing spear.
In wrath you strode through the earth
And in anger you threshed the nations.

The Time Of The END

You came out to deliver your people, to save your anointed one.
You crushed the leader of the land of wickedness (Satan),
You stripped him from head to foot.
With his own spear you pierced his head
When his warriors stormed out to scatter us,
Gloating as though about to devour the wretched who were in hiding.
You trampled the sea with your horses, churning the great waters.

I heard and my heart pounded, my lips quivered at the sound;
Decay crept into my bones, and my legs trembled.
Yet I will wait patiently for the day of calamity to come to the nation invading us.

Though the fig tree does not bud and there are no grapes on the vines,
Though the olive crop fails and the fields produce no food,
Though there are no sheep in the pen and no cattle in the stalls,
Yet I will rejoice in the Lord, I will be joyful in God my Savior.
The Sovereign Lord is my strength;
He makes my feet like the feet of a deer,
He enables me to go on the heights.

ZEPHANIAH SPEAKS OF THE TIME OF THE END

Warning Of Destruction Coming Upon The Earth (Zephaniah 1:3)

'I will sweep away everything from the face of the earth,' declares the Lord.
'I will sweep away both men and animals;
I will sweep away the birds of the air and the fish of the sea.
The wicked will have only heaps of rubble
When I cut off man from the face of the earth,' declares the Lord.

Be Silent Before The Sovereign Lord, For The Day Of The Lord Is Near (Zephaniah 1:7-13)

Be silent before the Sovereign Lord, for the day of the Lord is near.
The Lord has prepared a sacrifice (of all those who have rejected His Christ);
He has consecrated those he has invited.
On the day of the Lord's sacrifice
I will punish the princes and the king's sons and all those clad in foreign clothes.
On that day I will punish all who avoid stepping on the threshold (the superstitious),
Who fill the temple of their gods with violence and deceit.

'On that day,' declares the Lord,
'A cry will go up from the Fish Gate, wailing from the New Quarter,
And a loud crash from the hills.
Wail, you who live in the market district; all your merchants will be wiped out,
All who trade with silver will be ruined.
At that time I will search Jerusalem (and all the nations in The Time of The END)
With lamps and punish those who are complacent,
Who are like wine left on its dregs,
Who think, 'The Lord will do nothing either good or bad.'
Their wealth will be plundered, their houses demolished.
They will build houses but not live in them;
They will plant vineyards but not drink the wine.

The Great Day Of The Lord (Zephaniah 1:14-18)

The great day of the Lord is near—near and coming quickly.
Listen! The cry on the day of the Lord will be bitter,
The shouting of the warrior there.
That day will be a day of wrath, a day of distress and anguish,
A day of trouble and ruin, a day of darkness and gloom,
A day of clouds and blackness, a day of trumpet and battle cry
Against the fortified cities and against the corner towers.

I will bring distress on the people and they will walk like blind men,

The Time Of The END

Because they have sinned against the Lord.
Their blood will be poured out like dust and their entrails like filth.
Neither their silver nor their gold will be able to save them
On the day of the Lord's wrath.
In the fire of his jealousy the whole world will be consumed,
For he will make a sudden end of all who live in the earth.

Seek The Lord All You Humble (Zephaniah 2:1-3)
Gather together, gather together, O shameful nation,
Before the appointed time arrives and that day sweeps on like chaff,
Before the fierce anger of the Lord comes upon you,
Before the day of the Lord's wrath comes upon you.

Seek the Lord, all you humble of the land,
You who do what he commands.
Seek righteousness, seek humility;
Perhaps you will be sheltered on the day of the Lord's anger.

Gaza will be abandoned and Ashkelon left in ruins.
At midday Ashdod will be emptied and Ekron uprooted.
Woe to you who live by the sea, O Kerethite people;
The word of the Lord is against you, O Canaan, land of the Philistines.
'I will destroy you, and none will be left.'

The land by the sea, where the Kerethites dwell,
Will be a place for shepherds and sheep pens.
It will belong to the remnant of the house of Judah;
There they will find pasture.
In the evening they will lie down in the houses of Askelon.
The Lord their God will care for them;
He will restore their fortunes.

'I have heard the insults of Moab and the taunts of the Ammonites,
Who insulted my people and made threats against their land.
Therefore, as surely as I live,' declares the Lord Almighty,
The God of Israel,
'Surely Moab will become like Sodom, and Ammonites like Gomorrah--
A place of weeds and salt pits, a wasteland forever.

The remnant of my people will plunder them;
The survivors of my nation will inherit their land.'

This is what they will get in return for their pride,
For insulting and mocking the people of the Lord Almighty.
The Lord will be awesome to them

When he destroys all the gods of the Land.
The nations on every shore will worship him, every one in its own land.
'You too, O Cushites, will be slain by my sword.'
He will stretch out his hand against the north and destroy Assyria,
Leaving Nineveh utterly desolate and dry as the desert.
Flocks and herds will lie down there, creatures of every kind.
The desert owl and the screech owl will roost on her columns.
Their calls will echo through the windows, rubble will be in the doorways,
The beams of cedar will be exposed.

This is the carefree city that lived in safety.
She said to herself, 'I am, and there is none beside me.'
What a ruin she has become, a lair for wild beasts!
All who pass by her scoff and shake their fists.
[This is the attitude of Babylon, the Harlot of Satan, in The Time of The END.]

The Whole World Will Be Consumed
By The Fire Of God's Jealous Anger (Zephaniah 3:1-20)
Woe to the city of oppressors, rebellious and defiled!
She obeys no one, she accepts no correction.
She does not trust in the Lord, she does not draw near to her God.
Her officials are roaring lions, her rulers are evening wolves,
Who leave nothing for the morning.
Her prophets are arrogant; they are treacherous men.
Her priests profane the sanctuary and do violence to the law.
The Lord within her is righteous; he does no wrong.
Morning by morning he dispenses his justice,
And every new day he does not fail,
<u>*Yet the unrighteous know no shame.*</u>

I have cut off nations; their strongholds are demolished.
I have left their streets deserted, with no one passing through.
Their cities are destroyed; no one will be left—no one at all.

I said to the city, 'Surely you will fear me and accept correction!'
Then her dwelling would not be cut off,
Nor my punishments come upon her.

But they were still eager to act corruptly in all they did.
Therefore wait for me,' declares the Lord,
For the day I stand up to testify.
I have decided to assemble the nations, to gather the kingdoms
And to pour out my wrath on them—all my fierce anger.
The whole world will be consumed by the fire of my jealous anger.
Then will I purify the lips of the peoples,

The Time Of The END

That all of them may call on the name of the Lord
And to serve him shoulder to shoulder.
From beyond the rivers of Cush my worshipers,
My scattered people, will bring me offerings.
On that day you will not be put to shame for all the wrongs you have done to me,
Because I will remove from this city (and every city on the face of the earth)
Those who rejoice in their pride.
Never again will you be haughty on my holy hill.
But I will leave within you the meek and humble,
Who trust in the name of the Lord.
The remnant of Israel will do no wrong; they will speak no lies,
Nor will deceit be found in their mouths.
They will lie down and no one will make them afraid.

Sing, O Daughter of Zion; shout aloud, O Israel!
Bc glad and rejoice with all your heart, O Daughter of Jerusalem!
The Lord has taken away your punishment, he has turned back your enemy.
The Lord the King of Israel, is with you;
Never again will you fear any harm.
On that day they will say to Jerusalem,
Do not fear, O Zion; do not let your hands hang limp.
The Lord your God is with you, he is mighty to save.
He will take great delight in you, he will quiet you with his love,
He will rejoice over you with singing.

The sorrows for the appointed feasts I will remove from you;
They are a burden and a reproach to you.
At that time I will deal with all who oppressed you;
I will rescue the lame and gather those who have been scattered.
I will give them praise and honor
In every land where they were put to shame.

At that time I will gather you;
At that time I will bring you home.
I will give you honor and praise among all the peoples of the earth
When I restore your fortunes before your very eyes, says the Lord.

HAGGAI SPEAKS OF THE TIME OF THE END

In A Little While
I Will Once More Shake The Heavens And The Earth (Haggai 2:6-9)

This is what the Lord Almighty says:
'In a little while I will once more shake the heavens and the earth,
The sea and dry land.
***I will shake the nations**, and the desired of all nations (Christ) will come,*
And I will fill this house (the New Jerusalem, the Bride of Christ) with glory,'
Says the Lord Almighty.
'The silver is mine and the gold is mine,' declares the Lord Almighty.
'The glory of this present house will be greater than the glory of the former house,'
Says the Lord Almighty.
'And in this place I will grant peace,' declares the Lord Almighty.

The Lord Speaks To Zerubbabel (Haggai 2:21-23)

[In speaking to Zerubbabel,
God is speaking to all those who come out of the mixture of the world;
The confusion of the world and consecrate their lives to Him.]

The word of the Lord came to Haggai a second time
On the twenty-fourth day of the month:
'Tell Zerubbabel governor of Judah
That I will shake the heavens and the earth.
I will overturn royal thrones and shatter the power of foreign kingdoms.
I will overthrow chariots and their drivers; horses and their riders will fall,
Each by the sword of his brother.'

'On that day,' declares the Lord Almighty,
'I will make you my servant Zerubbabel son of Shealtiel,' declares the Lord,
'And I will make you like my signet ring,
For I have chosen you,' declares the Lord Almighty.

ZECHARIAH SPEAKS OF THE TIME OF THE END

The Man Among The Myrtle Trees (Zechariah 1:7-17)
On the twenty-fourth day of the eleventh month, the month of Shebat,
In the second year of Darius,
The word of the Lord came to the prophet Zechariah son of Berekiah,
The son of Iddo.

During the night I had a vision—
And there before me was a man riding a red horse!
He was standing among the myrtle trees in a ravine.
Behind him were red, brown and white horses.
I asked, 'What are these my lord?'
The angel who was talking with me answered, 'I will show you what they are.'
Then the man standing among the myrtle trees explained,
'They are the ones the Lord has sent to go throughout the earth.'

And they reported to the angel of the Lord,
Who was standing among the myrtle trees,
'We have gone throughout the earth
And found the whole world at rest and in peace.'

Then the angel of the Lord said,
'Lord Almighty, how long will you withhold mercy from Jerusalem
And from the towns of Judah,
Which you have been angry with these seventy years?'
So the Lord spoke kind and comforting words to the angel who talked with me.

Then the angel who was speaking to me said,
'Proclaim this word':This is what the Lord almighty says:
'I am very jealous for Jerusalem and Zion,
But I am very angry with the nations that feel secure.
I was only a little angry, but they added to the calamity.'

Therefore, this is what the Lord says,
'I will return to Jerusalem with mercy, and there my house will be rebuilt.
And the measuring line will be stretched out over Jerusalem,'
Declares the Lord Almighty.

Proclaim further; This is what the Lord Almighty says;
'My towns will again overflow with prosperity,
And the Lord will again comfort Zion and choose Jerusalem.'

Four Horns And Four Craftsmen (Zechariah 1:18-21)
Then I looked up—and there before me were four horns!
I asked the angel who was speaking to me, 'What are these?'
He answered me,
'These are the horns that scattered Judah, Israel and Jerusalem.'
Then the Lord showed me four craftsmen.
I asked, 'What are these coming to do?'
He answered,
'These are the horns that scattered Judah so that no one could raise his head,
But the craftsmen have come to terrify them
And throw down these horns of the nations who lifted up their horns
Against the land of Judah to scatter its people.'

A Man With A Measuring Line (Zechariah2)
Then I looked up—
And there before me was a man with a measuring line in his hand!
I asked, 'Where are you going ?'
He answered me, 'To measure Jerusalem, to find out how wide and how long it is.'
[This is the measurement that the apostle John is told to make in Revelation 11;
To measure the temple of God but to leave out the Outer Court..]

Then the angel who was speaking to me left,
And another angel came to meet him and said to him:
'Run, tell that young man
'Jerusalem will be a city without walls
Because of the great number of men and livestock in it,' declares the Lord,
And I will be its glory within.'
[This is the New Jerusalem, the Bride of Christ.]

'Come! Come! Flee from the land of the north,' declares the Lord,
'For I have scattered you to the four winds of heaven,' declares the Lord.

'Come, O Zion! Escape, you who live in the Daughter of Babylon!'
For this is what the Lord Almighty says:
'After he has honored me (Jesus)
And has sent me (Jesus) *against the nations that have plundered you--*
For whoever touches you, touches the apple of his eye--
I (Jesus) *will surely raise my hand against them*
So that their slaves will plunder them.
Then you will know that the Lord Almighty has sent me (Jesus).'

[Zion, the Israel of God and all the nations of the world
Will know that Jesus is the Messiah, the Christ, the Anointed One of God,
When He comes to rescue His people.]

The Time Of The END

'Shout and be glad, O Daughter of Zion.
For I am coming, and will live among you,' declares the Lord.
Many nations will be joined with the Lord <u>in that day</u> and will become my people.
I will live among you and you will know that the Lord Almighty has sent me to you.
The Lord will inherit Judah (the house of praise) as his portion in the holy land
And will again choose Jerusalem.
Be still before the Lord, all mankind,
Because he has roused himself from his holy dwelling.'

[At The Time of The END, Christ Jesus comes to live among His people in Jerusalem.
All mankind will know that Jesus is the Christ when He fulfills His Scriptures.
Christ Jesus gathers His people from every nation on earth,
His faithful ones, who do His will.]

The Angel Of The Lord, Christ Jesus
Puts Clean Garments On Joshua The High Priest,
Representing The Israel Of God,
The New Jerusalem, The Bride Of Christ (Zechariah 3)

Then he showed me Joshua the high priest standing before the angel of the Lord,
And Satan standing at his right side to accuse him.
The Lord said to Satan,
'The Lord rebuke you, Satan!
The Lord, who has chosen Jerusalem, rebuke you!
Is not this man a burning stick snatched from the fire?'

Now Joshua was dressed in filthy clothes as he stood before the angel.
The angel said to those who were standing before him,
'Take off his filthy clothes.'

Then he said to Joshua,
'See, I have taken away your sin, and I will put rich garments on you.'

Then I said, 'Put a clean turban on his head.'
So they put a clean turban on his head and clothed him,
While the angel of the Lord stood by.

The angel of the Lord gave this charge to Joshua:
'This is what the Lord Almighty says:
If you will walk in my ways and keep my requirements,
Then you will govern my house and have charge of my courts,
And I will give you a place among these standing here.

Listen, O high priest Joshua and your associates seated before you,
Who are men symbolic of things to come:

The Time Of The END

I am going to bring my servant, **the Branch** *(the Christ).*
See, the stone (Christ) I have set in front of Joshua!
There are seven eyes on that one stone,
And I will engrave an inscription on it,' says the Lord Almighty,
'And I will remove the sin of this land in a single day' (the last day of "time").

'In that day each of you will invite his neighbor to sit under his vine and fig tree,'
Declares the Lord Almighty.

The Golden Lampstand And The Two Olive Trees (Zechariah 4)

Then the angel who talked with me returned and wakened me,
As a man is wakened from his sleep.
He asked me, 'What do you see?'
I answered, 'I see a solid gold lampstand with a bowl at the top
And seven lights on it, with seven channels to the lights.
Also there are two olive trees by it,
One on the right of the bowl and the other on its left.'

I asked the angel who talked with me,
'What are these, my lord?'
He answered, 'Do you not know what these are?'
'No my lord,' I replied.
So he said to me,
'This is the word of the Lord to Zerubbabel:

Not by might nor by power, but by my Spirit,' says the Lord Almighty.

'What are you, O mighty mountain?
Before Zerubbabel (the people of God who have come out of the mixture of Babylon)
You will become level ground.
Then he will bring out the capstone (Christ) to shouts of 'God bless it! God bless it!'

Then the word of the Lord came to me:
'The hands of Zerubbabel have laid the foundation of this temple;
His hands will also complete it (it will be completed in The Time of The END).
Then you will know that the Lord Almighty has sent me (Christ) to you.

Who despises the day of small things?
Men will rejoice when they see the plumb line in the hand of Zerubbabel.
(These seven are the eyes of the Lord, which range throughout the earth.)'

Then I asked the angel,
'What are these two olive trees on the right and the left of the lampstand?'

Again I asked him,

The Time Of The END

'What are these two olive branches beside the two gold pipes
That pour out golden oil?'

He replied,
'Do you not know what these are?

No, my lord,' I said.
So he said,
'These are the two who are anointed to serve the Lord of all the earth.'

[The two olive trees are Joshua and Zerubbabel, one representing religious authority
And the other representing civil authority which have been melded into to one body,
The Israel of God, the New Jerusalem, the Bride of Christ.
They are achetypes of the two witnesses in Revelation 11: 3-4.]

The Flying Scroll (Zechariah 5:1-4)
I looked again—and there before me was a flying scroll!
He asked me, 'What do you see?'
I answered, 'I see a flying scroll, thirty feet long and fifteen feet wide.'

And he said to me,
'This is the curse that is going out over the whole land;
For according to what is says on one side, every thief will be banished,
And according to what is says on the other,
Every one who swears falsely will be banished.'
The Lord Almighty declares,
'I will send it out, and it will enter the house of the thief
And the house of him who swears falsely by my name.
It will remain in his house and destroy it, both its timbers and its stones.'

[This curse goes out over the earth and finds all who are thieves of any sort.
It also finds all who swear falsely concerning the Lord.
This includes those in the Church, as judgment begins in the House of the Lord,
And those outside, who use the name of the Lord in vain.
They will all be destroyed in The Time of The END.]

The Woman In A Basket (Zechariah 5:5-11)
Then the angel who was speaking to me came forward and said to me,
'Look up and see what this is that is appearing.'

I asked, 'What is it?'
He replied, 'It is a measuring basket.' And he added,
'This is the iniquity of the people throughout the land.'

Then the cover of lead was raised, and there in the basket sat a woman!

The Time Of The END

He said, 'This is wickedness,' and he pushed her back into the basket
And pushed the lead cover down over its mouth.

Then I looked up—and there before me were two women,
With the wind in their wings!
They had wings like those of a stork,
And they lifted up the basket between heaven and earth.

'Where are they taking the basket?' I asked the angel who was speaking to me.

He replied, 'To the country of Babylonia to build a house for it.
When it is ready, the basket will be set there in its place.

[The woman in the basket represents the fully mature, iniquity of the world,
Represented by the final Babylon, the harlot of Satan in Revelation 17.]

Four Chariots (Zechariah 6:1-8)
I looked up again—
And there before me were four chariots coming out from between two mountains--
Mountains of bronze!
The first chariot had red horses, the second black, the third white,
And the fourth dappled-- all of them powerful.
I asked the angel who was speaking to me,
'What are these, my lord?'

The angel answered me,
'These are the four spirits of heaven,
Going out from standing in the presence of the Lord of the whole world.
The one with the black horses is going toward the north country,
The one with the white horses toward the west,
And the one with the dappled horses toward the south.'

When the powerful horses went out, they were straining to go throughout the earth.
And he said, 'Go throughout the earth!'
So they went throughout the earth.

Then he called to me, 'Look, those going toward the north country
Have given my Spirit rest in the land of the north.'
[These are the same spirits that we see in Revelation 6.]

The Man Whose Name Is The Branch (Zechariah 6:12-13)
Here is the man whose name is the Branch (Christ),
And he will branch out from his place and build the temple of the Lord.
(The New Jerusalem whose architect and builder is God.)
It is he who will build the temple of the Lord, and he will be clothed with majesty

The Time Of The END

And will sit and rule on his throne.
And he will be a priest on his throne.
And there will be harmony between the two (the temple and the throne).
[This is a prophecy of what Christ Jesus will do at The Time of The END.]

The Lord Promises to Bless Jerusalem (Zechariah 8)
Again the word of the Lord Almighty came to me.
This is what the Lord almighty Says:
'I am very jealous for Zion; I am burning with jealousy for her.'
This is what the Lord says:
'I will return to Zion and dwell in Jerusalem.
Then Jerusalem will be called the City of Truth,
And the mountain of the Lord Almighty will be called The Holy Mountain.'

This is what the Lord Almighty says:
'It may seem marvelous to the <u>remnant</u> *of this people at that time,*
But will it seem marvelous to me?' declares the Lord Almighty.

This is what the Lord Almighty says:
'I will save my people from the countries of the east and the west.
I will bring them back to live in Jerusalem;
They will be my people,
And I will be faithful and righteous to them as their God.'

This is what the Lord Almighty says:
'You who now hear these words spoken by the prophets
Who were there when the foundation was laid for the house of the Lord Almighty,
Let your hands be strong so that the temple may be built.
Before that time there were no wages for man or beast.
No one could go about his business safely because of his enemy,
For I had turned every man against his neighbor.
But now I will not deal with the <u>remnant</u> *of this people as I did in the past,'*
Declares the Lord Almighty.

'The seed will grow well, the vine will yield its fruit, the ground will produce its crops,
And the heavens will drop their dew.
I will give all these things as an inheritance to the <u>remnant</u> *of this people.*
As you have been an object of cursing among the nations, O Judah and Israel,
So will I save you, and you will be a blessing.
Do not be afraid, but let your hands be strong.'

This is what the Lord Almighty says:
'Just as I had determined to bring disaster upon you
And showed no pity when your fathers angered me,' says the Lord Almighty,
'So now I have determined to do good again to Jerusalem and Judah.

The Time Of The END

Do not be afraid.
These are the things you are to do:
Speak the truth to each other,
And render true and sound judgment in your courts;
Do not plot evil against your neighbor, and do not love to swear falsely.
I hate all this,' declares the Lord.

Again the word of the Lord almighty came to me.
This is what the Lord Almighty says:
'The fasts of the fourth, fifth, seventh and tenth months
Will become joyful and glad occasions and happy festivals for Judah.
Therefore love truth and peace.'

This is what the Lord Almighty says:
'Many peoples and the inhabitants of many cities will yet come,
And the inhabitants of one city will go to another and say,
'Let us go at once to entreat the Lord and seek the Lord Almighty.
I myself am going.'
And many peoples and powerful nations will come to Jerusalem
To seek the Lord Almighty and to entreat him.'

This is what the Lord Almighty Says:
'In those days ten men from all languages and nations
Will take firm hold of one Jew by the edge of his robe and say,
'Let us go with you, because we have heard that God is with you.'

The Coming Of Zion's King (Zechariah 9:9-13)
Rejoice greatly, O Daughter of Zion!
Shout , Daughter of Jerusalem!
See, your king comes to you righteous and having salvation,
Gentle and riding on a donkey, on a colt, the foal of a donkey.

I will take away the chariots from Ephraim
And the war-horses from Jerusalem, and the battle bow will be broken.
He will proclaim peace to the nations.
His rule will extend from sea to sea
And from the River (the Euphrates) *to the ends of the earth.*

As for you, because of the blood of my covenant with you,
I will free your prisoners from the <u>waterless pit</u>.
Return to your fortress, O prisoners of hope;
Even now I announce that I will restore twice as much to you.
I will bend Judah as I bend my bow and fill it with Ephraim.
I will rouse your sons, O Zion, against your sons, O Greece,
And make you like a warrior's sword.

The Lord Will Sound The Trumpet In The Last Days
(Zechariah 9:14-17)
Then the Lord will appear over them; his arrow will flash like lightning.
The Sovereign Lord will sound the trumpet;
He will march in the storms of the south,
And the Lord Almighty will shield them.
They will destroy and overcome with slingstones.
They will drink and roar as with wine;
They will be full like a bowl used for sprinkling the corners of the altar.

The Lord their God will save them <u>on that day</u> as the flock of his people.
They will sparkle in his land like jewels in a crown.
How attractive and beautiful they will be!
Grain will make the young men thrive, and new wine the young women.

The Lord Will Care For Judah In The Last Days (Zechariah 10)
'Ask the Lord for rain in the springtime;
It is the Lord who makes the storm clouds.
He gives showers of rain to men, and plants of the field to everyone.
The idols speak deceit, diviners see visions that lie;
They tell dreams that are false, they give comfort in vain.
Therefore the people wander like sheep oppressed for lack of a shepherd.

My anger burns against the shepherds, and I will punish the leaders;
For the Lord Almighty will care for his flock, the house of Judah,
And make them like a proud horse in battle.

From Judah will come the cornerstone, from him the tent peg,
From him the battle bow, from him every ruler.
Together they will be like mighty men trampling the muddy streets in battle.
Because the Lord is with them, they will fight and overthrow the horsemen.

I will strengthen the house of Judah and save the house of Joseph.
I will restore them because I have compassion on them.
They will be as though I had not rejected them,
For I am the Lord their God and I will answer them.
The Ephraimites will become like might men,
And their hearts will be glad as with wine.
Their children will see it and be joyful; their hearts will rejoice in the Lord.
I will signal for them and gather them in.
Surely I will redeem them; they will be as numerous as before.

Though I scatter them among the peoples,
Yet in distant lands they will remember me.
They and their children will survive, and they will return.

The Time Of The END

I will bring them back form Egypt and gather them from Assyria.
I will bring them to Gilead and Lebanon,
And there will not be room enough for them.

They will pass through the sea of trouble; the surging sea will be subdued
And all the depths of the Nile will dry up.
Assyria's pride will be brought down and Egypt's scepter will pass away.
I will strengthen them in the Lord
And in his name they will walk,' declares the Lord.

In The Last Days All The Nations Gather Against Jerusalem And They Are All Destroyed (Zechariah 12:1-9)

This is the word of the Lord concerning Israel.
The Lord, who lays the foundation of the earth,
And who forms the spirit of man within him, declares:
'I am going to make Jerusalem a cup that sends all the surrounding peoples reeling.
Judah will be besieged as well as Jerusalem.
On that day, when all the nations of the earth are gathered against her,
I will make Jerusalem an immovable rock for all the nations.
All who try to move it will injure themselves.
On that day I will strike every horse with panic
And its rider with madness,' declares the Lord.

'I will keep a watchful eye over the house of Judah,
But I will blind all the horses of the nations.
Then the leaders of Judah will say in their hearts,
The people of Jerusalem are strong, because the Lord Almighty is their God.'

On that day I will make the leaders of Judah like a firepot in the woodpile,
Like a flaming torch among sheaves.
They will consume right and left all the surrounding peoples,
But Jerusalem will remain intact in her place.

The Lord will save the dwellings of Judah first,
So that the honor of the house of David and Jerusalem's inhabitants
May not be greater than that of Judah.
On that day the Lord will shield those who live in Jerusalem,
So that the feeblest among them will be like David,
And the house of David will be like God,
Like the Angel of the Lord going before them.
On that day I will set out to destroy all the nations that attack Jerusalem.

Jerusalem Will Mourn For The One They Pierced (Zechariah 12:10-13)

And I will pour out on the house of David and the inhabitants of Jerusalem
A spirit of grace and supplication.

The Time Of The END

They will look on me, the one they have pierced,
And they will mourn for him as one mourns for an only child,
And grieve bitterly for him as one grieves for a first born son.

On that day the weeping in Jerusalem will be great,
Like the weeping of Hadad Rimmon in the plain of Megiddo.
The land itself will mourn, each clan by itself, with their wives by themselves;
The clan of the house of David and their wives,
The clan of the house of Levi and their wives,
And all the rest of the clans and their wives.

The Lord Will Provide a Fountain Of Cleansing For Jerusalem
(Zechariah 13:1-6)
On that day a fountain will be opened to the house of David
And the inhabitants of Jerusalem,
To cleanse them from sin and impurity.
<u>*On that day*</u>*, I will banish the names of the idols from the land,*
And they will be remembered no more.

I will remove both the prophets and the spirit of impurity from the land.
And if anyone still prophesies,
His father and mother, to whom he was born, will say to him,
'You must die, because you have told lies in the Lord's name.'
When he prophesies, his own parents will stab him.

<u>*On that day*</u> *every prophet will be ashamed of his prophetic vision.*
He will not put on a prophet's garment of hair in order to deceive.
He will say, 'I am not a prophet.
I am a farmer; the land has been my livelihood since my youth.'
I someone asks him,
'What are these wounds on your body?' he will answer,
'The wounds I was given at the house of my friends.'

The Shepherd Struck, The Sheep Scattered
Two-Thirds O Mankind Will Be Struck Down (Zechariah 13:7-9)
'Awake, O sword, against my shepherd (Jesus),
Against the man who is close to me!'
Declares the Lord Almighty.
'Strike the shepherd and the sheep will be scattered,
And I will turn my hand against the little ones.'

'In the whole land,' declares the Lord,
'Two-thirds will be struck down and perish;
Yet one-third will be left in it.
This third I will bring into the fire;

The Time Of The END

I will refine them like silver and test them like gold.
They will call on my name and I will answer them;
I will say, 'They are my people,'
And they will say, 'The Lord is our God.'

The Day Of The Lord Is Coming (Zechariah 14)

A day of the Lord is coming when your plunder will be divided among you.
I will gather all the nations to Jerusalem to fight against it;
The city will be captured, the houses ransacked, and the women raped.
Half of the city will go into exile,
But the rest of the people will not be taken from the city.

Then the Lord will go out and fight against those nations,
As he fights in the day of battle.
On that day *his feet will stand on the Mount of Olives, east of Jerusalem,*
And the Mount of Olives will be split in two from east to west,
Forming a great valley,
With half of the mountain moving north and half moving south.
You will flee by my mountain valley, for it will extend to Azel.
You will flee as you fled from the earthquake in the days of Uzziah king of Judah.
Then the Lord my God will come and all the holy ones with him.

On that day *there will be no light, no cold or frost.*
It will be a unique day, without daytime or nighttime--a day known to the Lord.
When evening comes, there will be light.

On that day *living water will flow out from Jerusalem,*
Half to the eastern sea and half to the western sea, in summer and in winter.

The Lord will be king over the whole earth.
On that day ***there will be one Lord and his name the only name.***

The whole land, from Geba to Rimmon, south of Jerusalem,
Will become like the Arabah.
But Jerusalem will be raised up and remain in its place,
From the Benjamin Gate to the site of the First Gate, to the Corner Gate,
And from the Tower of Hananel to the royal winepresses.
It will be inhabited;
Never again will it be destroyed .
Jerusalem will be secure.

This is the plague with which the Lord will strike
All the nations that fought against Jerusalem:
Their flesh will rot while they are still standing on their feet,
Their eyes will rot in their sockets,

And their tongues will rot in their mouths.
On that day men will be stricken by the Lord with great panic.
Each man will seize the hand of another, and they will attach each other.
Judah too will fight at Jerusalem.
The wealth of all the surrounding nations will be collected--
Great quantities of gold and silver and clothing.
A similar plague will strike the horses and mules, the camels and donkeys,
And all the animals in those camps.

Then the survivors from all the nations that have attacked Jerusalem
Will go up year after year to worship the King, the Lord Almighty,
And to celebrate the Feast of Tabernacles.
If any of the peoples of the earth do not go up to Jerusalem
To worship the King, the Lord Almighty, they will have no rain.

If the Egyptian people do not go up and take part, they will have no rain.
The Lord will bring on them the plague he inflicts on the nations
That do not go up to celebrate the Feast of Tabernacles.
This will be the punishment of Egypt and the punishment of all the nations
That do not go up to celebrate the Feast of Tabernacles.

On that day *HOLY TO THE LORD will be inscribed on the bells of the horses,*
And the cooking pots in the Lord's house
Will be like the sacred bowls in front of the altar.
Every pot in Jerusalem and Judah will be holy to the Lord Almighty,
And all who come to sacrifice will take some of the pots and cook in them.
And on that day there will no longer be a Canaanite
In the house of the Lord Almighty.

MALACHI SPEAKS
OF THE TIME OF THE END

Who Can Endure The Day Of His Coming? (Malachi 3:1-5)

'See, I will send my messenger, who will prepare the way before me.
Then **suddenly** the Lord you are seeking will come to his temple;
The messenger of the covenant, whom you desire, will come,'
Says the Lord Almighty.

[The messenger the Lord is sending, to prepare the way for His second coming
Is the Bride of Christ.]

But who can endure the day of his coming?
Who can stand when he appears?
For he will be like a refiner's fire or a launderer's soap.
He will sit as a refiner and purifier of silver;
He will purify the Levites and refine them like gold and silver.
Then the Lord will have men who will bring offerings in righteousness,
And the offerings of Judah and Jerusalem will be acceptable to the Lord,
As in days gone by, as in former years.

'So I will come near to you for judgment.
I will be quick to testify against sorcerers, adulterers and perjurers,
Against those who defraud laborers of their wages,
Who oppress the widows and the fatherless,
And deprive aliens of justice, but do not fear me,' says the Lord Almighty.

In The Day When I Make Up My Treasured Possession
(Malachi 3:16-17)
Then those who feared the Lord talked with each other,
And the Lord listened and heard.
A scroll of remembrance was written in his presence
Concerning those who feared the Lord and honored his name.

'They will be mine,' says the Lord Almighty,
'In the day when I make up my treasured possession.
I will spare them, just as in compassion a man spares his son who serves him.
And you will again see the distinction between the righteous and the wicked,
Between those who serve God and those who do not.'

A Day Like A Burning Furnace (Malachi 4)

'Surely the day is coming; it will burn like a furnace.
All the arrogant and every evildoer will be stubble,

The Time Of The END

And that day that is coming will set them on fire,'
Says the Lord Almighty.

'Not a root or a branch will be left to them.

But for you who revere my name,
The sun of righteousness will rise with healing in its wings.
And you will go out and leap like calves released from the stall.

Then you will trample down the wicked;
They will be ashes under the soles of your feet
On the day when I do these things,' says the Lord Almighty.

'Remember the law of my servant Moses,
The decrees and laws I gave him at Horeb for all Israel.

See, I will send you the prophet Elijah
Before the great and dreadful day of the Lord comes.
He will turn the hearts of the fathers to their children,
And the hearts of the children to their fathers;
Or else I will come and strike the land with a curse.'

[Before The Great and Dreadful Day of the Lord,
The Bride of Christ comes in the Spirit of Elijah
To turn the hearts of the fathers to their children
And the heats of the children to their fathers.
All who will not respond to the ministry of the Spirit of Elijah
Will be cursed,
And the events of The Great Tribulation will fall upon them.]

THE PSALMS SPEAK OF THE TIME OF THE END

Why Do The Nations Rage (Psalm 2)

Why do the nations rage and the peoples plot in vain?
The kings of the earth take their stand
And the rulers gather together against the Lord
And against his Anointed One (Christ Jesus).

'Let us break their chains,' they say, 'and throw off their fetters.'
(These are the chains and fetters of God's righteous requirements)

The One enthroned in heaven laughs; the Lord scoffs at them.
Then he rebukes them in his anger and terrifies them in his wrath, saying,

'I have installed my King (Christ Jesus) on Zion, my holy hill.'

I will proclaim the decree of the Lord:

He said to me, 'You are my son;
Today I have become your Father.
Ask of me, and I will make the nations your inheritance,
The ends of the earth your possession.
You will rule them with an iron scepter;
You will dash them to pieces like pottery.'

Therefore, you kings be wise; be warned, you rulers of the earth.
Serve the Lord with fear and rejoice with trembling.
Kiss the Son, *lest he be angry and you be destroyed in your way,*
For his wrath can flare up in a moment.
Blessed are all who take refuge in him.

[At the Time of The END, all the nations rage against God and His Christ.
They resent the righteous requirements of God and want to thrown them off.
Under the deception of Satan,
They come together at the Battle of Armageddon and are destroyed.
God the Father has enthroned His Christ on an eternal throne.
The nations say to themselves,
"Let us break the chains of the law of God and the covenant of His Christ."
But the Lord simply laughs at them for the futility of their thoughts.

In The END Christ Jesus will rule the nations with His iron scepter.
Today, the nations have the choice of turning to Christ and be blessed,

Or succumbing to the deception of Satan and being destroyed.]

The Nations Have Fallen Into A Pit (Psalm 9)
I will praise you, O Lord, with all my heart;
I will tell of all your wonders.
I will be glad and rejoice in you;
I will sing praise to your name, O Most High.

My enemies turn back;
They stumble and perish before you.
For you have upheld my cause;
You have sat on your throne, judging righteously.
You have rebuked the nations and destroyed the wicked;
You have blotted out their name for ever and ever.
Endless ruin has overtaken the enemy,
You have uprooted their cities;
Even the memory of them has perished.

The Lord reigns forever;
He has established his throne for judgment.
He will judge the world in righteousness;
He will govern the peoples with justice.
The Lord is a refuge for the oppressed,
A stronghold in times of trouble.
Those who know your name will trust in you,
For you, Lord have never forsaken those who seek you.

Sing praises to the Lord, enthroned in Zion;
Proclaim among the nations what he has done.
For he who avenges blood remembers;
He does not ignore the cry of the afflicted.

O Lord, see how my enemies persecute me!
Have mercy and lift me up from the gates of death,
That I may declare your praises in the gates of the Daughter of Zion
And there rejoice in your salvation.

The nations have fallen into the pit they have dug;
Their feet are caught in the net they have hidden.
The Lord is known by his justice;
The wicked are ensnared by the work of their hands.

The wicked return to the grave, all the nations that forgot God.
But the needy will not always be forgotten,
Nor the hope of the afflicted ever perish.

245

The Time Of The END

Arise, O Lord, let not man triumph;
Let the nations be judged in your presence.
Strike them with terror, O Lord;
Let the nations know they are but men.

[At The Time of The END, God judges the nations of the world in righteousness.
They are struck with terror and destroyed because they are only men.]

Blessed Is The Nation Whose God Is The Lord (Psalm 33:10-19)

The Lord foils the plans of the nations;
He thwarts the purposes of the peoples.
But the plans of the Lord stand firm forever,
The purposes of his heart through all generations.

Blessed is the nation whose God is the Lord,
The people he chose for his inheritance
From heaven the Lord looks down and sees all mankind;
From his dwelling place he watches all who live on earth--
He who forms the hearts of all, who considers everything they do.
No king is saved by the size of his army;
No warrior escapes by his great strength.
A horse is a vain hope for deliverance.
Despite all its great strength it cannot save.

But the eyes of the Lord are on those who fear him,
On those whose hope is in his unfailing love,
To deliver them from death and keep them alive in famine.

The Lord Makes Wars Cease (Psalm 46:8-10)

Come and see the works of the Lord,
The desolations he has brought on the earth.
He makes wars cease to the ends of the earth;
He breaks the bow and shatters the spear,
He burns the shields with fire.
'Be still, and know that I am God;
I will be exalted among the nations,
I will be exalted in the earth.'

[At the end of The Great Tribulation and The Battle of Armageddon
The earth is desolate.
God causes wars to cease on earth forever.
He alone is exalted in THAT DAY.]

The Lord Comes To Judge The Earth (Psalm 96:12-13)

Then all the trees of the forest will sing for joy;
They will sing before the Lord, for he comes,
He comes to judge the earth.
He will judge the world in righteousness
And the peoples in his truth.

He will Judge The World In Righteousness (Psalm 98:8-9)

Let the rivers clap their hands, let the mountains sing together for joy;
Let them sing before the Lord, for he comes to judge the earth.
He will judge the world in righteousness and the peoples with equity.

The Day Of The Lord's Wrath (Psalm 110)

The Lord says to my Lord;
'Sit at my right hand until I make your enemies a footstool for your feet.'

The Lord will extend your mighty scepter from Zion;
You will rule in the midst of your enemies.
Your troops will be willing on your day of battle.
Arrayed in holy majesty, from the womb of the dawn
You will receive the dew of your youth.

The Lord has sworn and will not change his mind:
'You are a priest forever, in the order of Melchizedek.'

The Lord is at your right hand ;
He will crush kings on the day of his wrath.
He will judge the nations heaping up the dead
And crushing the ruler of the whole earth (Satan)**.**
He will drink from a brook beside the way;
Therefore he will lift up his head.

The Sentence Written Against The Nations (Psalm 149)

Praise the Lord.
Sing to the Lord a new song, his praise in the assembly of the saints.
Let Israel rejoice in their Maker;
Let the people of Zion be glad in their King.
Let them praise his name with dancing
And make music to him with tambourine and harp.
For the Lord takes delight in his people;
He crowns the humble with salvation.
Let the saints rejoice in this honor and sing for joy on their beds.

The Time Of The END

May the praise of God be in their mouths
And a double-edged sword in their hands,
To inflict vengeance on the nations
And punishment on the peoples,
To bind their kings with fetters,
Their nobles with shackles of iron,
To carry out the sentence written against them.
This is the glory of all his saints.

JUDGMENT COMES WHEN SIN IS IRREVERSIBLE

God Is Patient

All sin, personal and national, is against God.
God is patient with each one of us and with each nation.
However, there comes a time when the sin in a persons life
And sin in a nations life is irreversible.
Then all that remains is the judgment of God.

Biblical Examples Of Irreversible Sin

Noah's Day:
Irreversible sin occurred in Noah's day.
At that time the sin of mankind had reached the point where it would only get worse.
When this occurs the judgment of God is demanded.
As long as there is hope of repentance and turning from sin, God will wait;
But when the sin is irreversible
He is compelled by His holiness, to bring it to an end.
The flood of Noah's day destroyed all living things, except those in the Ark.
This is event foreshadows The Time of The END;
Virtually all of humanity will be killed except The Bride of Christ.
The whole earth will be devastated.

The Tower of Babel:
At the tower of Babel
God did not destroy the culture that had set itself against Him.
In this case He chose to simply disperse the people
By giving groups of them different languages
So that they could not understand each other and would be forced to disperse
And cover the earth as God had commanded.

Sodom and Gomorrah:
The sin of Sodom and Gomorrah had reached the point where it was irreversible.
It was getting worse by the day,
And God was compelled to act, and He did;
Because of its sin the whole area was destroyed except for Lot and his family.
He was saved because he abhorred the sin and believed God.

Egypt:
Egypt had made slaves of the Israelites and was treating them terribly,
Forcing them to kill their male babies.
God sent the Israelites a deliverer in the person of Moses.
Moses went to Pharaoh, king of Egypt and demanded in the name of the Lord,

That he let God's people go free.
When Pharaoh would not comply, he brought upon that nation the terrible plagues
That devastated the whole country.
In the end he was forced by God to let the Israelites go free.

The Nation Israel:
The sin of the nation Israel got to the point of no return
And God used the nation of Babylon to defeat them
And take them into captivity for seventy years.

The Nation Babylon:
When the nation Babylon became exceedingly wicked
God used the nation of the Media-Persia to defeat them
And bring them to permanent ruin.

The Nation Israel In The Time of Christ:
The nation Israel in the time of Christ Jesus had become wicked.
Jesus said that they were more wicked than Sodom and Gomorrah.
Because of this and because of the fact that they did not receive their Christ,
And had Him killed, they were destroyed as a nation in 70 A.D.

The History Of The World:
The history of the world from the time of Christ Jesus forward,
Is the story of kingdoms rising and falling,
Leading up to The Time of The END.
At The Time of The END, the wickedness of the whole world,
Under the deception of Satan is irreversible,
And God brings His judgment on the whole world,
Like in the days of Noah.
As was predetermined from before creation,
God puts an END to "Time;"
God is finished with His 6,000 years of dealings with mankind.
He has obtained a Bride for His Son
Which was His sole objective in creation.

What follows is 1,000 years of rest,
The final judgment and eternal bliss for The Bride of Christ.

A NEW HEAVENS
AND A NEW EARTH

'Behold, I will create new heavens and a new earth.'

'The former things will not be remembered,
Nor will they come to mind.'
(Isaiah 65:17)

The apostle John declares:
'Then I saw a new heaven and a new earth
For the first heaven and the first earth had passed away.'
(Revelation 21: 1)

Isaiah prophesies these great statements in Isaiah 65:17,
And the Apostle John sees them in Revelation 21:1.
Ultimately God does away with this corrupted world.
Not because it was damaged by mankind's lack of ecology,
Not by some unforeseen calamity,
But because of their sin.
In the eyes of God, sin is what corrupts the earth.
The earth is soaked in the blood of mankind and God's saints;
It is defiled.

Mankind did not ruin the earth ecologically but spiritually,
And before God all that matters is the TRUTH, which is spiritual.
Christ Jesus is the WAY, the TRUTH, and the LIFE;
He offered Himself to every person who ever lived
And most rejected Him.

The earth reals like a drunkard, it sways like a hut in the wind;
So heavy upon it is the guilt of its rebellion that it falls--
Never to rise again. *(Isaiah 24:20)*

Before God, nothing on earth is worth saving.
All the accomplishments of mankind are worthless before a Holy God;
And they are all destroyed.
The only thing that remains from the first earth
Are those who gave their lives to Christ Jesus,
And they do not remember anything about the first earth.
They have been made ONE with Christ Jesus for eternity.
They are given a new heaven and a new earth to live in;
A fresh, clean and holy place for a fresh, clean and holy Bride.

The Time Of The END

Those who gave their lives to Christ Jesus came to Him
And drank of the Living Water He offered;
They received the Anointing from The Anointed One.
They allowed Christ Jesus to put His law in their minds
And write them upon their hearts.
They were crucified with Christ and no longer lived
But Christ lived in and through them.
They submitted their will to His will;
They sought first and above all the Kingdom of God.
They asked but one thing: To live in the house of God!
They worshiped God in Spirit and in Truth.

They were water washed, blood washed,
Filled with the Holy Spirit and walked in the Light.

Hallelujah!

HOW TO BE READY FOR THE TIME OF THE END

[Christ Jesus said that we have one teacher, The Christ.
The following Scriptures represent some of what the Lord has taught us,
To be ready for His return.]

Repent

Christ Jesus said:
Repent, for the kingdom of heaven is near.

Believe

For God so loved the world that he gave his one and only Son,
That whoever believes in him shall not perish but have eternal life.
For God did not send his Son into the world to condemn the world,
But to save the world through him.
Whoever believes in him is not condemned,
But whoever does not believe stands condemned already
Because he has not believed in the name of God's one and only Son.

This is the verdict:
Light has come into the world,
But men loved darkness instead of light because their deeds were evil.
Everyone who does evil hates the light,
And will not come into the light for fear that his deeds will be exposed.
But whoever lives by the truth comes into the light,
So that it may be seen plainly
That what he has done has been done through God.(John 3:16-21)

What Works Must We Do?

The work of God is this: to believe in the one he has sent. (John 6:29)

Seek First The Kingdom Of God

But seek first his kingdom and his righteousness,
And all these things will be given to you as well. (Matthew 6:33)

You Must Be Born Of The Spirit To Enter the Kingdom of God

I tell you the truth, unless a man is born of water and the Spirit,
He cannot enter the kingdom of God.
Flesh gives birth to flesh, but the Spirit gives birth to spirit.
You should not be surprised at my saying,
You must be born again.
The wind blows wherever it pleases.
You hear its sound, but you cannot tell where it comes from or where it is going.

So it is with everyone born of the Spirit. (John 3:5-8)

Believers Must Worship In Spirit And In Truth
Yet a time is coming and has now come
When true worshipers will worship the Father in Spirit and truth,
For they are the kind of worshipers the Father seeks.
God is Spirit, and his worshipers must worship in Spirit and in truth.
(John 4:23-24)

Come To Christ And Drink His Living Water
Jesus said:
If a man is thirsty, let him come to me and drink.
Whoever believes in me, as the Scripture has said,
Streams of living water will flow from within him.
By this he meant the Spirit,
Who those who believed in him were later to receive.
(On the Day of Pentecost)
Up to that time the Spirit had not been given,
Since Jesus had not yet been glorified. (John 7:37-39)

The Truth Will Set You Free
If you hold to my teaching, your are really my disciples.
Then you will know the truth, and the truth will set you free. (John 8:31)

Christ Jesus Is The Resurrection And The Life
I am the resurrection and the life.
He who believes in me will live, even though he dies;
And whoever lives and believes in me will never die. (John 11:25-26)

You Must Love One Another
A new command I give to you: Love one another.
As I have loved you, so you must love one another.
All men will know that you are my disciples if you love one another.
(John 13:34-35)

Jesus Promises The Holy Spirit
If you love me, you will obey what I command.
And I will ask the Father,
And he will give you another Counselor to be with you forever--
The Spirit of Truth.
The world cannot accept him, because it neither sees him nor knows him.
But you know him, for he lives with you and will be in you.
I will not leave you as orphans; I will come to you.
Before long, the world will not see me anymore, but you will see me.

On that day you will realize that I am in my Father,
And you are in me, and I am in you. *(John 14:15-20)*

Enter Through The Narrow Gate
Enter through the narrow gate.
For wide is the gate and broad is the road that leads to destruction,
And many enter through it.
But small is the gate and narrow the road that leads to life,
And only a few find it. *(Matthew 7:13-14)*

Store Up Treasure In Heaven
Do not store up for yourselves treasures on earth,
Where moth and rust destroy, and where thieves break in and steal.
But store up for yourselves treasures in heaven,
Where moth and rust do not destroy, and where thieves do not break in and steal.
For where your treasure is, there your heart will be also. *(Matthew 6:19-21)*

The Golden Rule
In everything, do to others what you would have them do to you,
For this sums up the Law and the Prophets. (Matthew 7:12)

Those Worthy Of Possessing Christ
Anyone who loves his father or mother more than me is not worthy of me;
Anyone who loves his son or daughter more than me is not worthy of me;
And anyone who does not take his cross and follow me is not worthy of me.
Whoever finds his life will lose it,
And whoever loses his life for my sake will find it. *(Matthew 10:37-39)*

He Must Deny Himself And Take Up His Cross And Follow Me
If anyone would come after me,
He must deny himself and take up his cross and follow me.
For whoever wants to save his life will lose it,
But whoever loses his life for me will find it.
What good will it be for a man if he gains the whole world,
Yet forfeits his soul.
Or what can a man give in exchange for his soul? *(Matthew 16:24-26)*

He Who Is Not With Me Is Against Me
He who is not with me is against me,
And he who does not gather with me scatters.
And so I tell you,
Every sin and blasphemy will be forgiven men,
But the blasphemy against the Spirit will not be forgiven.
Anyone who speaks a word against the Son of Man will be forgiven,

But anyone who speaks against the Holy Spirit will not be forgiven,
Either in this age or in the age to come. (Matthew 12:30-32)

Your Words Will Save Or Condemn You
For out of the overflow of the heart the mouth speaks...

But I tell you that men will have to give an account of the day of judgment
For every careless word they have spoken.
For by your words you will be acquitted, and by you words you will be condemned.
(Matthew 12:34-37)

Act Justly, Love Mercy
He has shown you, O man, what is good.
And what does the Lord require of you?
To act justly and to love mercy
And to walk humbly with your God.(Micah 6:8)

The Lord Does Not Want Anyone To Perish
But do not forget this one thing dear friends:
With the Lord a day is like a thousand years, and a thousand years like a day.
The Lord is not slow in keeping his promise, as some understand slowness.
He is patient with you,
Not wanting anyone to perish,
But everyone to come to repentance. *(2 Peter 3:8-9)*

ABOUT THE AUTHOR

Tom Haeg is an architect, writer, song writer and musician
Who has been a student of the Bible for more than 25 years.
He and his wife Susan have been blessed
To experience the outpouring of God's Spirit called "Renewal"
And have witnessed the manifest presence of God.
Tom and Susan's lives have been changed forever
By this encounter with the Living God;
Changed by His grace, love and power.

They have led worship in small groups and larger services
Where God has poured out His Spirit in marvelous ways.
Through this outpouring they have seen God change lives.

Tom has read extensively about the history of the Christian Church
And the revivals that God has visited upon His people
Up to and including this present time.
He believes that the Final Revival lies dead ahead,
Where God is going to pour out His Spirit in a magnitude
That has never been seen before.
Tom believes that this outpouring will precede The Great Tribulation
Spoken of in the Book of Revelation.
He believes that soon there will be thousands upon thousands of Christians
Ministering Christ Jesus in the power and fullness of Christ.
The name of Jesus will be upon every heart, mind and mouth
Every man woman and child
In every nation on the face of the earth.

Christ Jesus will present Himself personally to every living person on earth.
Every person will be given the opportunity to accept Him
As their Savior, Lord and Anointing.

Tom's previous book is "Called By Christ To Be ONE", available at Amazon.com.
Tom's blog is calledbychristtobeone.blogspot.com.

CPSIA information can be obtained at www.ICGtesting.com
Printed in the USA
LVOW09s1933160914

404336LV00008B/560/P